PRAISE FOR THE

'This is a thoughtful under
by setting out his crec
republicanism. An Andersonstown uprising entitles him to
an opinion, while his capacity for insight ensures that opinion
will carry a good deal of weight. He is well equipped to
disentangle the various strands – the sense of grievance,
historical consciousness, tribal solidarity, self-interest, self-
delusion, self-perpetuating aggression and all the rest – which
make up the ideological clump . . . Succinct, courageous and
clear-sighted, *The Trouble with Guns* is a telling contribution
to the literature of Northern Irish politics.'

Patricia Craig, *Independent*

'His is no outsider's account contrived to confirm or deny a
preconception . . . However alienated from them he has
become, the people of whom he writes are his people. He
does not deny them, he recognises what some have suffered,
but he rejects absolutely what he calls their "mythology". . .
A fine, compelling and necessary book.'

Ian Bell, *Scotsman*

'This is one of the most valuable books to emerge from
Northern Ireland in recent years . . . O'Doherty's intellectual
clarity, moral and physical courage are never in doubt.
His book abounds with uncomfortable truths that would
enrage more than republicans . . . It is lucid and accessible,
and is the most subtle analysis of the modern-day
republican movement that I have read.'

Sean O'Callaghan, *The Times*

THE TROUBLE WITH GUNS

Republican Strategy and the Provisional IRA

MALACHI O'DOHERTY

THE
BLACKSTAFF
PRESS

BELFAST

First published in March 1998 by
The Blackstaff Press Limited
3 Galway Park, Dundonald, Belfast BT16 2AN, Northern Ireland

This book has received support from the
Cultural Traditions Programme of the Community Relations Council,
which aims to encourage acceptance and understanding of cultural diversity.
The views expressed do not necessarily reflect those of the
NI Community Relations Council.

Reprinted May 1998

Typeset by Techniset Typesetters, Newton-le-Willows, Merseyside

Printed in Ireland by ColourBooks Limited

A CIP catalogue record for this book
is available from the British Library

ISBN 0-85640-605-8

to Maureen

CONTENTS

PROLOGUE

One night in May 1995 in the Felons club, in west Belfast, an IRA man called Bobby Storey directed me into a corner for a quiet word. Bobby Storey is about six foot four and I am five foot two so I wasn't about to argue. He was a human tower, and the hand he pressed against my chest was nearly as big as my chest itself. I have been asked many times if I am not afraid of being duffed up by the IRA for all the rude things I have said about them. I generally expect they won't respond to me like that, but at that moment I was contemplating that this might be a breach with tradition.

'I am not going to hit you, but I want to tell you that you are a slug,' Storey said.

I started to reply but he asked me to apply my energies instead to a consideration of the merits of his statement. 'Shut your fucking mouth,' he said.

Bobby was angry with me because of a piece I had written for BBC Radio Ulster's *Talkback* programme. The piece had described him as a former gunman, but did not name him. I wrote it as a follow-up to an article published by Liam Clarke in the *Sunday Times*. Liam had written that Bobby Storey had been given the job of policing the IRA ceasefire. He had been sitting in on the edges of meetings of Sinn Féin sceptics, listening to their reservations, and making it clear to them that the ceasefire was to hold. Where Liam or others got this story from, I don't know.

After I had read it, I searched the available literature for information on Bobby Storey. Bowyer Bell (1993) wrote that the police nicknamed Storey 'Brain Surgeon'. Normally this would be a way of saying he was stupid. He's not stupid. BS, Bobby Storey,

Brain Surgeon. The initials matched, and presumably the nickname appealed to some policeman's sense of humour.

Bowyer Bell was given access for his research to all levels of the IRA by its army council, but this detail seems to have come directly from the Royal Ulster Constabulary (RUC). How else would Bowyer Bell have known a code name used in police communications? Bobby Storey, I presumed, would have read the book himself, or at least flicked through the index for references to himself, and learned what was in the public domain about him. Apparently he hadn't.

My point was to argue that the ceasefire that we depended on was itself dependent on people like Brain Surgeon. That was the reality we lived with. How did we like that? I wanted to ask if this was an inevitable part of any peace process, that we would become dependent on the disciplinary machinery within paramilitary groups themselves for public order.

This idea had been mooted some years before, in September 1988, by Frank Wright and John Lampen (*Fortnight* 265). They contrived a sketch in which various parties, including Sinn Féin, and the British and Irish governments, discussed the possible steps towards a British announcement of intent to withdraw from Northern Ireland, and towards a ceasefire by the IRA. In the sketch, Sinn Féin complained that making an IRA ceasefire a precondition for Sinn Féin being given a place at talks imposed on them the responsibility for curtailing or disowning all republican violence. Wright and Lampen were dealing with political pragmatism, however, not with the moral question of how a state or its people might become dependent on law-breakers, and potentially on law-breaking, to maintain the peace.

That question arose again in May 1997, when John Alderdice of the Alliance Party argued for the removal of loyalist parties from talks because of violence coming from groups that those loyalists claimed they were not linked to. Billy Hutchinson of one of those loyalist parties, the Progressive Unionist Party, reminded a BBC audience (*Good Morning Ulster*, 27 May 1997) that, the year before, Lord Alderdice had been similarly critical of the loyalists when they had issued threats to try to keep loyalist dissidents in line. The implication seemed to be: either the Alliance Party should accept that loyalists had to police their ceasefire, or it could not penalise them for failing to do so.

A ceasefire is a military operation. The authority of military leaders is required to maintain it. Those leaders may be people who are enemies of the state; they may be people who have ordered or conducted the murders of hundreds of people in terms that we would wholly abhor, but when they have taken on the job of containing their own murderous followers, through the authority they have acquired over those people by leading them to murder, then our interests in them are reversed. We are concerned now that they should succeed.

Brain Surgeon was working for us now.

'You got all that shit from the police,' he said.

'No, I read it in a book.'

'Shut up. I have got the text of what you wrote.'

'I know, I sent it to you.'

One of Bobby Storey's friends had told me that Bobby was angry with me, and I had passed the script on to him so that he could see that the piece was at least a thoughtful one. I don't mind debating my points with people, if they will listen, and I have often trusted republicans to listen and argue back without losing the rag. For example, I had written previously that the notion of the republican community as disempowered was nonsense, since the whole world was waiting for it to make its mind up. 'Actually, that is right,' one republican said to me, 'though I never thought of it like that; but where you always go wrong, Malachi, is that you make no allowance for circumstance. You talk as if republicans contrived all this themselves.' Storey was in no mood for a debate.

A few weeks later another journalist was talking to one of Storey's friends and asked him why Storey had leaned so heavily on me. Storey's friend said, 'I guess Bobby doesn't like Malachi thinking he is free to come and go in this area when he knocks the Provies so much. Coming from the area, people would expect him to have a bit more understanding.' I have heard this before. It tires me. It presumes that anyone who grew up around the IRA, or with

3

the IRA around them, would learn to see things their way. Either they would cease to rest their political convictions on moral principles, in the same way we all did when we relied on Brain Surgeon to police the ceasefire, or they would find moral certainties of a new kind, that would allow them to stand shoulder to shoulder with the killers. Either they would discover that there were no rights and wrongs and that IRA members were at least no more reprehensible than anyone else, or they would find a greater evil in the state than it normally displays in middle-class areas, and would understand how the options of republicans were limited to the tragic but self-sacrificing course they had taken.

I hadn't bought either of these propositions. There was an obvious paradox for me in that it was usually apologists for the IRA rather than the IRA themselves who argued that they had no choice but to conduct themselves as they did. It became part of the common lore that these were people who had suffered, been humiliated and angered, and who were striking back out of their hurt and rage at the British army or the RUC. Rarely did republicans make such a case for themselves. They didn't want to be pitied as victims; they wanted to be regarded as politically astute and purposeful. So they rode on a support base that had a contrary image of them to the one they indulged themselves.

The meeting I had gone to in the Felons club, that night, showed just how reasoned and methodical republicans were in their approach to politics. In a club like this one, which you could only be a full member of if you had served a prison sentence for the republican cause, members of Sinn Féin and the IRA spoke openly, expecting to be answered only by people who were broadly in sympathy with them. Republicans were asserting their commitment to their cause and weighing the political demands of the moment against their need to conserve their resolve. They were going to be pragmatic in their dealings with others, but they were going to stick firmly to basic principles. They were going to form political allegiances to serve their own advantage, but they were not going to let others set the pace of change for them. Nor were they going to accept anything that smacked of defeat.

4

The main speaker at the meeting was Gerry Kelly, there to present a lecture to the Bobby Sands Discussion Group. Kelly was a leading member of the Sinn Féin and IRA talks team that had been meeting with government officials and ministers for six months now. A former jailbreaker who had been extradited from Amsterdam with Brendan McFarlane, Kelly had a reputation for sitting in on those meetings with the British and saying nothing. People said he was scary.

His lecture that night was like an exposition of holy writ. He took the famous lines from Bobby Sands the hunger striker: 'Everyone, whether republican or not, has his or her own part to play.' They are mundane words, the sort of thing a team coach would use, but Kelly derived from them the authority of the republican movement to work alongside constitutional nationalists in the SDLP. Spoken by Sands, the words sounded as if they were meant to extend campaign inclusiveness to the weak and the weary. They said, You don't have to be a street fighter or a political wizard to take part, because every little bit of effort helps. They said also: This campaign is bigger than the republican struggle, so even those who disagree with us should get involved for the sake of saving lives. We are doing God's work here, and even if you can't measure up to our commitment you should give us some little bit of help. Kelly was using the words to explain something that Sands could never, in his day, have envisaged. At the end of the hunger strikes, with Sands and nine other hunger strikers dead, the IRA prisoners described the SDLP as 'imperialist lickspittles' who had 'occupied their time trying to make political gain by attacking those who did genuinely endeavour to end the issue honourably' (Campbell, McKeown and O'Hagan [eds.], *Nor Meekly Serve My Time*, 1994). But now, in 1995, Sands's words offered the key to explaining to republicans that working with the SDLP need not amount to a sellout.

Kelly spoke also about the talks with British officials around the demand for a decommissioning of IRA weapons. He said that he would be going back up to Stormont, the talks venue, again the following week. He would be putting on that coat again, he said. That got a laugh. He always wore a trench coat reminiscent of the traditional image of an IRA man, and the joke and its response acknowledged that he and his audience enjoyed the symbolism. There would, he said, be no decommissioning, of any kind. That was his frank promise to the audience.

Several questions were raised from the floor, some of them by people anxious that republicans were diluting their old tradition, and Kelly did his best to assure people that nothing of the kind was happening. I was looking for some sense that republicans were preparing the minds of their followers for the inevitability of a political compromise, but I got no sense of that at all. I knew other journalists there who believed the ceasefire was the end of the IRA's campaign. They believed that the people of the Falls Road and other republican areas were being deceived by the IRA about the scale of the real political prospects before them; that the republicans' new political allies in the SDLP and the Irish government had got it right, but that nobody had had the heart to admit openly that the party was over. As far as I could see, people were being given an unrealistic sense of what was available to them, and would be outraged with those who blocked the way to it, rather than with those who had fostered their high expectations.

Maybe republican leaders had accepted by the time of the 1994 ceasefire that the campaign had run its course, but had found a new vitality and a new value to the violence as the peace process advanced. The bomb at Canary Wharf which in February 1996 ended the ceasefire had far more impact than any bomb before it, and the force of that impact derived from the shattered hopes of millions. No bomb before had ever darkened the hearts of so many people. It was the peace prior to it that had made it so powerful.

There were sceptics in the audience that night, but they were not doubting the will of the IRA to sustain a ceasefire; they were doubting that the current strategy would produce a British withdrawal. None of these sceptics seemed deterred by the fact that Brain Surgeon, the policeman of the ceasefire, who had been named in the *Sunday Times*, was present at the meeting, drinking with friends at a neighbouring table. Whatever dark thoughts troubled his mind about the journalist a few tables away, many people there felt free to air their doubts, perhaps for the first time, before the republican dignitary on the platform. Was this strategy taking us to a British withdrawal? Could the SDLP be trusted not to ditch us? Would the people be humiliated? If I had been an IRA leader in that hall I might have been angered by all these theorists in a bar, debating whether I should go on risking my neck. Bobby Storey there had just been released from a long sentence, and was still on licence. Eighteen months later he would be arrested for allegedly bombing Thiepval barracks, an attack which brought the IRA campaign back home to Northern Ireland. Was he not wondering why he should be throwing his own life away, let alone so many others', for these critics of the movement? There was some organic connection between these speakers and the IRA, so that republicans sympathised with the fears of speakers from the floor, and speakers from the floor easily assumed the right to require further violence from the IRA, if they thought that was in order.

Not that the audience could be perceived as a strong moral pressure on the IRA to stick to its guns rather than settle terms short of a united Ireland. It was hardly representative of anything more than a sympathetic base. People with opinions strongly divergent from those of the republican movement were not expected to be there, certainly not in significant numbers, though there were often journalists or members of other political groups at meetings like this. Some republicans, like Bobby Storey, presumably thought that critics of the republican movement should be told to stay away. That was why he had me in the corner. What right had I to be there if I was only going to go away and criticise?

Republicans have mostly accepted that they have no power over some people. Their control is geographically circumscribed. What Storey did in attacking me was exceptional behaviour. For instance, once I was recording interviews in Newry near a republican parade against crime in the area. It was a transparent propaganda stunt. Two men who had been ordered out of the town under threat of a kneecapping had taken sanctuary in the cathedral. The republicans were out to show that they held the moral seniority. I moved with a tape recorder among the women supporting the parade, but no one

7

would speak to me because a tall thin man in a brown leather jacket hovered over me wherever I went.

'You are preventing me from doing my job,' I said.

He bent over and yelled at me: 'You are an anti-republican.'

'Since when was that a crime?'

I walked over to the Sinn Féin man who had organised this parade. He was one of the smart young ones. He looked like a student. I told him I was being harassed and asked him to call off the thug. The student explained that people were very angry about an article I had written. I accepted his criticism and he assured me there would be no further trouble. That is their way of doing things, usually. That afternoon I was walking through Newry when I was suddenly surrounded by police asking for ID. They had clearly been concerned to find out who this little man was who mingled with republicans and who barked back at tall threatening people.

There was no point in trying this on with Bobby Storey. He would have hit me hard if I had answered him back, at least that's what he said he would do, and I believed him. So I stood back against the wall, and held my peace while he told me what rubbish I was. Someone walked past and glanced at me to see what was going on, then either thought better of intervening or trusted that if matters were in Bobby's hands then all was as it should be. Bobby told me that I was taking information about him from the police. I was one of a group of slugs, and he named two others, who were in the pockets of the police. Then he told me he wasn't going to hit me, but he wanted me to know what he thought of me. I soon did.

And I felt small and humiliated. Intimidation works: it makes you timid. I have known this since my schooldays. Anyone who ever said, 'I'll wipe that silly grin off your face, O'Doherty', usually did. Violence awakens the self-accuser. It sets your mind to absolving the abuser and to finding flaws in yourself that explain his behaviour. And in that state of mind – as you do – I asked myself if I was wrong. I don't feel that every turn of my life that directed me away from joining the IRA is to my credit. I have been pulled from my house and kicked down through the garden by a soldier. I saw that soldier standing in our living room screaming back at my

8

mother who was screaming at him, she in her nightie, he in a uniform with a rifle and a blackened face. I had been stupid. I was drunk and blew a whistle out the window to alert the neighbourhood that this man and his men were crawling through our garden. I should have had more sense. He kicked the door in. Why did I not resolve to kill him or his kind afterwards? Was it because I was wiser and could grasp the larger context, or was it just because I had a job to go to the next day? Was it because I had a perverse and squirming obsequious streak in me that would own up to my own awfulness and defer to authority rather than accept the burden of knowing that some people should have their power taken away from them?

After my encounter with Storey, I walked down the Falls Road feeling I had hacked at my own roots, deserted my own people to violence and disgrace, even joined in berating them, all for a failure to remember where I came from and to identify with what they had suffered.

Next day I pulled myself together. Isn't it awesome how a fright will shake your convictions?

1 PERSONAL AND POLITICAL BEGINNINGS

This book attempts to unpick some of the mythology of republicanism. Its conclusion will be that the success of the IRA has been in the prevention of agreement between the SDLP and the Ulster Unionist Party. Republicans have not succeeded in creating a united Ireland, but they have succeeded in closing off, until now, all other options for settling the constitutional problem and bringing peace.

Republicanism was an unfortunate development, an anachronism, the wrong course for dealing with Northern Ireland's problems, because it was absolutist and because it shut off for far too long the prospects of compromise. Gerry Adams has frequently explained that the ceasefire of 31 August 1994 was brought about as a *quid pro quo* for talks, and he blames the then British government of John Major for the failure to initiate talks in the months that followed that ceasefire. One of the obstacles to talks had been the set of preconditions established by republicans before they would sit down, so the hedging over creating a talks process was at least as much Sinn Féin's as anyone else's. They only wanted talks that had the potential – they would say the 'dynamic' – to end partition – they would say 'to move the situation forward'. We will come back to this.

Before I get to that point I want to look back at some moments in the history of the Troubles and pick off a few other myths: the myth of the IRA as a defence force for Catholics; the myth that the IRA is a guerrilla army engaged in war; the myth that they are the voice of a community; the myth that there is tension between the political project of Sinn Féin and the military enthusiasm of the IRA. This book will not be a history, but a discussion of purposes at different stages.

Before I go further, I have to go back. This is to sort out my own feelings, so that you, as reader, can at least separate out what you think is reasonable from what you think is unreasonable. If you know my baggage, and the inclination of my prejudices, then you can take them into consideration in weighing up my ideas. I won't pretend to have no such prejudices, but I will make an honest effort to disclose them.

I have a long annoyance with the IRA for the way they treated nonmembers like me in the housing estates of west Belfast. I resented wee lads of sixteen, moving into safe houses near me, taking me out of a car at night, sometimes with a gun in their hands, to demand to know where I lived and who was with me. I resented the pressure to take part. A couple of days after that incident in which a soldier kicked in our back door and dragged me down the garden, a local IRA man approached me and said, 'You know, Doc, some people here are saying you're not pulling your weight.' I loathed the thought of entering hierarchies in which gruff people could tell me what to do. Others of course were completely at ease with that. Being part of an organisation that gave them a gun made them important.

I feared and detested the army more than anyone, but I thought that the best way to get rid of them was to stop shooting at them. There was at least a selfish logic in that.

And I was at an awkward age, anyway, when all this started. Many of the new IRA were younger than me. Those who led them were a little older. I wanted girlfriends. I wanted to work. And my politics were about shaking off the influence of traditions impressed on me, including republicanism and Catholicism. I had already started working some things out in my head, and this revolution round me was irrelevant to any of it.

Anyone who wants to try to explain how Northern Ireland turned so violent after 1969 has to take into account the fact that it was not violent before that. I will try to recall the feel of those peaceful days through a little autobiography.

I was brought from Ballycastle to Belfast as a small child. Riverdale, where we lived then, was a mostly Catholic housing estate close to the Protestant Finaghy Road. When we arrived there, the estate still showed traces of the Second World War. There were Nissen huts at the end of the street. There was a filthy grey waterhole that the children of the area called the Dam. My brothers and I soon pressed down a safe passage through massed coils of barbed wire between the Dam and the fields, and we would scramble through to tease the odd tethered goat.

Life was peaceful then, but there were clues to the problem that were conspicuous enough for a child to pick them up. Life was normal enough for the several policemen who had been housed in our street to travel to work on bicycles. They all left when the Troubles started. My naïveté about sectarianism frequently embarrassed my mother. I remember once coining a cowboys-and-Indians game around the IRA and the Black and Tans. She hurried me into the house to instruct me in the basic rule of life that you don't do that kind of thing in front of Protestant neighbours.

It was Belfast that taught me that being a Catholic with an Irish name would be a problem. Sometimes we would go down the Falls Road, either to meet friends of my father's or later when I helped the local milkman. The common remark of older people when told my name was, 'Sure the wee lad would be better off with a number.' It was an elementary item of folk wisdom that you would be discriminated against when you were older and went looking for a job. Similarly, people would frown on my ambitions for education by saying, 'Sure, in this place it's not what you know but who you know.' We learned an early sense that we had a right to be wary of the state, and not just because it was a Protestant state, but because those Catholics with power couldn't be trusted either.

The Derry republican Mitchel McLaughlin has spoken of his sense that he was discriminated against as a child within the Catholic education system. He was a bright, lazy child, he says, who passed his eleven-plus without exertion, but that in itself did not prepare him for the grammar school. In an interview with me he said, 'The thinking was that I would be wasted in the grammar school, that I would be better off with the Christian Brothers; that they would knock some discipline into me. And as a result of that, some other boy, who was not so bright, had the way cleared for him into grammar school, perhaps to become a teacher or a priest. I have always resented that.'

The working-class people of the Catholic areas were stratified by the Catholic education system. Families that were noted as good families that produced vocations, for instance, would have the way smoothed for them, perhaps at the expense of the rougher families. Father Michael Collins, who was parish priest in the Bogside in Derry at the Long Tower church, and had a number of confrontations with Mitchel McLaughlin over issues like funerals of the IRA dead, admits to being from the other side of that Catholic social divide. 'I became a priest,' he told me, 'almost because it was expected of me. I was from one of those families that produced vocations. I would say the question was almost not even asked of me. I just followed a course that was laid out in front of me.' I was streamlined too, away from the danger of having to do an apprenticeship, away from resentment, perhaps away from a future inclination to political violence. Whoever chose to put me in the 'A' stream of a secondary school effectively determined that I would one day vote for the SDLP.

McLaughlin reflects intensely on how it was that he as an intelligent child had his life mapped out in front of him towards manual work and long periods of unemployment, and he leaves no doubt that it is in large part his anger at that which made him a revolutionary. I was brought up to believe that study would clear a way for me, and that the disadvantage facing Catholics could be defeated with hard work and application. In that sense, I was being conditioned towards accepting Northern Ireland and playing a part in it, rather than towards resisting it or begrudging it. At home, we did not talk much about the cause of Ireland or discrimination in the North of Ireland. I think there was a sense that Catholic disadvantage was an embarrassing truth. If you dwelt on it too long, you would do something rash and be even worse off. We would be brought up to try and get ahead without paying any attention to this problem. Others, of course, would be left behind.

There were times, however, when we had a very clear sense that we were at odds with the state, and even at risk from it. I remember once the police coming along and telling me to put out a smoky grass fire in our front garden. My father asked afterwards what they had wanted: 'Why don't they mind their own bloody business,' he said. On another occasion, when we were small, on a trip to Donegal we approached a checkpoint of B Specials at the border. The B Specials were a reserve constabulary, heavily armed but regarded as less professional and more tetchy and sectarian than the ordinary police. My father turned round and told us to sit quietly and say nothing. He was afraid that some smart-aleck remark from me or my brother would land us all in trouble. It was all right to be sceptical of the state when you were at home or in safe company, it was quite another to challenge it directly.

So you might play with the policeman's son but you acquired an early sense that he had no automatic right to intrude in your life when he had his uniform on. One child of a policeman took me up to the family's back bedroom and together we tried to fire his father's pistol into the back garden, but with no luck. I remember that I was disappointed to see that the hammer of a real gun was pointed, not flat like that of my cap pistol.

My mother's view would have been that you must always respect the law, even when you knew it was Protestant and dis-criminatory. It was better than having no law at all. She would probably have been a law-abiding person if she had lived in Iraq, and she would have expected her children to be the same. She had been a smuggler in her youth, but now saw it as one of the respon-sibilities of motherhood to inculcate a respect for order and authority.

In many ways the boys I grew up with were like the generation of 1916, the Christian Brothers boys working as clerks who felt entitled to run the country, but who would never get a chance.

Tom Garvin has written the best book on this theory, that status envy was the motive force behind the Irish revolution – status envy combined with the machinery of the Irish Republican Brotherhood (IRB), which had then been in place for fifty years. It was the tradition of the Brotherhood that gave shape to the aspiration of the clerks and shopkeepers and which defined their goal as a republic. It was that commitment to a republic that ensured that they would never get all they wanted. It was a goal pitched impossibly high, yet its very unattainability would preserve that Brotherhood into successive generations, to be born into a sense that the job was still unfinished. Pegged to the impossible, they survived. Movements that get what they want, or lower their standards, fade away.

The potential for revolution in the 1960s seemed dead. There was an IRA, but it was small. A republican culture lapped around us and fired up momentary enthusiasms, but I don't think it was a directing influence in my own life. As a small child I wrote to the Pope and asked him to pray for Irish freedom. He didn't reply. When I read boys' comics with their stories about plucky squaddies in the Western Desert I wondered why there were no stories about the Boys of the Old Brigade.

I did not acquire much republicanism at home. Some relatives who visited us occasionally were very committed to the idea of a future united Ireland, and scoffed at the British, but mostly at the Protestants and the Stormont government. We read old songbooks and tried to put tunes of our own to songs about dying rebels and comely Irish maidens rejecting the advances of British soldiers. This wasn't politics. It didn't translate into anger. It contained a suspicion of the state, but that was tempered by wishfulness and ambition. Things had to be changing in our generation. We had to believe that this was possible and to take the opportunities that arose and not question them too closely.

In our last year at primary school, our teacher marked time by filling us in on some Irish history. I was very keen and wanted to bring in some books I had read, Dan Breen's *My Fight for Irish Freedom* and an account of the life of Seán Treacy. My mother said I shouldn't; these weren't significant figures. She thought they were more of a disgrace to Ireland. They were the men who went out and shot Royal Irish Constabulary (RIC) men in the back. They were contemptible, not like Collins or de Valera, who were heroic figures. Even I could have told her that Collins wouldn't have got far without the hit men.

As a boy, I would make my own gunpowder. It was very rough stuff. I didn't get the proportions right or grind it properly, so it never exploded; it simply flared for a while. I made Roman candles rather than bangers. Other boys told me they knew how to make a proper explosive mix. They knew yet another boy who could make a bomb. He was in the Fianna, the youth wing of the republican movement from which members of the IRA were recruited. The formula was exchanged around the street, and I decided to try it. I bought the main ingredient, in a white paper bag, from a chemist's shop on the Andersonstown Road, for the price of a quarter of brandy balls. The man who owned the shop was well used to providing for chemistry sets. I mixed the stuff with sugar. A few of us lit a fuse to it at the foot of a tree in a field beside Finaghy Road North. The mix burned for ages. I watched and wondered if the tree would burn through and fall over. In the end there was a thick effervescent sludge. Several of the boys I went to school with later joined the IRA. I doubt if any, except perhaps one, could have foreseen that. One or two others joined the British army or the RAF.

When I was twelve, at the end of my first year at the Christian Brothers secondary school on the Glen Road, I went to the Gaeltacht with boys from school and shared a small bedroom with seven others in bunk beds. One night the discussion turned to de Valera and Michael Collins, and I argued for Collins against a boy who said he had sold out. We were contesting the principles that drove the Civil War, forty years after it had ended. I must have absorbed my arguments at home from someone. I said that de Valera had sent Collins to do what had to be done, and without having the stomach to do it himself. I remember the *bean an tí* was very pleased with me. My mind was made up on the anti-Treaty Provisionals well in advance of them.

Many loyalists have spoken of their sense that they were

hoodwinked by the Unionist Party into voting for people who had little interest in their material welfare. Glenn Barr has said, 'They could have sent a donkey down the Shankill with a Union Flag wrapped round it and we would have voted for it.'

I think Catholics should acknowledge where they were hoodwinked too. While kids in English schools at our age were being told that their education was a right won for them through working-class struggle, we were being assured that it was a privilege bestowed on us by the Catholic Church, to which we would always be indebted. The fact is that the Catholic Church colonised the provision of education for the perpetuation of the faith, and in some sections of it, for the perpetuation of nationalism. We weren't given the option of free education that left you free to make up your own mind about your place in the world. We were conned. Education for us was not a liberation but an enslavement.

It is impossible to quantify what effect the Christian Brothers had on the fostering of a republican culture and the actual creation of the Provisional IRA. In the research into the spread of militant republicanism in Ireland at the start of the twentieth century, many writers have wondered what made the difference between areas of concentrated activity and areas that were relatively dormant. Peter Hart's article 'The Geography of Revolution in Ireland, 1917–1973' says that one of the best positive correlations he found with militancy was the percentage of boys in each county being taught by the Christian Brothers. This point is aired by Joost Augusteijn, in *From Public Defiance to Guerrilla Warfare*, as if it is merely a quaint anomaly in the statistics, proving nothing. Maybe that is what it is, but the same correlation would undoubtedly show up in any study of the first generation of Provisionals in Belfast.

Brother Walshe teased us all for being West Britons, not really Irish at all. On one of those school occasions when you have to bring in your birth certificate, he pointed out the harp on the top of mine and presented me to the others as the only real Irishman there besides himself. Many of the Christian Brothers were republicans, and they taught a simple nationalist version of history. Patrick Pearse, the martyr who anticipated his own blood sacrifice in the Easter Rising, was indistinguishable from the saints in the way he was revered. The paradox, as I recall, was that the boys of unfree Ireland were held in some contempt by the republican Brothers, who you might have expected, given their worldview, would have pitied these unfortunate children, and bolstered their morale for a future struggle against discrimination. There was a feeling that those boys who sang songs about Raglan Street, or even the belle of Belfast city, were letting themselves down. It's shocking to think now that people who grew up in the city and loved it were being sneered at for their mannerisms, their dialect, and their delusion that the Irish revolution would not be over until it included them. That's how it was.

Brother Gibbons was a sickly thin man with a voice like a crow's. He would vacillate unpredictably between warm humour and vicious temper. We were always wondering what mood he would be in. It was taken for granted with him and others that mood could change like the weather. Gibbons was an actor, who affected a bent, stalking posture, who loped around the classroom with his stick, berating us in Irish. We were *amadáin* or *lúdramáin*, fools and idiots. He taught religion, Latin and maths, and he was an absolutist. There was one true faith; to discard it was a certain path to hell. He, more than anyone, imposed a total ban in the school on what he called 'foreign games'. He would watch from the window when he saw boys chasing a ball in the yard to make sure that they kicked it up into their hands every so often, and didn't just play at ground level. He would have gone out to them with his stick if they didn't handle the ball. The man was a lunatic.

Wee dark Brother Beausang directed a huge effort to turn all Christian Brothers boys into Irish speakers. He ran the Fáinne meetings at the Ard Scoil on the second Sunday afternoon of each month. The Ard Scoil was a musty hall in Divis Street. We would sit in rows in front of him at each meeting and he would talk virtually unintelligible Irish at us, and we would pretend to each other that we understood more than we did. We were made to stand and sing the same two or three songs as if they were hymns, and then we were let loose on each other for the second half of the meeting which was always a *céilí*. A little man with a limp called Ducky Mallon would weave among us and teach us the steps. I only remember one word from these *céilís*: *luascadh*, 'swing'. Ducky would lurch to one side of himself and point us towards our partners, then with his arm out and his finger to the floor he would jerk a circle in the air as if he was trying to flip us into motion the way you would spin a top, or crank the engine of an old car.

I was keen to speak Irish. By the age of fourteen, I had a silver Fáinne, and I had been to the Gaeltacht and got to a level where I could converse roughly. And I loved to dance. I met my first girlfriends at the Fáinne meetings and the *céilís*. A paradox, looking back, is that the Christian Brothers turned out to be so helpful in arranging for us to meet girls, though the sexual morality they espoused was completely unrealistic.

Wee Brother Beausang, or Wee Bo, did not espouse radical republicanism. If anything, his agenda was to make us feel more Irish by getting the language and culture into us, rather than to turn us into revolutionaries. He had a favourite speech about how a nation was not really a nation without its language. France had a language, England had a language, but what about Ireland? *Gan teanga, gan tír,* without its tongue it could not be regarded as a country. We probably took him very seriously then, with his unthought-out notions that state boundaries should follow linguistic boundaries, and that the way back to statehood for orphaned nations of old was to relearn the language of the past, already a failed experiment within the Irish Republic. Most of those who went to the Fáinne meetings, being serious, bookish teenagers, went on to teacher training colleges in Belfast and Manchester, and if they came back they probably formed the backbone of the SDLP, rather than of the republican movement.

But for the Christian Brothers schools to have an effect in moulding a future generation of republicans, it wasn't even necessary that those schools taught the traditional yearning for a revolution against British rule; there was already a marked correspondence between traditional Catholicism and republicanism, as if they shared the same template.

Republicanism and Catholicism are both about the reward for sacrifice. The true Catholic and the true republican give up their ordinary lives to heroic self-sacrifice for the attainment of a promised land. For the Catholic the promise is of an eternity of bliss, for the republican the promised land is the republic, a new Ireland which is imagined to be the restoration of a pure and ancient Ireland, uncontaminated by British influence. For the Catholic, particularly the pre-Vatican Two Catholic of the generation that educated the current republican leaders, and for the republican, the goal of the promised land can only be attained through a complete rejection, on principle, of compromise. Compromise is defeat or surrender, it is never a path to victory.

The senior leaders of the IRA in 1972 were men of strong Catholic conviction. Billy McKee, Seamus Twomey and Seán Mac Stiofáin belonged to a generation that was nurtured in its faith at a time when Roman Catholicism regarded itself as the one true faith. The younger members of the leadership, Gerry Adams and Martin McGuinness, were Catholics educated by the Christian Brothers.

You have only to watch Gerry Adams in operation at a Sinn Féin *ard-fheis* (annual conference) to see the mannerism of a Christian Brother on him. He walks in and the crowd noise falls to a hush. He says, 'Would someone at the back open a window please, it's a bit stuffy in here.' He holds himself with the stiff bearing of a Christian Brother and speaks direct from his script. His first few paragraphs are in Irish, as a mark of homage to the language itself. Then he repeats the point in English. He delivers with gravity and a wooden bearing. When he diverts from the script he stumbles. Occasionally he fires out a caustic line to the side of him, perhaps at the reporters. He allows himself to make some tritely absurd points: as when he said that Sheena Campbell, shot dead by loyalists in the bar of the York Hotel in Belfast, had, 'make no mistake about it, been killed because she was a woman'.

He has the moods of a Brother Gibbons: game to spar with words sometimes, determined to let you know another time that you cannot depend on any familiarity. Other republicans might meet you at eleven in the morning with the smell of stale drink on their breath. Adams is not like that. He is the massgoer, the clean and tidy one, the head boy, the one whose roots in the republican movement precede the upsurge that drew in the mass of angry young lads. He has inherited the faith. Gerry Adams is a working-class romantic. He lives in a fantasy world in which the poor are an ideal and noble people like his brave mother. He wrote in *Before the Dawn* that he sees Ballymurphys wherever he goes. 'They all have one thing in common. Hardworking parents, even when unemployed, doing their best to give their children the best possible opportunities.' This is the working class that Gerry sees around him, the people who rise above the problems of poverty and preserve their dignity. The people who lose their dignity, or who see little choice but to squander it, are invisible to him. The thieves and alcoholics are not real, and they are certainly not part of the real community.

Republicans regard themselves as fundamentally decent, community-minded people. They have become the arbiters of who really belongs in the community, in a very real way: if you don't belong they put you out. They are great believers in punishment too. Many accounts of kneecappings tell of young men lined up in a queue, waiting for their bullet, or reporting to the Sinn Féin office to be dealt with. The similarity between this treatment and the form of discipline imposed by the Christian Brothers is inescapable to anyone who knew it. The worst of being caned by Gibbons was the wait for your turn as you watched bigger boys before you crumple weeping over their thrashed red hands.

Both republicanism and Catholicism in their histories of martyrdom accept that death can be part of the struggle. Failure is negated, because to die in the assertion of your belief is to advance your cause. The enemy is cheated just as sin is cheated, or the devil is cheated. Both are perfect counters to any worldly realism that says that what you believe is irrelevant and what you do is unproductive. Both are immune to the suggestion that compromise would be more expedient, because both gain more in total defeat than in compromise. In fact, for each, compromise is surrender, and death on a point of principle is victory. There is no argument against those

21

who believe that, and no price that is high enough to buy off their commitment.

Catholicism and republicanism offer a form of immortality in the memory of those who honour the martyrs. Many republicans in Belfast wear medallions engraved with the image of Mairead Farrell or other republican martyrs, as other Catholics wear similar medallions bearing the image of the Virgin Mary or one of the saints. There is always a community of practice and ritual which supports the believer. Bobby Sands became a virtual saint, as Patrick Pearse had seven decades before him – proof that the old ways of transforming someone into a memory in the hearts of millions were still functioning. They have to function. Republicanism sustains itself, in part, for the work of respecting the dead. It knows the need to do that. If the cause collapses, there may be no one left to tend their graves or honour their memory. Conversely, if people forget to honour the dead, the cause will collapse, and scepticism is as close as a neighbour.

Though republicanism and Catholicism both sustain a core belief, founded on inflexible principle, they both draw allegiance from a wider range of people who do not adhere strictly to that principle and who are not even expected to. The faith in the republic or the afterlife is regarded as fundamentally true, and those who stray from it are regarded as fallen, deluded or lazy, but they are not disowned. To a republican, a constitutional nationalist is merely an imperfect republican who might yet return to the fold, just as for a priest a lapsed Catholic or a sinner is merely a stray who can be brought back in. For the apostate republican as for the apostate Catholic, there is always a community that understands better where you truly belong.

Republicans are the holy orders of nationalism. Those who attain to that status make sacrifices for the others, as the most devout of Catholics retain the purity of the faith that the others observe less strictly. The constitutional nationalists are trusted at least not to be ungrateful for the sacrifices of the republicans. They may not be able to share in the ardour and principle of those who are prepared to kill and die, but they are believed to retain in their hearts an undeniable attachment to those who do. They are all one family. The degree of annoyance created by condemnation of the IRA is an indication of this. Many people regard such condemnation as one-sided and hypocritical, and they see it as lending succour to the political enemies of all nationalists.

In 1966, when I was fifteen, there was a big revival of interest in republicanism, awakened around the fiftieth anniversary of the Easter Rising. Many of our neighbours hung out the Irish tricolour. We had a moth-eaten cotton tricolour in a drawer upstairs, and I wanted to hang it from a window, but my mother wouldn't allow that. It would spoil all our chances of getting jobs, was I a fool altogether?

On Easter Sunday I stood on the stand at Casement Park, above what had been my classroom some years before, and waited to watch the parade arrive. Some of my schoolmates were down on the field. One was running about waving a big tricolour. This was great mischief, to be running wild with a flag that was illegal outside that ground. The green, white and orange tricolour, ostensibly representing peace between nationalism and unionism, was regarded as provocative and dangerous in the little northern Orange state. My schoolmate saw me and waved up at me, and started to chant his rebel instinct. 'Celtic! Celtic!' he shouted.

I was a more bookish republican and I hadn't a clue what this was that was coming out of him, or why he should link the fight for Irish freedom to a football team, let alone a Scottish one. There was nothing about this in anything I had read.

Around the time of the 1966 celebrations there had been small bomb and petrol bomb attacks by the IRA in Belfast. The IRA had released a statement announcing that they would light 'fifty candles' to commemorate the Easter Rising. One of these candles was a petrol bomb thrown at a police car in Commedagh Drive, Andersonstown. Another was a small bomb thrown, for symbolic effect, at the Belfast GPO. The man who threw that bomb was a British army deserter who later told me that he had intended becoming a Christian Brother; on his way to do this, he had passed an army recruitment office, and on an impulse he had walked in and joined up. His father had been a republican, but he rebelled against that. In fact, he says he was not a member of the IRA at the time he threw his bomb but joined when he met Joe McCann and others in prison.

What has amazed me over the years about the boys who joined the IRA was that the influence of the Christian Brothers seemed to be all over their language and ideas. Reading Gerry Adams's *Cage Eleven*, and coming across accounts of the men in the Long Kesh internment camp singing the Irish-language children's songs we were taught at school, was like discovering an immediate connection with their lives and mine, except for one glaring fact: that many of the men who took the language seriously in prison were among the ones who were least interested in paying attention to the Brothers in school. It was the ones who had confronted the Brothers and defied them who went into the IRA, which I suppose is another way of saying that it was the ones with gumption.

It was as if the arrival of the Troubles awakened some delayed emergence in them of the effects of the conditioning drilled into them at school, at a time when others, like me, were leaving it behind.

In 1968, the first generation of boys in the school I went to were leaving for their first jobs. They became clerical assistants at Stormont or in the City Hall. They became telegram delivery boys for the GPO, and they were very proud of their little red motorcycles. Their brothers had apprenticeships to plumbers and sparks or publicans, but they were like a generation that expected more. They could imagine that they had entered a huge government structure where work was secure and promotion potentially endless. The places where they were going to work were government places, the last places their families expected them to thrive in. They were to be Castle Catholics. They would come home from work to tell tales at the dinner table about whole days spent shuffling paper or counting paper clips, and everyone around them from their younger brothers to their grannies would tell them they were codding themselves if they thought they would ever be given responsibility or power. 'They'll give the real jobs to their own.'

The boys told stories about the 'saved' people they shared offices with. The 'saved' fascinated them. For one thing, they broke the first rule that the boys had learned at home, that you don't discuss religion with people from the other side. The saved were people who had seen the light and knew they were going to go to heaven when they died. I doubt if any of us, in our Catholic environment, had ever considered that other Christians held beliefs so far removed from our own. For one thing, we had been taught that Protestants were people of lesser religious commitment, not greater. Our religious culture taught that you got into heaven by doing good to others. The saved seemed crafty skivers who bypassed the need for that. They were regarded as perverse and arrogant. At work they were crawlers.

My mother started work at about this time as a nurse in the City Hospital, picking up a career she had left to have children. One day she came home in a state of fatigue more fraught than normal. Later, nearly in tears, she blurted out what had happened. A patient had pushed her away with the words, 'You can get off me, for you've the mark of the beast on your brow.'

This was just puzzling. She might as well have been a returned missionary reporting on a completely alien culture. On another occasion I asked her to tell me more about these people who could spot the mark of the beast even on a washed face.

'I'll tell you this, I never met one of them but wouldn't court a brush,' she said.

The saved had come to be easily castigated among us in the way that foreign cultures are, particularly when they are perceived to be at an advantage within the system. They added to the impression, or at least served to embellish an impression, that the world of available work was an inhospitable, alien place. The stereotypical saved worker in the office seemed to be saying, I've got my promotion already, because God's looking after me.

The boys in work didn't complain about getting a raw deal. Most of them were disposed to think well of their new circumstances and bragged to those of us who stayed on at school about the money they now had.

What was happening in the working class of Britain at this time was that education was splitting communities and families. The process is described in Richard Hogarth's *The Uses of Literacy*. The educated child had interests that the parents could not follow. The father, as much as he had studied himself, had been helped by his own father, but children were now learning more than their parents ever did at school. There was a fissuring of the working class, not just between children and their parents, but between brothers and sisters who went different ways. One brother would do the apprenticeship that was expected of him or take that civil service job, while the other prepared for university and a profession.

In Northern Ireland this fissuring was delayed, at least among Catholics. Young people started off towards the changes that education brings, and they stalled. A generation was spared the normal fissuring caused by education, and many of the bright boys became the articulators of working–class anger, while staying with the less ambitious and even giving them work to do for the cause. The generation after that broke through the barriers against them, and suddenly there was a profusion of young Catholic solicitors.

There was a bottleneck in the promotion of young Catholics. Many eagerly sought out the jobs that education would give them and were horrified by the sectarian culture that this admitted them to. Others simply balked at the prospect of a life of humiliation. Gerry Adams was one of the boys who squandered his education and settled for a job without prospects. He was a grammar school boy who became a barman, as Martin McGuinness, clearly destined to be the master of many, became a butcher. Mitchel McLaughlin went to work in a factory. That whole first generation of Provisionals was full of men who had already undersold themselves, probably for lack of faith. Richard McAuley, who later became the press officer of Sinn Féin, is clearly as competent in the eyes of the world media as the press manipulators of any multinational company, political party or government. Even the rebellious ones outside the republican movement like Eamonn McCann and
26 Bernadette McAliskey, though conspicuously educated and

thrillingly eloquent, had disappointing experiences of the academic world and left without degrees. I speak in sympathy with that experience because I went through it too.

A sanely organised society would have had room for these people in the running of its universities, its broadcasting companies and its civil service. They were told by the Christian Brothers and others to shape up and get on with it. The undercurrent of the culture they lived in was the incessant message that they hadn't a chance.

Most of the first generation of IRA men active in the present Troubles joined only after the violence on the Falls Road in August 1969. Few had foreseen a career in republican activity, but some had. These were the boys who had been with the Fianna scouts for years. Gerry Adams was one of these, and he describes some of the Fianna camps in his autobiography *Before the Dawn*. Gerard McAuley, one of the first to die, had been a Fianna boy.

There was a boy called Brendan in our class who was a republican. He was probably a couple of years older than the rest of us. He had black hair and dark shadowy down on his face when he didn't shave. He was more a man than a boy. Another older boy called Peter and I were his closest friends at school. Brendan was a very serious and competent man, even at seventeen. He had the air of someone who had trained. He was physically very fit. We often skived off classes to go to the Farmers' Inn up the Glen Road for a drink. You would ask him what he wanted and he would say, 'A beer'. And I thought him very cool for not expressing a preference. Brendan had a little car with a sticker on the rear window that read SHJC. I asked him what it stood for. Sacred Heart of Jesus Christ, he said. In fact, it stood for Sammy Houston's Jazz Club. One day in the study room during a free period I made some mocking remark about republicanism, thinking he would go along with it, and he turned on me and said I didn't know what I was talking about.

After the conflagration of August 1969 he turned up at my home with Peter and took us to the Felons club for a drink, the old Felons club down a lane near Milltown Cemetery. No one had seen Brendan for weeks. In the club he was received like a hero, by many other people who had not seen him recently either. They came over and shook his hand, they hugged him and they congratulated him. Somehow in the previous weeks, Brendan had won the admiration and affection of Belfast republicans. I could only guess at how.

Then there was Tony Henderson. Tony had been in the same class as me since we were eleven. His nickname was Hen. I got a good laugh at his expense once in the gym, waiting for him to take his turn in front of me swinging on a rope. 'Come on, Hen, or are you chicken?' We were put in the same room together in a house in Donegal when we went to the Gaeltacht. Tony's mother had died about that time, and he was very low. I was homesick, and getting a lot of sympathy from the women in the house, while Tony was sulking away down the garden at the back, much more in need of a hug than I was.

Hen transformed himself over one summer and came back to school with winklepicker shoes on, ready to fight everybody and getting no takers. He left school as soon as he could, and sometimes I would meet him on the road and chat to him, and his talk was all about girls and drinking. I got evening work in bars in town, and on the bus I would see him and his friends going off to a pub for a few drinks before going on to the Marquee dance club. I doubt if there was anything remotely political about him then.

I should have gone to his funeral. It was one of the first appearances of an IRA escort accompanying a funeral cortège. Tony died in a shooting accident in a training camp in the Wicklow hills. I don't know the details, but Hen was a hero and at his funeral an escort including old classmates, in black berets, marched in formation with his cortège. A Sinn Féin *cumann* in Lenadoon was named after him.

I did not comprehend the changes that were taking place in Belfast. Many of the people closest to those changes were close to me also, and I was familiar with the cultural context out of which they emerged, so perhaps I should have known. I understand A.T.Q. Stewart's point. He says that the return of sectarian violence in 1969 was like the crashing of a leviathan from the nineteenth century up through the brickwork of the Falls Road. I associated my incomprehension then with the feeling I had had since I was five years old, that I was an outsider in the city, but there was more to it than that. There is a part of this that an outsider to the republican movement cannot be expected to understand: how a small number of people in a virtually dormant republican tradition provided the pattern for a huge sustained response to events, so that they themselves became the central problem which all political effort afterwards would try to solve.

Gerry Adams has given his own account of that transition period in his autobiography and in some of his short stories. He, like Brendan, was one of the pre-1969 men. The amazing thing about him and the closest people to him is that they started the Provisional project as little more than boys, and that they stayed in control of it for three decades at least. Men born to expect discrimination and a life without shape or purpose made their own purpose and worked long enough at it to earn the company clock.

It was soon clear that violence generated violence. Every calamity produced the anger and hurt that would fire the next. The shock of the police attack on the Derry civil rights march of 5 October 1968 produced the eagerness among many to participate in the student march to the centre of Belfast the following week. The disillusionment with the police led to them being seen as an irritant at parades rather than an agent for order. A year elapsed between the first parades and the arrival of the army, and in that year the trouble round parades got progressively worse, so that by the end of it the Catholics and the Protestants and the police had all drawn guns on each other.

This process began with a levity that now seems almost impossible to recapture. It was exciting to be challenging the state and testing limits against it. It was an extension of the normal youthful challenge to parents, teachers and Church. Catholics did not know what they were up against. They did not know that Protestants would not come out and join them; many thought they would. Paisleyism, as it was called then, was encountered with the

29

presumption that it was a form of quaint lunacy. With a wave and a laugh it would all be dispelled.

But the crisis deepened in horribly foreseeable stages. I was at a rally on the Falls Road one day around April 1969. Afterwards, as people straggled home up the road, someone in the crowd said that two policemen had been beaten up. There were attacks on post offices because, as in the 1966 attack on the GPO, these were symbols of British rule, all that could be found of an imperial presence at that time. An ambulance inched up the road through the crowd and a man in a frantic state lunged forward near my shoulder and heaved a lump of stone through the front windscreen, cutting the driver's face. For what? Someone said the ambulance was being used just to smuggle peelers into the area. I don't know. There is always a rationalisation available for lunatic actions. There always would be. People would learn the habit of trawling their minds for a reason for the most unreasonable things, so that nothing would be left unaccounted for that might warrant a moral judgement against the angry violent people.

After the Apprentice Boys parade of 12 August in Derry, there was intense fighting between the police and many people in the Bogside area of that city. Old footage of this makes it look more like an intergang riot than a dispassionate effort on the part of the forces of the state to restore order. The best accounts of it are in Niall Ó Dochartaigh's book and in Eamonn McCann's *War and an Irish Town*.

It spread to Belfast. I had a Protestant girlfriend at the time, called Jackie. I set off into town with her to see her onto her bus out to Rathcoole. Because of the disturbances, our bus was re-routed down the Grosvenor Road away from the lower Falls. Our minds were on anything but the rioting, and when we walked along King Street and saw a water cannon, with slats for windows, lumbering along Divis Street and turning, I think it looked absurd to us.

We stood and looked up Divis Street at the riot outside Hastings Street police station. Jackie was contemptuous. I said she had to understand the background to it. She laughed at me. People did this kind of thing because they wanted to and because they thought they could get away with it; it was as simple as that. I left her at the bus station and walked up Divis Street, closer to the riot. There was an audience already in place, so I just had to take a position at the edge of it.

We watched a gang of young people throwing stones and bottles and petrol bombs at the police guarding the police station. The police were responding in two ways. First, Shorland armoured cars would wait in side streets while the attacking gang grew more confident and inched closer to the police station in a group. Then the cars would spin out from the side streets and weave among the rioters. A snatch squad would dash forward and grab at any of the men running for cover. The rioters had their own tactic for drawing the police towards them and into danger. Groups of them stood on the roof of Divis Tower, a high block of flats, with petrol bombs. As the snatch squads dashed forward, these groups on the roof would drop bottles of petrol to flood the tarmac and light the vapour with a single petrol bomb following on.

I saw the B Specials arrive with their rifles in a civilian grocery van and go into the police station. A senior officer came out and told those few dozen of us watching that he could not guarantee our safety and that we should go home.

I couldn't get up the Falls Road, so I went down Durham Street and up the Grosvenor Road onto the Falls that way. A group of Americans stopped me. They said they had come from Ardoyne and asked me if there had been any shooting here yet. I said, absurdly, that I thought I had heard people firing blanks. The notion that real guns would come into play just seemed daft.

When I reached the Falls on the other side of the riot I heard a sudden rage of rapid fire. I was walking along the front of the Royal Victoria Hospital, and I thought the first bursts were coming from the roof, though when I had heard shooting a few more times I realised that it's not easy to pinpoint it. Probably what I heard was one of the machine guns mounted on the police armoured cars. I crouched against the wall, then when the shooting stopped got up and ran. A car stopped alongside me and a man pulled me in and drove me home. Further up the road we saw people still waiting at bus stops.

The tactical objective of the attack on Hastings Street was to overstretch police resources so that they would have to withdraw from the Bogside. Gerry Adams gives an account of the thinking behind this in *Before the Dawn*. A meeting, he says, had been called by the leadership of the Northern Ireland Civil Rights Association in the Wellington Park Hotel in Belfast and a tape-recorded appeal from Sean Keenan of the Derry Citizens' Defence Association was played, calling for demonstrations to draw police attention away from Derry.

Adams organised the protest on the Falls Road, to the Springfield Road police station and to Hastings Street on the night of the 13th. He says the Hastings Street protest turned into a riot after it was attacked by the police. Patrick Bishop and Eamonn Mallie, in *The Provisonal IRA*, say that the protests on the Falls were led by a group of civil rights members who were defying a ruling by their leadership that they should not organise demonstrations to overstretch the police. By their account the first use of arms was a grenade thrown by people within this group at Springfield Road police station.

The young people supporting Adams's protest erected barricades and lit fires from kindling that had been gathered for the traditional 15 August bonfires. This, Adams says, was all to draw the police out of the Hastings Street police station. Adams says four or five IRA men with guns were on the streets that night to defend the rioters, and that he personally thought this was madness, because he was afraid that republicans would end up shooting at each other in the dark. The first shooting that night, he says, came from the police on the Springfield Road.

The second night, the one Jackie and I watched the start of, was the more chaotic. Adams himself had gone to work that morning in the Duke of York pub, and left at 11.30 a.m. because the IRA wanted his help with 'defensive arrangements'. Again, he says, he argued against the use of guns because the whole thing would descend into a gunfight which the RUC would inevitably win.

The turning point, in Adams's account, was the descent of

loyalist mobs led by B Specials onto the Falls Road, petrol-bombing houses as they came. The question of whether the IRA should use guns had been superseded by the shooting that came from the police. No one, not even Adams himself, seems to have considered that returning fire would exacerbate things and further endanger the people of the area.

That night and the following day were a horror for thousands of people. Hundreds of homes were burned or damaged by petrol bombs. Refugees from the lower Falls flocked to the suburbs, and schools were turned into relief centres for them. Eight people died, most of them shot by the police. Several others were wounded. (Later, I knew a man from that period, Rocky Wyley, who had taken a bullet through his neck. He was proud to show off the marks on each side.) The army was sent in to restore order: on 15 August young soldiers in helmets and with bayonets fixed marched onto the Falls Road and started laying down coils of barbed wire. That night Bombay Street was burned out. The soldiers were there in time to prevent the burning of Bombay Street but didn't.

That was the psychological starting point of the Provisional IRA campaign, even though the organisation itself did not yet exist. Catholics in Northern Ireland felt suddenly that the terms on which they lived in the Northern Ireland state were made brutally clear to them. For some, the experience of August 1969 is a legitimation of the Provisional IRA campaign; for others that experience at least explains the driving passion behind the campaign, the hurt and the anger and the sense that Catholics had lost their place.

2 FIRE IN THE STREET

We are myth makers. History happens, and we weave it into our understanding of who we are and where we are. The events themselves bewilder us, the story we tell of them is of our own creation. Sometimes this is wilful: a political party determines its line and repeats it until it is accepted as the truth. Every IRA bomb is proof, for the DUP, of the need for tighter security, for Sinn Féin of the need for inclusive dialogue. Words like 'security' and 'dialogue', when used by different parties, have different meanings too, taking us further away from anything like an objective significance of something, if there is such a thing.

Sometimes the story we create from events is an act of faith; people infer from events, and many people infer in the same way at the same time. Why did the IRA call a ceasefire in August 1994? Well, they wanted off the hook, didn't they? Why did they kill two policemen in Lurgan in June 1997, on the eve of an opportunity to get into talks? Well, there must be a split. Why doesn't Gerry Adams condemn the violence? Well, he can't, can he?

The 1994 ceasefire came, some say, because the IRA had had enough, had seen that violence was going nowhere. They had decided to replace the armed struggle with a political strategy. Many fine decent people had come together to show them that there was a political way to achieve their goals; they accepted their word and chose to follow that political course.

Here I want to discuss the myth surrounding August 1969. One of the key questions hanging over it is whether a republican conspiracy moved secretly through the street politics that preceded it to

stimulate a predictable crisis. Niall Ó Dochartaigh's book *From Civil Rights to Armalites* offers much evidence that this is what happened, yet he interprets that evidence with a subjective weighting to tell us that events spun out of control as the state machinery of the police, and later the army, made stupid and brutish decisions. There is a very strong argument that the simple untenability of a divided society became obvious in August 1969. The IRA of 1970 did not exist in 1969, though many of its leaders were active. The embryonic core did not have the power to control and direct events, but it did have the power to influence them. It had rewards to reap from crisis, however, and so it headed wilfully towards crisis rather than resolution.

The turmoil of August 1969 is remembered by Northern Irish Catholics as if it had a clear meaning. That meaning is accepted not just by republicans but by many who oppose them yet who trust themselves to understand the fundamental anxieties that perpetuated the IRA campaign. The meaning of August 1969 by this view is that Northern Irish Catholics need defence against Protestants and against the state. The rioting of those days is recalled as a pogrom in which the state, supported by loyalists, ran wild and attacked and murdered innocent Catholics: August 1969 proved the untenability of the Northern Irish state; it legitimated protest to bring it to an end and armed organisation to defend those trapped within it. It was, in a sense, the Big Bang which generated three decades of warfare.

In 1995, when republicans were asked to begin to disarm at the start of political negotiations, the argument was made, by Father Des Wilson and others, that it was absurd to expect the IRA to leave the Catholic community defenceless; history had taught Catholics that they could not trust the state to protect them. Who else could they rely on, then, but the IRA? But many Catholics – most Catholics – made no effort to arm themselves for defence against loyalists and the state, even after August 1969. The conclusion that some had no choice but to arm themselves seems less simple and obvious in the light of that.

The republican interpretation of August 1969 relies on simplifications. The unproblematic conclusion that the IRA had inevitably to arm itself for the defence of Catholics depends on a reading of those events as a simple clash of Protestant and Catholic, evil and good, strong and weak. In a history written from a position sympathetic to the IRA, Ciarán De Baróid, in *Ballymurphy and the Irish War*, tells the story of those days in a way that extrapolates the lessons that republicans claim to have learned. It is an account of the clash of opposites, of civilised people confronted by barbarians. By De Baróid's account, the rioting on the Falls Road grew out of a spontaneous mustering of people in solidarity with the Catholics of Derry's Bogside. Streetfighters there, organised by the Derry Citizens' Defence Association, had been fighting the police for days. 'The city [of Derry] was burning. The RUC and loyalist mobs had the Bogside under siege . . . poised for what looked like an impending massacre of the people behind the barricades.' The only grounds De Baróid appears to imagine for the loyalists and police wanting to enter the Bogside would be to kill everyone there. Protesters on Belfast's Falls Road sought to lift the pressure of the police assault against the Bogside. They went first to Springfield Road police station, from which they were sent to Hastings Street by the officers in charge, who said that a more senior officer there could receive their complaints. There, armoured cars were pitted against the stone throwers. The protesters returned to Springfield Road. Shots were fired by the police in the police station. Shots were fired at the building by members of the IRA, but the first night of trouble settled down. On the following day, writes De Baróid, the B Specials were mobilised and a mob gathered on the Shankill and invaded the Falls Road through Percy Street and Dover Street. What followed was a concerted assault on Catholic areas, which the people were ill equipped to defend themselves against.

My own observation was that there were several hours of rioting outside Hastings Street police station before the B Specials came on the scene. It was at that point that a senior officer came out of the station and warned spectators to disperse because he could not be responsible for their safety. What was significant about these events, in De Baróid's view, was that the IRA, not the RUC, had failed to protect the people. Out of that failure, it is said, republicans learned that they could never risk leaving the Catholic people without protection again.

The political repercussions of the violence would include calls both for a reform of the RUC, so that they could maintain order, and calls for the IRA to reorganise and provide defence. The more significant of these, by De Baróid's view, was the call on the IRA.

For a republican, this need to defend Catholics is predictable, as the violence itself was predictable. De Baróid claims that two years earlier, some members of the Civil Rights Association had foreseen that their campaign would culminate in a clash over national rights, and that loyalists and the B Specials would turn on them. The invasion of the Falls Road, as he sees it, was the fulfilment of that fear. That loyalists were ambushing in response not to a civil rights protest but to a sustained and concerted attack on a police station seems irrelevant to him. He appears to think that Catholics had as much right to try to burn down police stations as they had to sit in the middle of the road and sing 'We Shall Overcome'. In this book, the nationalist people are viewed as being capable of no wrong, while the entire Protestant working class is regarded as the enemy.

Myth making like De Baróid's is transparent. The flaws are obvious to a critical reader, but it is not written for the critical reader. It is written for the people who see things that way already, to mirror a community's established mythology. But there is a gap in the record of that period in both the popular and academic literature, though those violent nights are detailed in the Scarman report. The prevailing assumption in most accounts is that the IRA had little or no part in the fighting. The IRA of that time was small and ill-armed and it was overwhelmed by the momentum of sectarian violence. These are not flat, meaningless facts, however, but elements of the myth making. The reported lack of arms makes two points: that the IRA cannot be regarded as having tried to lead an insurrection, for to do so they would have had to put more men and guns into the effort, and that they were ill equipped to defend the area, and therefore were right to reorganise afterwards. Both these points absolve the IRA in the popular lore, and in many of the written accounts. They support the argument that republicans were born out of the volition of history and they dispense with the conspiracy theory, much loved by unionists and the RUC of the time, that the IRA planned the whole thing in advance.

The lessons of the period are widely regarded as obvious and in little need of scrutiny. In Tim Pat Coogan's *The IRA*, for instance, the nights of mayhem in August 1969 are passed over in a sentence, as if they simply establish the inevitable cracking of a divided society along an ancient fault line. Most writers, acknowledging that August 1969 was the turning point, see the most significant change as having happened in the minds of the Catholic people of west Belfast. The received conclusion is that these people simply realised that they were defenceless and open to attack from Protestants and the state. Therefore they needed the IRA, and the IRA needed guns.

Brendan O'Leary and John McGarry, in *The Politics of Antagonism*, are among those who see the violence as a further stage of things spinning out of control. Any volition that they see in it comes from 'Protestant mobs and the police [who] attacked Catholic areas, the latter killing six people on 14 August'. The writers say that 'strategically minded Catholic actors' played these events to their own advantage, either to discredit the Northern Ireland state before the British government and the world audience or, if they were republicans or socialists, to deepen the crisis. It seems to me to be a purely subjective judgement whether events are seen as running out of control or whether those who 'play them to their own advantage' are seen as stimulating them. It is impossible to know now if a combined force of police and loyalist mobs would have attacked the Falls Road, had hundreds of people there not been organised by republicans into overrunning the police, but it seems unlikely. Just reflecting on that consideration alone, however, lends some weight back to the discredited conspiracy theory. I will return to this conspiracy theory in Chapter 3.

Paul Arthur, in *Political Violence: Ireland in a Comparative Perspective*, has described the violence of August 1969 as a 'republican debacle'. Certainly it was a debacle for the old guard who had wanted to move into socialist politics and away from the prospects or dangers of a sectarian war in the North. Regarded in strictly military terms it was a debacle for the new generation too, because they were over-run. But assessing success or failure for republicans on the basis of their physical gains and losses is to regard them as an ordinary army at war and to misunderstand their objectives and methods. They may have been surprised by the scale of violence in August 1969 and the political results, but they were to go on to appropriate the dominant interpretation of the crisis and to launch a rapid expansion of their movement on the back of it. This is not what most people think of as failure. Usually an event which provides such enormous validation and stimulation of a new movement is regarded in terms of achievement, victory and rebirth.

Republicans have dwelt on this themselves, through the imagery of a phoenix rising from the flames, and through the slogan that it is not those who inflict the most, but those who endure the most, who prevail. The IRA has long understood that a military defeat can have huge political rewards. Did the ill-armed and exhausted republicans of the Falls Road in 1969 walk away from the wreckage, as the army came in, feeling disconsolate and confused, or were they cheered to see that their interpretation of the Northern Ireland political context was being reaffirmed on the streets, and that they had the makings of an enormous political and military project before them?

They had awakened violence which J. J. Lee described as looking 'dangerously like the genocidal impulses of the Shankill and the Specials'. Lee appears to take his chronology from Coogan and has Protestants rioting in Belfast in response to a claim by Taoiseach Jack Lynch that the South would not stand by, and Catholics attacking police stations after this. The arrival of the army frustrated the 'incipient pogroms'. Lee attributes the extraordinary scale of the murderous response from Protestants, in part, to the demographic spread which put more Catholics at risk.

Coogan returned to the details of those days in his history *The Troubles: Ireland's Ordeal 1966–1995 and the Search for Peace*. He gives his chapter on this the typically florid title 'Letting Slip the Dogs of War'. The centrepiece of this chapter is the text of a sermon given to the confraternity at Clonard monastery recounting the events of 39

15 August 1969, when the streets around the monastery had come under attack from Protestants. In this sermon, Father Paudge Egan describes his increasingly futile attempts to get the police and the army to come to Clonard to protect the church and the people.

Father Egan says that he came upon a man being arrested (probably the IRA leader Frank Card) and that he stood by and watched to be sure that no violence was used against him. The frightened people around about told him afterwards that he had taken his life in his hands; the B Specials might have shot him dead. Five people had already died in the violence of the previous night. Father Egan would have heard the machine guns of the police armoured cars roaring through the neighbouring streets, but he starts his account after that.

'I don't believe that there was the slightest danger of my being shot,' Father Egan said. 'But when I thought about that remark I felt that it was typical of the lack of confidence so many of our people have in the forces of law and order.' He seems not to have shared the perception of others that the Catholics of the Falls were under immediate threat from the police and B Specials, though he was talking about the day after the worst of the killings in what republicans remember as 'pogroms'. He gives another unconscious insight into a prevailing normality on the Falls Road that day before a large Protestant mob assembled in Cupar Street. 'At this particular time of day, three o'clock approximately, the men of the area were at work, as you would expect. So the defence of the area was left to a handful of teenagers, and they did a grand job.'

Father Egan was in the monastery when he heard the first shots of that afternoon. Gerald McAuley lay dying on the road, and Father Egan anointed him. Gerald McAuley is remembered as the first IRA casualty of the Troubles. Bowyer Bell says he was killed in an exchange of fire. Coogan says he was helping to move refugees, and Gerry Adams says he was defending the area. Father Egan's greatest anger was at the Stormont administration, which had apparently advised the army to expect attacks from the Falls Road, and had left the Clonard area with no defence other than 'the local lads who, totally unprepared and ill equipped, and comparatively

40

speaking defenceless, fought against terrible odds, and saved this district from complete destruction'. From this experience, however, Father Egan concluded, not that Catholics needed their own militia, but that they needed to demand justice from the government. He emerged from the experience, that is, thinking like a moderate SDLP voter.

Both Protestants and Catholics remember that period as the realisation of old fears that the other community was organising for war. The Protestant perception of Catholics rising up against the state had calamitous effects. The RUC and the government believed that this was the whole nature of the crisis, and responded to Catholic neighbourhoods not as places in equal need of protection but as revolutionary bases.

Bowyer Bell's later account of the fighting in *The Irish Troubles: A Generation of Violence* attributes it to fantasies enjoyed on both sides: police and Protestants imagining that they were facing an IRA-led rebellion; Catholic stone-throwing youths imagining that the IRA was at their back, when the IRA was a force that was so small it could have paraded in a pub. Misapprehensions, Bowyer Bell believes, prolonged the violence in Derry on 12 August, and misapprehensions caused the escalation in Belfast. In Derry, police insisting on restoring order were perceived as attacking. They either hadn't the sense to see that they could have defused the problem by falling back, or they were determined not to be humiliated in that way, whatever the cost. In Belfast, the Protestant mobs thought they were doing a constructive day's work in supporting the police and B Specials as they descended on the Falls.

It may have been naïve, but it was not wholly irrational for Protestants to suppose that they were faced with a dangerous uprising, when Adams and his friends were besieging police stations. Paddy Devlin believes that the violence from Protestants is explained by their belief that a large-scale IRA insurrection was under way. Ian Paisley approached the Stormont government and offered to put his Ulster Constitutional Defence Committee (UCDC) at its disposal, if it should find that the terms under which it might have to accept army intervention were unacceptable. The government 41 declined the offer, and the Scarman report conceded that there was no indication that the UCDC had participated in the violence which followed. An internal police memorandum indicated that the police at a high level also believed that an IRA uprising was imminent and that they would have to take extraordinary measures to deal with it. Inspector General Peacocke had reported that he had information that armed units of the IRA were about to infiltrate from the South 'to escalate the degree of control over inward-bound traffic' – whatever that means. The support of mobile armed units would be of material assistance in countering these subversive activities, he said.

A view of the Belfast violence from the Protestant side is contained in Steve Bruce's book *The Red Hand*. Bruce's view is that two communities clashed with each other, rather than that one ambushed the other while the latter was ambushing the police. He quotes from an account of the attack on Bombay Street on the evening of 15 August, written by a man who later held a middle ranking position within the UDA. He makes the contentious claim that Catholics fleeing their homes there in fear were the first to set them alight. The sight of this was the signal for an attack.

> The rest of the night was spent burning rows of terraced houses in Cupar Street, Bombay Street and the surrounding areas. The police were powerless to prevent the raging mass's rampage of burning and destruction. I saw one young fellow smash the front windows of a tiny kitchen house with a flag pole and light the billowing curtains. Soon the place was ablaze.

Where this man thought that the police were powerless to hold back his mates, Father Egan saw an army, with orders not to fire, turned towards the Falls because that was where they were told the insurrection was coming from.

Social scientists don't like conspiracy theories, and it runs counter to their thinking to attribute mass movements to the leadership of individuals. The motivation for a Protestant backlash, as understood by Bruce, was a combination of the tension of the night and the growing sense that a republican revolution had been gaining ground through the civil rights agitation, which the government was losing ground to rather than confronting. He might have added that the government and police experience to date was that they lost ground anyway, even when they did confront the civil rights movement, as if their own energies inevitably worked against them. The state, when prompted to show force, always lost the moral argument. That had been the lesson of the first civil rights parade in October 1968, and in many ways that was the basic model that future confrontations followed, whether by contrivance or incidentally, including the one in August 1969. Swarms of Protestant rioters lunging towards the Falls Road that night could only damage their beloved Union and discredit the police force they thought of as their own.

The question arises whether there is any evidence that such an insurgency was under way or in preparation at that time. Most nationalists say confidently that there was no organised insurgency, and they feel that the conspiratorial elements spotted by Cameron and Scarman were too small to be significant. The conspiracy theory is regarded as simple unionist propaganda. It absolves the RUC and the B Specials. It also denies the experience of the thousands of innocent people who were driven from their homes. The conspiracy theory seems to imply that those people were in the wrong from the start, that the blame for the burning of their homes rests with themselves and their neighbours, rather than with the mobs who actually attacked them.

There is, however, a tendency to explain all violence in Northern Ireland as if it emerges simply from the unstable mix of intercommunal chemistry, without anyone actually being responsible. That is as simplistic and shallow an explanation as pure conspiracy theory itself. The appropriated version, though, was not cynically contrived by political manipulators and imposed on a credulous people; it felt close enough, for many, to the truth of what they had experienced. The word commonly used in republican literature to describe what happened is 'pogrom'. This term was not applied at a much later stage by people trying to rewrite history; it was, in fact, used in much of the underground literature produced at the time. Small, single-issue newspapers circulated to promote political 43 interpretations of events, but also to fill a need for a fuller journalism of a community's experience. Much of this journalism, and many of the people who read it, accepted that what had happened was that an armed alliance of police, B Specials and Protestants had attacked the Falls Road and Ardoyne, that those who had suffered on the Catholic side had merely been ambushed. They believed that in so far as Catholics had instigated the violence in Belfast, they had merely been responding to a crisis, building up in Derry, which would have overtaken them anyway.

In some ways it is understandable that innocent Catholic victims would remember the events in that way. They had kept to their homes, waiting for the battle to blow over, and their first experience of it was the attack on their homes by Protestants. There is a painful irony about this too; these were people who were least sectarian among the Catholics of west Belfast, for they had taken housing in mixed streets between the Shankill and the Falls. They were the ones who were least inclined to pose a threat to Protestant neighbours and who had shown no wariness of living among them; yet they were the first to be burned out of their homes and to be forced to seek refuge in school halls in Andersonstown where they would exchange stories of the horror of what had happened to them. Their experience was one, as they felt it, of deep disillusionment.

The Finucane family of Percy Street was an example. They tell their story in Kevin Toolis's book *Rebel Hearts*. The children had been merely puzzled when bigger boys abused them on the street for playing hurley. Their memory of the violence of August 1969 is that the Protestant neighbours simply turned against them.

For much of the previous year, I had been working with my father in a pub on Agnes Street, which runs between the Shankill and Crumlin roads. I was still studying, but I helped out in the evenings and at weekends.

The pub belonged to a Catholic family who lived on the Malone Road. There was nothing to distinguish it from a Falls Road bar but the predominance of people called Billy and the shortage of Seans. The regulars spent all of their Saturday afternoons between the pub and the bookie's. The pub was a second home to them.

On the afternoon of 15 August we discussed closing the bar and getting out of the area. Most of the customers, many of whom had joked and chatted with us on other days, declined now even to speak to us, other than to order a drink. My sister Brid and I walked down the Shankill Road together, taking in with some strange elation the changed character of the city. We went into another pub and had a drink. We wandered freely along the road. We asked directions to the Falls without fear when we missed a turning. The man we spoke to was disproportionately friendly, as if determined to emphasise that he was no threat to us. We stood at the bottom of the Falls Road and watched a detachment of soldiers with helmets and fixed bayonets arrive in Durham Street. Brid said they looked like boys. That night someone burned the pub in Agnes Street to a shell. For years, my father kept a photograph of the burning bar. It had been published in *Paris-Match*.

There were rumours everywhere. People said the ambush on the Falls had come prematurely, that the real plan had been to burn the whole road to the ground on the day of the All Ireland football final when the men would be gone. How would anyone have known that? Who on the Falls would have had such access to the conspirators? After the Shankill bomb of October 1993, I was told in all seriousness by Protestant friends, 'The IRA sent Begley the bomber out with a short fuse because they wanted him to die. They set him up to die with his own bomb. They wanted rid of him.' The lore that gathers round such events always serves to rationalise them in someone's favour, usually that of the people telling the story. Pick out the implications and you can see whose advantage is served by the story. The one about the secret plan to attack during the All Ireland final implies that the men of the Falls did a good job of defending their road against the Protestant hordes, for it tells you that things would have been worse if the men had not been there. It tells you also that the attackers understood this well, that they had not wanted to face the men but hadn't the patience to wait. It deals with doubts too, for it implies that the rioting by Catholics on the Falls Road, that started off the events of that night, was productive: it coaxed the Protestants into launching their planned attack on the wrong day. And you can't say the whole thing wouldn't have happened but for the violence from the Catholics, since it was going to happen anyway. You can't say that the men of the area wouldn't be up to the job of protecting it, should their activities trigger another clash, when even the Protestants knew it was safer for them to wait. They would have cleared the Catholics off the road but for the resistance they met.

Who was to contradict the mythologies that explained the need for an IRA defence force and for a concerted political campaign for justice? There are simple reasons why nationalists of all shades leave the apparent legacy of August 1969 unchallenged. Constitutional nationalists and republicans are traditional rivals, but each find affirmation of their position in the events of August 1969. Constitutional nationalists do not contest the details of the events but point to that and later violence as evidence of a fundamental political malaise, for which they prescribe the solution. That solution is not the simple one of a British withdrawal or the abolition of the RUC such as republicans prescribe. Constitutional nationalists say there must be an impetus for political change, of a more complex nature, but also based on an understanding that the state is fundamentally flawed in ways that produce violence. The party is hardly going to question the evidence for those problems existing, if their political agenda is based on the acceptance of that evidence, is based on the sense that Northern Ireland has lost its legitimacy to function in the old way, and if refuting it would undermine their rationale for political action.

This may sound cynical. It presupposes that political parties enjoy the quagmires which they offer to dig us out of. It's not that simple. Politics is about defending an analysis and converting others to a plan of action based on it. The SDLP has no political incentive to detract from its own analysis by rethinking its understanding of what happened when the civil rights campaign evolved into sectarian civil war. Privately, some members may deride the sectarian passions among working-class Catholics that helped to produce August 1969 and, with less embarrassment, the same people will assert their defence of policing; but they will tend to evade both issues in public. They are kept in line by the moral force of the tradition that the Catholics are victims and the police are monsters. They feel perhaps that they would lose working-class support if they seemed to be soft on these issues.

Nearly every political force in Northern Ireland today, including the modern RUC, was born out of the seismic eruption of August 1969. When it was founded, the SDLP was a coalition of political forces, fired with the need to reform Northern Ireland into a place in which Catholics could be secure and have political dignity. The Provisionals are viewed as a product of the same felt need. They are a product of circumstances, by this view, and whatever else they may be blamed for, they are not to be blamed for the conflagration within which they were conceived.

Both strands of northern nationalism have passed down a mythology about August 1969. Both are unconscionably lazy, at least, in how they recall that period.

John Hume gave a summary of the events of August 1969 in his address to the annual conference of the SDLP at Cookstown in November 1993. This was less than a month before the signing of the Downing Street Declaration by Albert Reynolds, the taoiseach, and John Major, the British prime minister. Hume's point in referring back to those days was to reinforce the argument that the Provisional IRA were not criminals or evil, but had been born out of the violence of that time. He was making his point 'not to concentrate on the what-aboutery of the past, but to point out to those masses of Unionist people who want peace, the hypocrisy of those Unionist politicians who say that they refuse to talk to the SDLP because I am talking to Gerry Adams'.

Hume was not simply reinforcing the fundamentals of his political philosophy by garnishing it with a flimsy dash of history. He was attempting to persuade Unionists of the meaning of the events of August 1969, so that they would understand why he had to negotiate with Gerry Adams and why they should also negotiate with himself. He said he was also restating history to show that unionism had had its own relationship with violence, and one that was very different from his own because it was for destructive rather than for constructive purposes. He wanted his own association with republicans to be seen as a creative initiative for peace, founded on the realities of Northern Ireland's past.

History, for Hume, is part of the political discourse, so why does he allow himself to get it so horribly wrong? His restatement of history, in his appeal to the unionist people over the heads of their hypocritical leaders, was this:

> When Terence O'Neill moved gently towards a more just society in Northern Ireland, the first violence of the last quarter of a century emerged to bring him down. The Ulster Protestant Volunteers did so with the use of bombs – the Silent Valley, Ballyshannon, etc., and the first member of the RUC to be shot, Constable Arbuckle, died on the Shankill Road. Then in 1969 during the Civil Rights Movement when the Official IRA declared a total abandonment of violence, a DUP Member of Parliament came with a mob onto the Falls Road, burned Bombay Street to the ground and killed nine innocent Catholic residents. Out of that shameful attack was born the Provisional IRA.

The chronology and weighting of events is skewed here. Does it matter that there was no DUP in 1969, or that Victor Arbuckle was killed after the burning of Bombay Street? It does, if the point in mentioning it is to add to the list of atrocities contained within the Protestant reaction to the civil rights movement. It's clear enough – isn't it? – that when Hume refers to the Official IRA, he is actually referring to the pre-split IRA, and not to the section that became known as the Officials after 1970. Neither of those groups, though, ever declared 'a total abandonment of violence'. And, of course, no one died in Bombay Street, but several died in the rioting that preceded the burning of that street, one of them only hours before it.

When Hume is convinced of the central importance of these events and of their lasting significance, why does he summarise them so inaccurately? It is almost as if they have so comprehensively passed from history into mythology that the actual details are unimportant compared to the retained meaning. You would think from this account that unionists alone were to blame for all violence that preceded the creation of the Provisional IRA, and that they were to

48

blame for the start of the IRA campaign too. Even when attempting to address unionists and invite them to face the past out of which modern problems grew, John Hume insisted on a version of history that apportioned blame to one side only. Of course, in arguing from myth like that he was doing nothing unusual in the context of Northern Ireland politics.

3 BACK TO THE CONSPIRACY THEORY

I cannot counter myth with truth. The greater certainties that I have are about things that I have seen, but even the meaning of these has changed on reflection. For instance, I was astonished and puzzled by the emergence of political violence. Others older than me, with a memory span that went back to previous episodes of sectarian warfare, predicted with ease what would happen, found it all familiar. It is strange to think that some folk memory was at work to bring it all about, and it is strange to try to reconcile that with the fact that so many of the people who joined the mayhem were so young. Carlo Gébler has written of his sense that modern people in Northern Ireland are well clued into the violent ways of past generations. Things were handed down. A.T.Q. Stewart writes of the same phenomenon. Once things got out of hand, people seemed to know what to do.

Part of this handing down is the political tradition of republicanism. The links are easily traced. Tom Clarke, who helped lead the Easter Rising of 1916, was an old Fenian from the 1880s. IRA men active in the years following the revolution of 1916 went on to guide campaigns in the 1930s and 1940s. Men of the 1940s campaign guided the young Adams, took to the rooftops of the Falls Road with what guns they had.

The stepping stones back into the origins of republicanism are not difficult to trace either. The methodology of republicanism is familiar to anyone who reads the history of the Whiteboys (the agrarian bandits of the eighteenth and nineteenth centuries), the Land War or the war for independence. The consistent element is usurpation of the state through imitation of the state. Whether it was a Whiteboy by night imposing an oath of loyalty and secrecy on a farm boy, or the audacious de Valera asserting his right to the presidency of the republic imagined by Pearse, the common thread was a style of mocking and disabling the established authority with parody.

Provisional republicans recall events within the context of a longer freedom struggle dating back a century and a half. Where John Hume might say that the Provisional IRA was born of the ashes of Bombay Street, Provisionals themselves are more likely to say that a longer-term revolutionary effort, which had been almost dormant, was given a new direction or impetus by the lessons of August 1969.

In much of the literature of republicanism, the Provisional IRA's revolution is viewed as continuous with the preceding civil rights campaign. The claims of unionists that there was a republican agenda to the civil rights campaign are not refuted within the republican tradition but endorsed. Critics within nationalism of the republican movement would say that the republicans are claiming the credit for something they only played a small part in, and validating their struggle by claiming wider populist roots for it. Unionists make the connection between republicans and the civil rights campaign for a different reason. They see the connection as discrediting that campaign and proving that there was a secret agenda all along. The violence of August 1969, say republicans, crystallised the issues, but since it was a unionist response to demands for civil rights, it was but a battle along the way. That is how Gerry Adams recalls things in his autobiography.

A simpler republican account of events is contained in Sinn Féin's 'History of the IRA', published on the Internet. This traces the progression from the civil rights movement to the IRA campaign:

> The emergence of the civil rights movement in the mid-1960s was to transform the political situation ... In Belfast and Derry in 1969 nationalist districts were attacked by the state police, the RUC, and by unionist mobs ... Once more the peaceful pursuit of change in the form of the civil rights movement had been met with violence

from the British state and so it was that the armed struggle gained predominance again as the republican strategy.

So, had the civil rights movement met with success and reforms been granted within Northern Ireland, had the Protestant invasion of the Falls and Ardoyne not shaken republicans to the core, there would, by this version, have been no re-emergence of armed struggle. The fight for a united Ireland would have continued, of course, because the meeting of civil rights demands would not have fulfilled the republican aspiration, but that fight would not have been fired in the same degree by anger and humiliation. The question that arises here is whether the sectarian riots of August 1969 were provoked by republicans, more intent on fostering civil war than they have ever admitted, or whether the validation of a return to armed struggle that they found in those events was something they stumbled on inadvertently while attempting a peaceful transition to a new form of agitation.

The pre-split IRA is remembered by Provisionals as having diverted its energies into socialist politics and agitation for civil rights. De Baróid and others who recall that period are clear that the IRA then had no intention of entering an armed revolt. Yet that same IRA was growing and training more energetically than at any time since the end of the fifties campaign. How is that fact to be reconciled with their having been taken by surprise, unarmed and unready, in August 1969? Was the IRA genuinely caught on the hop? The riots had grown out of protests initiated by republicans in Belfast. They were predictable, to a degree, in that previous protests and managed riots had drawn in loyalists before. Not to have foreseen the possibility of a huge escalation seems to have been incompetent and irresponsible. That, of course, is the case made against the IRA by the defectors who formed the Provisionals.

According to Adams, the impetus for the Belfast protests of 13 August was an appeal from the Derry Citizens' Defence Association. But the call was made by Sean Keenan, a well-known local republican: thus, the call for the protest had come from one republican and was heard by another republican. Moreover, Eamonn

McCann, who was a member of the Derry Citizens' Defence Association, says in *War in an Irish Town* that he was annoyed that the association had been set up by republicans and that they had hogged all the positions of leadership before inviting others to join. So the plan to organise protests in Belfast was hatched within the republican movement and the leadership of the protest was provided by the republican movement. It's not hard to read some kind of plot into that.

Niall O'Dochartaigh says that the republican commitment to preventing violence was minimal, as indicated by their failure to provide stewarding for their protest against the Apprentice Boys parade that started things off. He writes: 'It does not seem unreasonable to suggest that they saw 12 August as an opportunity to bring the very existence of Northern Ireland into question.'

In a current edition of *War and an Irish Town*, Eamonn McCann says that the objectives of the defence association were to keep the peace, or to defend the area if the peace broke, but in 1969 he wrote in his *Barricade Bulletin* that a victory had been won over the Unionist government. McCann wasn't one of the republican organisers of the protest, but he was close to them as a member of the Derry Citizens' Defence Association. He seems to have had little sense of the implications of involving other areas in the fight. He says that he took it as encouragement that fighting had broken out in Belfast and elsewhere. Later when he heard the details of the carnage he wrote: 'It sounded very different from Derry, inconceivably horrific.'

The IRA was clearly not initiating a war that it had any power to fight. It was provoking disorder in the hope that someone else would sort it out. Clearly they must have had a strategy – either that or they were fools – but there can have been no place in that strategy for an open clash of arms with the RUC or with the British army, otherwise they would have had more guns on hand.

The opportunity that had presented itself, or that seemed to have presented itself, was to bring the Irish army into the North. Bowyer Bell notes that the Irish government had suggested, in Taoiseach Jack Lynch's speech, that should events cross a certain line into deeper crisis, his government would take action. There were also suggestions in the air that United Nations forces might come in. Either way, there appeared to be a huge prize available to the insurgents for extending the rioting in Derry and beyond. Bowyer Bell declines to reason from this that some people leading the rioting might well have felt that there was here a tenable prospect of overthrowing the Stormont government.

Many of those rioting in Derry believed that Irish troops would come over the border to relieve the Catholics and confront the RUC. That appeared to be a tenable objective after Lynch's speech. It seems reasonable to assume that some people at least could have taken that as an invitation to extend the rioting. McCann writes:

> On the evening of the 13th Mr Jack Lynch appeared on television and said that he could not 'stand idly by'. Irish troops were to be moved to the border. This put new heart into the fight. News that 'the Free State soldiers are coming' spread rapidly.

The prospect may have been a long shot, but even a republican who seriously doubted Lynch's rash words would have been tempted to take a chance on a sudden and unprecedented opportunity to revive the historic enmity between Ireland and Britain. None of this suggests that the civil rights campaign was part of a protracted strategy for bringing the Irish army into the North, but after that year of deterioration, a moment arrived when it seemed possible to do it. You don't need a long-term conspiracy theory to explain why the IRA might have taken the initiative to push Northern Ireland to the brink of chaos when half a century of southern Irish indifference had seemed suddenly to start evaporating.

Conspiracy theories suggesting a longer-term preparation for war were revived at the beginning of 1997 with the publication of cabinet papers under the thirty-year rule. The disclosure of Stormont government papers from 1966 showed that the RUC Inspector General, Sir Albert Kennedy, had been warned of likely attacks by the IRA. Republicans had been expected to sow confusion during the 1966 Easter Rising commemorations and to shoot members of the Crown forces. A letter by Brigadier Bill Magan congratulated the RUC for managing the danger well and averting a crisis.

Magan said that movement of weapons in the previous year, 1965, had indicated preparations for a period of violence. One of the measures he thought had averted serious trouble was the closure of the border on Easter Sunday 1966 and the cancellation of the morning train. This seems naïve. What sort of revolution comes by train and is stymied by a change in the timetable? If Magan regarded the IRA as so incompetent that they needed public transport to function, he also seems to have overestimated their military capabilities.

Nationalist politicians at Stormont were highly sceptical of statements from government about the danger of an IRA uprising, but in 1966 the intelligence reports made available to the British government by its intelligence services carried the same message, that the IRA was reorganising and rearming. On 7 April 1966 the government in London was presented with a six-page report detailing the level of IRA threat. Scotland Yard had estimated that three thousand members or supporters could be drawn upon by the IRA in an emergency. British army units would have to be on hand to respond to IRA violence around the Easter commemorations, or in the weeks after them, and the danger for government was that they would be wrong-footed into acting like the instigators of trouble. Troops were moved to Northern Ireland, but the government was anxious that this move should not be seen as provocative. The government at the time was drawing on reports also from the office of Terence O'Neill, the Northern Ireland premier. O'Neill's office had notified the Home Office of thirty-four IRA training camps allegedly in existence in the South, half of which had been established in the previous eight months. O'Neill did not believe that the Irish government could be ignorant of these camps, and he wanted the Home Office to call on the Irish to do something about them. If these assessments were realistic it is difficult to accept that the IRA was winding down and that it was virtually unarmed three years later.

The split that was to follow the August 1969 riots was already in progress before the riots. It was a clash of personalities within the IRA army council and a clash of ideologies, with some members coming under the influence of communist advisers and others, more traditionalist, insisting on retaining the old goals and methods, and with deep animosities opening up between the two factions. Bishop and Mallie say, however, that there were only about sixty IRA members in Belfast at the start of 1969. That's half the figure that Henry Patterson offers as an assessment of IRA strength at the time. A former British soldier who provided arms training for the IRA members in Belfast says that there were thirty IRA members at most. 'And I should know, because my job was to get round them all.'

Patterson is sceptical of the common dismissal of the IRA under Goulding's leadership as deluded by socialism. He says the IRA, as Goulding envisaged it, would be 'the armed guarantor of the social and political gains of a revolutionary popular movement'. The IRA, therefore, wasn't going soft, or losing sight of the need to hold weapons and train guerrillas. It was, however, committing itself to working for social transformation through legal political means, with a view to having a military role afterwards. It was losing members who were bored by the political training and was learning that military exercises were necessary to keep new members interested.

This was a period in which the IRA was recovering from its decline and enhancing recruitment, though many of those who joined and took training did not stay with the IRA for long because they did not get what they were hoping for, a war to fight. In that the IRA was expanding and the leadership had conceded the need to keep recruits fresh with gestural violence, Brigadier Magan's assessment was a sensible one. It included the observation that such violence as might come would be sporadic, rather than the commencement of a new campaign.

If the IRA in the mid-sixties was not demilitarising then demilitarisation cannot have been the grounds for the disillusionment of Northern members, as was suggested by Ciarán De Baróid and by Danny Morrison in his book *West Belfast*. Patterson suggests that the point of disagreement was not over whether the IRA had an armed role to play, but over what that armed role would be. The

IRA's leadership was concerned not to get drawn into a sectarian war in the North. Des O'Hagan of the Workers' Party, whose sympathies went with the Officials after the split, says, 'This is what the hatred of Goulding was all about. By standing up and saying, We are not going to get involved in the North, he was annoying the bigots. There is no way Cathal was going to introduce a new campaign in Northern Ireland.'

Some republicans undoubtedly saw the prospect of greater violence in Northern Ireland as providing an armed role for the IRA. O'Hagan argues that the development of the Provisionals started before August 1969. Ruairí Ó Brádaigh agrees that the broad outline of the division within the IRA was clear from about 1965. In fact he claims that the training camps in 1966 that alerted the Stormont government and British intelligence to the danger of renewed IRA violence had actually been established to help restore morale after those divisions had become visible around a debate on abstentionism. The former soldier who provided arms training for the IRA in Belfast says that he was one of those who saw the danger of a conflagration and urged the IRA to prepare for it. 'There were people with a bit of foresight, and I would consider myself one of them. I could also foresee that the message wouldn't be lost, and our word would be put across, because the media were showing interest. Even before August '69, there were a few individuals you could predict would not stay with the leadership.'

De Baróid says that in the summer of 1969, as the rioting increased in regularity and intensity, 'community leaders' again approached the Belfast IRA to ask for assurances that their people could be defended. He claims that the Belfast IRA turned to Dublin and were told that no weapons were available because they had been sold to Welsh nationalists. This showed the decline of the IRA under the influence of communists, he believes.

Ó Brádaigh says that there was debate on whether or not the IRA should work for the immediate overthrow of Stormont. 'There was a feeling within revolutionary theory, that Stormont was like a rotten door that only needed to be kicked in. Its day was past. It had not renewed itself. Goulding and the others did not want to overthrow Stormont but to work for reform as a phase of the struggle.'

Stormont would be overthrown through political action which exposed its contradictions. Might those who advocated this course not be tempted to draw Stormont and the RUC into a fight to expose their brutality and sectarianism? 'No,' says Ó Brádaigh. 'That would have been a political course. Military action would have been seen as work for another day, in providing defence for the Catholics if that was what was needed.' He says that he was one of those who anticipated that such defence would be needed, and that he understood this from drawing on the lessons of the 1920s as passed on to him by older members. In the spring of 1969, he says, he had asked Goulding what could be done to defend Catholics. Goulding, to his horror, had said he would 'put that up' to the British army and the RUC.

Ó Brádaigh insists that he and others did not see the need for violence to advance their political programme, but they did want greater military preparedness for the violence that would be directed against Catholics if their political programme continued. The fact that disillusioned republicans provoked an armed response from the RUC and the loyalists, thereby advancing the political programme of disgracing Stormont and the RUC is, he claims, no evidence that this is what was planned or intended. What is his response to the suggestion that that would surely have been a good day's work for the IRA members who were disillusioned by their leaders? 'That was just the momentum of events.'

The former British soldier who had been involved in the fighting on the Falls Road – 'serving the man with the sten gun at St Comgall's school, changing his magazines and chucking petrol bombs' – says the new IRA evolved without central direction, as the coming together of many people acting on their own initiative. 'It grew so fast out of necessity. Defence had to be prepared for. A lot of individuals procured weapons on their own, with the attitude that they would never be left unarmed again. I was one of those people, because even though I was a member of the IRA, I had no faith that the leadership would look after us.' The perceived need for defence, by his account, was not just the rationalisation afterwards of political operators taking over the IRA, it was the very engine driving their accumulation of weapons and providing the material out of which the Provisional IRA campaign would be built.

Joe Cahill, cited by Robert White in *Provisional Irish Republicans: An Oral and Interpretive History*, claims that the arms produced by republicans on the Falls Road in August 1969 belonged to a group of auxiliaries, ex-prisoners who had anticipated this trouble and were disturbed by the IRA's failure to prepare for it. This version diverges from that given by Gerry Adams in *Before the Dawn*, where he implies that the few weapons in the hands of republicans were under the control of battalion staff. Ó Brádaigh says that the weapons were probably the basic stock that would have been made available to a country unit for training, one of each type: 'One rifle, one Thompson, one Sten, one revolver and one automatic pistol.' Bishop and Mallie say that the most effective shooting from the Falls was conducted by a group of older IRA men, 'forties men', who had left the movement disillusioned with its political course but who intervened that night for the protection of the area. According to Bishop and Mallie, the first shooting, from Springfield Road police station on the night of the 13th, was a response to a violent protest led by Gerry Adams, Joe McCann and others. Two people were wounded, and later shots were fired over the heads of the mob besieging the station to disperse them.

The legacy of August 1969, as claimed by republicans and left relatively unquestioned, is the lesson that Catholics needed defence and that the IRA had to rearm to provide it. Joe Cahill told White that people on the Falls Road had been deeply disillusioned by the IRA's failure to defend them. He says he was spat at in the street by people who recognised him as a republican and who felt that the IRA should have done more to protect the area. This lore entails the assumption that most Catholics trusted that the possession of guns by the IRA would make Catholics safer and that the absence of guns would put them in greater danger. But Henry Patterson concludes from an interview with Liam McMillen that the IRA leadership in

59

Belfast was aware that the use of guns would exacerbate the violence rather than protect Catholics. This contrasts with the view of Adams: in his book there is little sense that return fire against the police could be anything but legitimate and productive. Patterson writes: 'The IRA's use of guns contributed powerfully to the remorseless intensity of the Protestant onslaught in these areas. It was therefore merciful that the IRA's resources were so pitiful.'

It is usually assumed that the violence of August 1969 was not a tenable insurrection because there were too few guns available. It cannot therefore have been the intention of the IRA to overthrow the government. This argument overlooks the fact that a number of revolutionary objectives were available simply as rewards for prolonging the violence. Niall Ó Dochartaigh suggests that the Irish government had intimated that the point at which it would intervene would be after the first outbreak of gunfire – a grand incentive to any IRA man to reach for his weapon. The United Nations had been called on by the Irish government to send in a peacekeeping force. Neither of these prospects was fulfilled, but they had appeared to be within reach; it is therefore reasonable to assume that intelligent leaders of the rioting would have set their sights on them. Did Gerry Adams and Joe McCann think that the Irish army was as good as at their back when they attacked Springfield Road police station and went to war with the RUC? Other objectives within reach were foreseeable and achieved. The police were disgraced, and the state of Northern Ireland was exposed as deeply riven. The government of Northern Ireland was exposed as unable to maintain order or retain the confidence of a huge section of the population. The British army was drawn in, and from then on the republican assessment of the problem as imperial would be easier to demonstrate. All of this may have happened without anyone foreseeing it or having any sense of control over it, but had there been thoughtful instigators at work, a productive course was open to them, and they would have had every right to feel by the end of that week that their efforts were well rewarded.

Another possible conspiracy theory is that the riots organised on the Falls Road by local republicans amounted to a coup within the

IRA. The modernising leadership who were averse to a sectarian war were to have the reins of influence snatched from them, and a sectarian war dropped in their laps.

Little of all this is contained in the myth memory of those days. The central meaning of those nights in August 1969, in the memory of Catholics, is the lesson that they need defence. Still, even in the nineties, it is virtually taken for granted by most political analysts that one of the main reasons the IRA cannot disband is that the people of west Belfast and other areas won't let them: those people would be left exposed to further pogroms, and until the state has changed and there is a system and a police force that those people can trust, they will always need to have men of their own with guns in their midst who can repel the police or the army or the Protestants, should they ever turn against them again.

There was another lesson. Republicans learned again that crisis in Northern Ireland provokes the political imagination of Britain in the search for solutions to the cause of the crisis. That lesson is the most meaningful legacy of that period. Anyone who thinks that the IRA discovered the need to defend Catholics has only to examine how well that job was done in the years that followed.

4 DEFENSIVE OPERATIONS?

The violence of August 1969 was followed by a rapid growth in the IRA. People who had had little conditioning into a republican ethos became committed members of the movement, ready to fight and die for Ireland. The old ideological inheritance of past upheavals was available to explain what had happened now. An old war that had died out in 1962 for lack of interest was almost ripe for resumption. That cannot be explained without reference both to the personal experiences of those who took up arms and to the political context in which violence had erupted. The reaction of the young men with guns was a personal reaction, but it was made possible by an organisation that was in place and ready for them to join. That organisation had very definite ideas about how to use the rage and hurt of the angry boys. The tendency of much comment and journalism is to interpret the whole thing as a social phenomenon, driven by fear and humiliation within whole communities. This is naïve, as naïve as assuming, as some do, that all those angry boys were simply manipulated and intimidated into war.

One of the things that decided some boys to join the IRA was the behaviour of the soldiers. When they came onto the streets of Belfast and Derry, most people were taken by the novelty of it. I was fascinated by the sight of guns. When a foot patrol was stationed near the Autolite factory at Finaghy, a lot of the local children went out and gathered round the soldiers. I was there too, and I asked one of them to show me the naked bullets in the magazine of his SLR, his self-loading rifle. His accent was almost as strange to me as his gun. The soldier seemed puzzled by our curiosity. Perhaps from the start he expected us to hate and fear him. Perhaps he was just bored, or lost for cues from his mates on how to respond.

Many people have written of that early period before the rift between the Catholics and the army. Eamonn McCann says that in Derry, Catholic women squabbled over whose turn it was to make the soldiers their tea. It was the only year in which it happened. Paddy Devlin says that the Catholic people were 'drowning the soldiers in tea, soup and sympathy', and that they felt they were safe without their barricades while the soldiers were there. It was to be a short-lived sensation.

Gerry Adams writes:

> They were 'welcomed' initially because they were seen as relieving a siege ... but it was an uneasy welcome. They got tea in only a few households ... They antagonised whole communities by their behaviour and especially by their attitude to womenfolk. So, while there were initially mixed feelings about the British army, once it became apparent what their role was, all ambiguity went out of the window.

The image of women bringing tea to the soldiers has survived into the nineties with an almost iconic significance. It sums up that moment between the eruption of crisis and the discovery that our whole lives were to be defined by the routine violence of the Troubles; this was a happy period when we felt that we had suffered a shock but might get over it. I can understand why Gerry Adams would want to contest the significance of that image. He wants to say that the revolution was unfolding, that the need for Catholic defence was already clear, that the legitimating circumstances for an IRA revival and the start of a northern war were already in place, and that only a few people were silly enough not to see that. The women with the teapots who linger in the memory still say that, just then, when Adams thought we were faced with the need for war, the common feeling of his neighbours was that the war was already over. The women with the teapots would take some persuading that their sons and husbands had to be armed and trained and sent to shoot the soldiers. They had no immediate sense that 63 any such prospect was remotely justified. Twenty-five years after the IRA first offered itself as the defender of the North's Catholics, Gerry Adams still had to confront the women with the teapots and try to revise them out of history.

When people did begin to suffer doubts about the army, the popular lore says that the women put ground glass in the sandwiches and caustic soda in the tea. All that tells you is that, even then, some women were still giving the soldiers tea and that the political cynics were still trying to rationalise the fact away. It shows that the woman with the teapot had already become the symbol of Catholic acceptance of the army, and that feelings for the soldiers were turning very nasty, but that some tolerance of the army, and the sense that it was needed, worked itself out as sympathy for the bored young men in uniforms who should have been at home.

The disillusionment with the army hit different people at different stages. It had settled on a lot of us well before the violent clashes of the spring and summer of 1970. There were early stresses that would have shown through had the IRA done nothing. Republicans had to work to make sure that the disintegration of relations would fulfil a traditionalist republican vision of the relationship between the British army and the Irish people, but the army would do its own work to show that blithe amity could not last.

I was walking home from a Sunday night dance in St Louise's school on the Falls Road in September or October 1969. We walked in groups because there were often a few rough boys around who picked fights after these things. We were drawn to the sound of shouting up ahead. It was a group of soldiers taunting some of the others who had also come from the dance. I heard the soldiers calling them 'stupid Micks'.

I found that incomprehensible at the time. I had not yet been to England and had rarely been called a Fenian, let alone a Paddy or a Mick. I simply didn't know that kind of racism existed, and nothing in my frame of understanding could explain why it should. Later I would experience much worse encounters with soldiers, and the routine of gruff body searches by men who were sometimes drunk and usually pig ignorant. Those don't stick in my mind so much, perhaps because I felt you could make allowances for men who were afraid and openly at odds with so much of the population. For them to have turned nasty before all that, just for the fun of it, seemed to say something fundamental about the untenability of using these men to bring peace. It seemed a betrayal that when there were problems of social order it was rabble like this that the government sent to sort them out.

The soldiers had come and I had been amazed. On the first days of their being here we had driven down the Falls Road just to look at them. Now, English soldiers calling Irishmen 'stupid Micks' seemed to confirm the republican notion that there was old bad blood at work here; that people who thought like me had come late to this quarrel and were unqualified to pronounce on it.

While the army was disclosing its incompetence to people on the streets, their senior officers, government ministers and media commentators perpetually affirmed the patience and nobility of these fine men. The more the soldiers clashed with the people, the more their virtues were praised in newspapers and in parliament. The product of that was a succinct lesson in what liars these institutions are. It was a quare dousing for youthful idealism.

As the transition to greater violence continued, I felt myself losing my own moral bearings. By 1971 I could, for instance, have been well able to point the police towards men on the run and to the likely positions of stores of arms and explosives. I didn't do that because I didn't trust them to come in and deal fairly. I wasn't siding with the IRA, but I wasn't siding with anybody.

In that period, there emerged a conviction among republicans, I believe, that they could establish moral certainties and moral seniority over the enemy they were dealing with. That sense of moral seniority was always to be a comfort to them. The community in which they were to move would be more amenable to them precisely because it agreed that there was no obviously consistent British moral position. Only the British would ever claim to be in a morally superior position, and the obvious hypocrisy of that would serve almost to absolve those who were more honestly brutal. A condemnation of the IRA couched in hypocrisy and deceit did little to detract from IRA support and much to disappoint and disillusion those who would otherwise have agreed with the need to curtail republican violence.

After August 1969, defence was an obsession. I was at a meeting in Milltown in early September 1969 where public speakers were urging the people to participate in defence. A man approached the platform and whispered to the main speaker. The speaker then announced that 'they are now up as far as Beechmount'. This supposedly meant that Protestant hordes, fighting from street to street up the Falls Road, were getting closer. After the meeting, I walked with friends down the Falls Road, past Beechmount, where there was no sign of any trouble.

The IRA split in two after August 1969, the socialists under the old leadership coming to be known as the Official IRA, and the dissidents becoming the Provisional IRA. There are two versions extant of why they called themselves the Provisional IRA: one says that the word refers to the fact that they were, for a time, a makeshift, literally provisional, handover group, awaiting legitimation, the other says the word is used to claim continuity with the Provisional Government of the Irish Republic declared by the rebels of Easter 1916 in a quixotic unilateral declaration of independence from Britain.

The Provisional IRA claimed in the two years following the arrival of the army that it would not attack British soldiers, other than to retaliate against their abuses of the people. This point was made by a Provisional IRA spokesman in March 1971, and was quoted in the *Irish Times*. It was only later, in a statement from the army council published in *Republican News*, on 30 October 1971, that Provisional IRA chief of staff Seán Mac Stiofáin announced that the movement had formally entered its 'third phase', all-out resistance to British forces.

In the early days of the army's presence in Northern Ireland, the IRA had not felt that its support base would sympathise with them if they opted for war against the British, no matter how well this might have been rationalised in terms of anti-imperialism. The Provisionals also needed time to prepare themselves logistically for what they saw as an armed engagement with the British army, and they did not want to start killing soldiers until they felt that they could maintain a rate of killing and survive. Their antagonism to the army was expressed at this stage through rioting and the tarring and feathering of women who had relationships with soldiers.

Their rationale that the British were imperialist invaders was in place long before events began to confirm it. There were limits to how much hostility they could express against the army on behalf of their community. At this time, they were competing with other defence groupings for support. Until relations between Catholics on the Falls Road and the army turned sour, the IRA would present to its sceptical community its vision of the army as an invader, and for a time that vision would look dangerously eccentric.

By June 1970 posters were erected on the Falls Road warning people not to fraternise with the soldiers. These followed serious rioting in Belfast: in Ballymurphy in April 1970, and on the Falls Road itself when a curfew was declared. De Baróid gives a description of the Ballymurphy riots which is sympathetic to the Provisionals. He describes the behaviour of the local army commander, based at the Henry Taggart Memorial Hall. Major James Hancock had presented himself at the Ballymurphy barricade on three successive days to speak to residents' representatives, and twice he was turned away.

> He met with a number of people operating a relief centre for incoming refugees at St Bernadette's School in the centre of the estate. From then on Hancock liaised with the Ballymurphy community through its leadership [sic] and managed to sustain a cordial relationship with the estate's residents.

The turning point, as De Baróid sees it, was an approach by the army to the residents to inform them that an Orange parade would be escorted through the area. The residents were outraged, and the army tried to assure them that the event would be controlled. When the Orange parade appeared, however, it played loud party music and a Catholic threw a stone at a drummer. 'The events that would lead to an all-out offensive by Irish nationalists against

British occupation forces in Ireland had been sparked off by a single reckless act that had just taken place on the perimeters of Ballymurphy.'

By this understanding of events, the violence was not the product of anyone's planning, but merely an eruption from a community that was handled badly by the British army at a sensitive time. The British, by implication, should have fully accepted the 'leadership' of the community and acted on the instruction from that leadership that the Orange parade should not be allowed through. The response of the army to the attacks on the parade is regarded by De Baróid as an invasion of Ballymurphy.

The community, as described by De Baróid, is a volatile entity which can only be spoken for or controlled by its leaders. It is a seething miasma of violent passions which must be mediated with, through those who understand its passions. Outsiders have no role to play in this. The state's legitimacy is not even open to consideration. The leadership appears to be something that appoints itself, unelected, and is validated by its own assertion that it is attuned to the needs of the community.

The British media, attempting to understand the rioting in April of 1970, suggested that local boys were annoyed that the soldiers had become rivals with them for the local girls. The press also seemed loath to identify political motivation or systematic planning behind the riots. (That tendency to attribute political violence to emotion rather than premeditation survives in the media still. Even twenty-five years later, during riots over the release of the paratrooper Lee Clegg who had been convicted of murdering a joyrider, the *Guardian* was giving credence to the view that the violence was triggered by the summer heat.) Ó Dochartaigh describes the rioting that developed in Derry as a procedure that politicised the young men and directed them towards joining the IRA. I suggest that reading these events as social upheavals without crediting them to some political direction is just as naïve as crediting them entirely to conspiracy without taking social forces into account. The IRA would gain nothing by refuting this thinking which displaces responsibility from the leadership of the rioting to the imagined spontaneous passion of the community. It has been a central part of the Provisional IRA's project to represent its own operations as the passion of the community, and to present itself as the body best qualified to mediate those passions.

Between August 1969 and April 1970, the Catholics of Belfast turned away from the army. This was largely the army's own fault. In the same period, the Provisional IRA armed and organised itself. When attacks on the army grew and the Provisionals and others armed themselves, the friction between the army and the community worsened. Army violence against the IRA and the rioters always had the paradoxical effect of turning against the army those people who had opposed the original violence. That is because the army was excessive. It was murderously brutal.

Gerry Adams traces the disaffection of the community with the British army to 'racism', the army's treatment of 'womenfolk' and their failure to intervene to protect Catholics during attacks by Protestants, on Bombay Street in August 1969 and Coates' Street in October 1969. However, since the initial amity between the British army and the Catholics survived into the autumn of 1969, the burning of Bombay Street, at least, cannot plausibly be accounted a major factor in this disaffection, much as it fits in retrospect into the pattern of disillusionment.

The failure of the army to protect Catholics attacked in Coates' Street was interpreted by nationalists as a lack of will to protect, but others saw it as an indicator that the army was ill-equipped to deal with riotous behaviour. The only tool the soldiers had in their hands at that time was the rifle. Military leaders and politicians discussed just how soldiers were to be armed for confrontation with civilians, if they were to have the power to restrain them by any other means than by shooting them dead. The early answers to that problem were CS gas and rubber bullets.

This was a time in which many community leaders were asking Catholics to take down their barricades, erected during the rioting of August 1969, to put their trust in the protection of the army, and to allow a more normal atmosphere to return to the city. Paddy Devlin was arguing for this, while others were arguing that the army could not be trusted and that the barricades should remain in place.

After August 1969, defence for Catholics was soon on offer not only from the British army, but also from defence committees, from the two wings of the IRA and from the Catholic Ex-Servicemen's Association. The Provisionals would come to gain most support among the civilian groups, and the others would fall away. Most writers on that period accept that the IRA earned its legitimacy from the community through a more credible offer of defence than was available elsewhere. The fact that the Provisionals killed so many Catholics themselves, and endangered their communities by drawing violent forces into further conflict with them, seems not, in the eyes of many, to qualify this simple assessment of the Provos as 'defenders'. In strict literal terms, I think you can only judge the Provisionals as having provided defence if you can argue that more Catholics would have been killed by Protestants and the army if there had been no IRA.

Yet many writers readily accept that the strategic objectives of the Provisionals honestly included the protection of the Catholic community through a readiness to repel any attack on it. That fits with how the IRA leadership presented things too. After the Provisional IRA was established, it defined itself initially as defensive. Seán Mac Stiofáin, chief of staff of the Provisional IRA, wrote:

> It was agreed that the most urgent priority would be area defence ... as soon as it became feasible and practical the IRA would move from a purely defensive position into a phase of combined defence and retaliation. Should British troops ill treat or kill civilians, counter operations would be undertaken when the republican troops had the capability. After a sufficient period of preparation ... it would go into a third phase, launching an all out offensive action against the British occupation system. It was also agreed that selective sabotage operations would be carried out.

It is part of the declared ideology of provisionalism that a republican army must always be ready to defend Catholics, and it is readily accepted by many external commentators that this preparedness to defend Catholics gave the IRA a moral authority or at least won it support from Catholics – this despite the fact that its actual record as a defence force is demonstrably a poor one. In *Fighting for Ireland* the strategy analyst M.L.R. Smith writes:

> PIRA's stock within the Catholic community rose in proportion to the decline in the army's popularity as the movement increasingly made its name as an energetic defence force. Understanding PIRA's defensive role helps to explain how it was able to mount such a formidable politico military challenge in the years to come. The Provisionals derived genuine popular kudos from fulfilling such a *practical* function. [emphasis mine]

C. Townshend shares this view that the validation of the IRA in the eyes of the Catholic community was their ability to provide effective defence in response to a clear demand from the community that it should perform that role: 'The Catholic community recalled the IRA to Defenderism by the unanswerable device of mockery. Wall graffiti simply accused the organisation of cowardice.' This is a bit simplistic. It is inconceivable that the republicans were more moved by what they read on the walls than by what they had experienced in August 1969, or by their life experience of political activism. Defenderism in Townshend's usage refers to the culture of communal warfare going back to the eighteenth century. He is not, strictly speaking, saying that the Provisionals became effective defenders in the military sense, but that they came to function like the old Defenders, representing Catholics against Protestants.

Certainly the IRA must have fulfilled some need in the Catholic community in order to win support from it, but at times the ease with which writers conclude that the need fulfilled was defence betrays a failure to question the matter. Smith recalls Conor Cruise O'Brien's view that the IRA campaign of the early 1970s thrived on 'its simple relevance to the situation'. Yet Smith also notes:

> Some Catholics suspected that the Provisionals were not really aiming to keep away the security forces at all, but were more interested instead in drawing them into Catholic areas so that PIRA could mount attacks, using the population as a shield, while

benefiting politically from the army's successes which the Provisionals themselves had partly provoked.

Smith offers no evaluation of the strength or validity of this argument, referring only to Frank Burton's view, in *The Politics of Legitimacy*, that the IRA might have been able to resolve the apparent contradiction by defining defence in terms of working to get the Catholics into a united Ireland where they would be safer. This is not, however, a strategic understanding of defence. Nor is it the understanding of defence that republicans convey in their own literature. It is wrong to suggest that republicans presented the notion of defence as anything other than the protection of Catholics.

Providing defence as a stage in the development of strategy was to be a means of consolidating a support base from which the state could be attacked. Republicans reasoned that once the Catholic community was secure against Protestants and the British army, the IRA would be free to go on the offensive for a united Ireland. But this only made sense if the community actually feared the army and if Catholic areas could be made impregnable to army intrusion. Bringing the army into closer conflict with the people was easy through provocative action, but physical defence was something the IRA was never able to achieve. Nor, having presumed the need to achieve this as a prelude to an offensive, did their failure actually inhibit them.

It seems the IRA was prepared to accept the increased endangerment of Catholics, and the attendant loss of life, in the furtherance of its political objectives. If defence is protection, marked by the reduction of casualties – and this would seem to be a simply obvious condition of defence – then what the IRA did for the Catholic community was the precise opposite, for it plunged Catholics into a war with the British army and escalated the sectarian tensions in Belfast, putting them in danger from murderous loyalists. Republicans might argue that if they had not been in place, the British army and the loyalists would have swept into the streets around the Falls Road and slaughtered everybody there. That is not an argument that has been seriously made by anyone else in mitigation of what they did.

The fact is that the Provisionals articulated not defence but defiance, and the cost of that defiance was increased casualties among the Catholic working classes. There were times when Catholics in certain areas were angry enough to pay that price for the freedom to lash out at loyalists or the state. The inconsistencies in the IRA's claim to be a defender of the community are evident in the words of IRA man Seamus Finucane, talking to Kevin Toolis for his book *Rebel Hearts* about the events that motivated him in the early days of the campaign.

> The campaign was very destructive with little direction that I would have understood at the time. I would not have been able to understand why the IRA were bombing Belfast city centre, killing Brits or killing policemen. But I knew that the IRA were our defenders, looking after our interests, fighting for our rights. There was a great sense of anger ... There was a sense that this was a time to change things and stop being pushed around, stop being downtrodden.

Seamus Finucane 'knew' the IRA were his community's defenders because they were asserting his community's rights, not because they were taking effective measures to reduce his community's casualties.

Martin Finucane said of his brother John, who died in a car crash while on a mission for the IRA:

> I was very proud of my brother because he had given up so much of his life not only to protect me but to protect his community. He spent many nights patrolling the estate with a rifle in case anything happened say from a loyalist attack. He manned checkpoints and foot patrols in his own community and I respected that.

By this view of events, the IRA is not a producer of violence but a force for tempering the violence of others. The reality is that loyalist violence against Catholics increased as IRA violence against the police and army and commerce increased, that there was something more like a symbiotic relationship between loyalists and republicans than is implied by a simple vision of one as a restraint on the other.

It is widely agreed, among writers on republicanism, some of whom also accept that the IRA defended Catholics, that clashes between the IRA and the army were sought out – 'goaded' is Tim Pat Coogan's word. M.L.R. Smith regards it as a widespread perception of the time that the IRA was trying to drive a rift between the nationalist people and the British army. Coogan thinks the goading of the army by the IRA was not necessary to break the relationship between the people and the army, but he acknowledges that it was a feature of IRA strategy: 'The mere fact of having troops on the streets in such a highly charged atmosphere would have brought the honeymoon period to an end, one way or another.'

Without the IRA influencing events and appropriating the interpretation of them, the outcome would not have been the same as it was. Certainly there was a waking from the honeymoon after people got acquainted with the army and the tension they introduced, but is it really likely that there would have been spontaneous armed attacks on the army by aggrieved and abused young men, acting on their own initiative, if the Provisionals had not been in a position to inspire and direct them? If that had been possible, the Provisionals would only have had to wait rather than invest their energies and weaponry in a goading exercise. They did not wait. They took on the political task of exacerbating the tension between the army and local people, and attempting to provide an interpretation of this that would prevail.

They drew the army into situations that appeared to confirm the republican analysis. Republicans said the army were an occupying force. They set out to demonstrate that the army could behave with the brutal detachment of an invader. They constructed a drama on the streets in which the army played the role of an invading force and the IRA presented themselves as the defender. They did not, of course, contrive this out of nothing – though it is not difficult, if you are armed, to invite the armed forces of the state to come and engage with you. The law requires that they must.

Two early clashes between the British army and the IRA are remembered as occasions on which the IRA came out to defend the Catholic communities. These were the fighting during the Falls Road

curfew in July 1970 and the response to the introduction of internment in August 1971. Weapons were fired and lives were endangered on both occasions. It would be possible to pick out many
events during that period in which the IRA fought either the army
or loyalists, and to show that the IRA's role was not tenable defence
but something much different, and that the motivation cannot
plausibly have been to protect people and save lives. These two
events are significant for their almost mythological importance in
republican history. They show that the widely held perception that
the IRA functions defensively is ill-founded.

The month before the Falls curfew, in June 1970, the Labour
government was replaced by Conservatives led by Edward Heath.
There had been increasing street violence in Belfast in the previous
months, particularly in Ballymurphy. Over three nights at the end
of June, the army fired 1,600 canisters of CS gas. The death toll
soared. Between an accidental bomb explosion in Derry on 26 June
and a night of sectarian exchanges in Belfast on the 27th, twelve
people died.

June 27 was a particularly violent night. The IRA claims that it
proved its defensive potential by repelling a loyalist attack on
St Matthew's chapel on the lower Newtownards Road. One of
the leaders of the Provisionals, Billy McKee, and two others
exchanged fire with loyalists, killing two of them and losing one
of their own men. Four other killings occurred that night on the
Crumlin Road and Springfield Road, on the other side of the city.
The exchanges at St Matthew's are remembered by republicans as
proof that the IRA could provide defence when Catholics were
under attack and the army stayed away. They are remembered by
loyalists as evidence that the IRA was being allowed a free hand to
arm and to act. The common element in both versions is a perception that the army stayed out of it.

At the end of that week the army moved to disarm the Official
IRA in the lower Falls area. It was met with attacks by both the Officials and the Provisionals. They responded by imposing an illegal
curfew on the whole area and searching every house for arms. They
found fifty-two pistols, thirty-five rifles, six automatic weapons   75

and fourteen shotguns, as well as ammunition and explosives.

Anyone reading an IRA conspiracy into the curfew has to make allowance for the fact that it was the army who picked the timing for this raid. The Provisionals would probably have preferred to wait longer before confronting the army like this. To describe the IRA response to the curfew of 1970 as merely defensive, however, is to overlook the complexity of the interactions between the British army, the Official IRA and the Provisional IRA. As a defensive operation, its goal would have been to save the lives of people under attack, in this case by British soldiers. This also presumes that the objectives of the soldiers were to kill or abuse residents of the area. The army had been received initially with the presumption that they were not sectarian, but in republican eyes they were presenting themselves as more eager to confront Catholics than Protestants. An assault to recover guns from the Official IRA just days after the Pro-visionals and loyalists had been running wild after each other does seem to indicate a loss of focus.

The army operations of that day began as a search for arms. The curfew was an extension of the raid, imposed after soldiers came under fire. I remember seeing a young man who looked like a stu-dent or a teacher walking down Albert Street with the barrel of a rifle poking out from under his coat. He was surrounded by a group of local people. They hedged close to him to hide the gun, while escorting him to a firing position. He looked like an outsider, and from what I saw of the gun it was polished and new and of low calibre. I took him for a middle-class man out with his own gun, perhaps someone with family in the area, who had come to help out.

There was almost a festive air during a lull in the rioting. Women brought buckets of water mixed with vinegar to their doorsteps so that people could soak their hankies in the mixture and mask them-selves against the CS gas, which created a sensation like a bar pressing against the front of the chest.

The curfew remains potent in the mythology of republicanism because of the scale and vigour of the army operation. Every home in a square-mile area of the lower Falls was searched, and many of them were damaged by the soldiers. It is also important to the Provisionals in that it gave them a chance to upstage the Officials. Later accounts by Provisionals or their supporters write the Officials out of the story altogether. So though the response to the curfew raids is presented as an important example of republican defence and a crucial moment in the disillusionment of the people with the British army, it is relished in the memory of Provisionals as a point scored against their paramilitary rivals on the Falls Road, who were other republicans claiming to offer defence.

The Provisionals did not score their point against the Officials by providing better defence than they could, however. During the curfew, two unarmed people were shot dead by the British army and one man was killed by an army vehicle. No soldiers were killed. That is to say, no one was killed at all in an exchange of fire. It was not therefore a gun battle in the ordinary sense, for neither one of the IRA factions nor the British army sustained fatal casualties. Such offence as was directed by the army against the IRA resulted in no IRA deaths. The IRA at least managed to stay out of the direct line of fire. In that sense they defended themselves, if not the community. It could be argued that the army was clearly attacking the community, rather than the IRA, since the victims were all noncombatants. It is difficult to argue, however, that the IRA – either the Officials or the Provisionals – with their own guns did anything practical to reduce the loss of civilian life.

Gerry Adams in *Before the Dawn* claims that Provisionals engaged the British army for the first time during the curfew, though outside the Falls area, in Andersonstown. There is no record of either Provisionals or British soldiers being killed in that engagement either. Adams says this was 'quite a sizeable gun battle ... which was a bit of a botched operation'. He says its purpose was to draw attention away from the lower Falls: as if he imagined that a second commotion would overstretch an army.

The military advantages of the curfew went to the British army, who recovered more guns than they would have captured in their initial raid alone. The attack on them during that raid both alerted them to the presence of other weapons in the area and gave them the excuse to extend their operation. Adams and others write that the curfew was a pivotal event in the relations between the British army and Catholics. In the days after the curfew a new poster appeared on the walls, reading 'Don't Fraternise'. The propaganda advantage had gone to the Officials and Provisionals who demonstrated that the army was brutal and hostile. No contribution was made, however, to the security of the people of the lower Falls.

The Provisionals and Officials both claimed to have reaped advantages from the curfew. The accounts of the progress of the battle vary markedly too. Adams gives no indication that any Provisionals participated in it. Bishop and Mallie, in *The Provisional IRA*, say that the Officials had eighty or ninety men at their disposal. The battle was fought by twelve Provisionals with a 'car boot sale armoury', according to a review in the *Andersonstown News* of a commemorative video of the curfew, released in 1995. The review describes the engagement as 'a triumph of community will and spirit over military might'. The review makes no mention of the efforts of the Official IRA, or of their loss of weapons to the British. In retrospect the incident was regarded as having a major propaganda advantage, presenting a demonstration of community cohesion. Its failure as a military engagement was regarded as unimportant.

Coogan writes: 'The two IRAs fought back with guns, petrol bombs and nail bombs. Civilians used stones or their bare hands.' This image of a brave and plucky working-class people taking on the British army overlooks the fact that in military terms their efforts, if they were in fact as Coogan describes them, were entirely pointless. H. Patterson, in *The Politics of Illusion*, records that the Official IRA, who were prominent in the exchanges with the army during the curfew, were proud of their achievements. They regarded themselves as having proved their mettle sufficiently to assume the right to operate in Ballymurphy, a Provisional area controlled by Gerry Adams, and Patterson says this caused intense annoyance among Provisionals there. This suggests another predictable advantage reaped from their escalation of the engagement: to test the courage of volunteers, most of whom would only have joined one or other IRA in previous months.

Mallie and Bishop give a different version of the state of Official IRA morale after the curfew. They report that the Officials felt they had been tricked into a battle with the army after a member of the Provisionals threw a grenade at the British army raiding party in Balkan Street. The Provisionals would have had much to gain from bouncing the Officials into a gunfight. They provoked a raid that cost their rivals much of their weaponry, and they created an opportunity to assess the tactics of the British army in an area in which they themselves would not be the direct targets of army attention. They also reinforced their own presentation of the problem as British occupation, and left it to the army's rough tactics to convert others to that view. Whether any of that was foreseen in a rational way can only be guessed at, however.

Bowyer Bell writes: 'In the drift towards the war the Provos sought, the Falls Curfew was a steep upward jag in the needed alienation of the Catholic community, the discovery that the British were the enemy.' The Bishop and Mallie version acknowledges that the engagement was a military defeat for the Official IRA. They had lost weapons and been reduced in strength. Adams claims that many of the weapons belonging to the Officials in the area were smuggled out by women in prams and handed over to the Provisionals. Danny Morrison's fictionalised account, *West Belfast*, makes the same claim.

The response to the curfew, though it features in the republican mythology as an example of a defensive operation, and is regarded as such in the literature on the IRA, was disastrous in those terms, but it served other propagandist and tactical objectives. These other plausible objectives are sufficient to explain why the IRA might have stimulated and participated in such an event. It isn't necessary to claim that the area was under attack by the army and that the defence-less civilians called on the IRA to protect them with their guns. It is more unlikely still, given the IRA's failure in defence, that the Catholic community learned from the experience of the curfew raids that it needed the IRA as defenders and could rely on them.

A purely defensive operation by the IRA would have set its goals   79 as the preservation of weapons, of the lives of the people in the area, and of the integrity of their homes. The IRA response was to fight, when these goals might have been more practically met by tactical acquiescence. It was inherent in the understanding of August 1969 as a failure of the republican will to defend, that the new republicans would have to show that they would not shrink away. They had to make the point that they were different from what went before.

Even the Officials, who had wanted to avoid confrontation in the North, felt they had to accept this fight and engage in it. From their point of view, it had the merit of not being a sectarian fight, unlike the clash at St Matthew's a few days earlier. It gave them the opportunity to show the newly emerged Provisionals that they were game. It seems fair to suspect, however, that protection of life, property and weapons was far from the minds of the Provisionals and Officials who fought the army that day, and that they were both more interested in showing their mettle and in rallying their people.

They were not just having a whack for the hell of it. They were also perhaps exercising the standard guerrilla tactic of inviting repression to demonstrate the brutality of the enemy so that the people could hate the army more. The people did hate the army more when it was over. Their homes had been overrun and ransacked. They had been insulted and abused. Newspaper stories followed, telling of how the English soldiers were shocked at the filthy state of the houses the people of the Falls Road lived in. There would be no more tea. That was a good result for republicans.

Little more than a year later, in August 1971, the IRA responded to the introduction of internment and the first internment raids by engaging British troops in exchanges of fire. Ostensibly, these were gun battles. These battles, however, were not contests of strength, nor were they defensive operations with the potential to restrain army operations. In a sense they were not military operations at all, because they were not up to the job of producing a physical result. They could not reduce casualties, prevent arrests, slow down the army, reduce the physical potential of the armed forces or impose the will of republicans on the British state. The use of weapons by the IRA in those circumstances cannot really be understood at all as the pitting of one army against another for the sake of coercing an enemy with physical force. That simple model of warfare just is not applicable.

The gun battles were a type of propagandist theatre. The IRA were playing at warfare, or acting out a semblance of warfare. At the simple level, they were presenting an image of exacerbated crisis to disgrace the government which had discarded normal legislative procedures to intern people without trial. They were making the statement that internment could not restore order. They were doing this by providing visible proof that disorder had grown and spread. They were showing that the government had created chaos, and that an army could not be deployed against civilians without reducing itself to barbarity.

Brian Faulkner, the Northern Ireland prime minister, said at the time:

> I have taken this serious step solely for the protection of life and the security of property. We are, quite simply, at war with the terrorists and in a state of war many sacrifices have to be made, and made in a co-operative spirit.

What did he mean by war? If Faulkner thought that he could overcome the IRA through deploying superior force against them, and then providing the legal means for containing them once they had been overcome, his thinking was operating on a very simplistic level. He was treating the IRA as a physical threat that could be restrained with physical measures. No doubt many in the IRA thought they were fighting a war in the same sense, pitting force against force, with the political prize going to the winner. Circumstances had already decided that no such war between the two was possible. The IRA would only get stronger if it was physically suppressed. No such physical suppression would have been possible anyway without damage to the wider Catholic community. This damage would inflame them with an anger that would convert into support for retaliation. A moral advantage would always go to victims of the state.

To gain the political advantage on the day internment was introduced, the IRA only needed to demonstrate that it had survived. It
could do that by shooting into the air. Later there would be no-go
areas behind barricades. The police and the army would stay out of
those areas – not because they hadn't the physical resources to storm
them, but because the resultant loss of life would have been politically unacceptable.

Whether political and military leaders of the time ever admitted
it or not, another complicating consideration was that some soldiers
appeared to relish opportunities to open fire on civilians. When
such soldiers were deployed, casualties would be higher than necessary, and the political embarrassment would be greater than might
be predicted. In the television footage of the shooting on Bloody
Sunday, 30 January 1972, the officer in charge can clearly be heard
calling on his men not to open fire until they had identified a clear
target. He would not have been saying that if he hadn't feared that
he was losing control of them. The common theory among nationalists about the shooting on that day is that the army had been given
free rein to punish the people by killing a few of them. The officer
shouting at his men is apparently trying hard to impose legal limits
on them to the use of force, as his men slip from his grasp.

When soldiers who relished killing were brought into play, the
political advantages went to republicans, because the behaviour of
those soldiers confirmed the interpretation of events that republicans offered. Several former members of the Parachute Regiment
and the Special Air Services (SAS) have written books about their
experiences, which depict the British soldier, in some regiments at
least, as a callous adventurer who thrills in killing. In *The Killing
Zone*, Harry McCallion, who served in the Parachute Regiment,
the SAS and the RUC, claims that when he was first with the Paras
in Belfast, the men pooled together a prize of £200 that would go
to the first one among them to get a kill. He describes how one of
the Paras kept a piece of the skull of a man shot dead on the Springfield Road and used it for years afterwards as an ashtray.

The army was clearly using excessive firepower on 9 August
1971, the day that internment was introduced. Many of those killed

by British soldiers that week need not have been shot. I was in Riverdale when Frank McGuinness was killed. I did not see the actual shooting, though I was only yards from it. What preceded it was this. We woke up to the news that internment had been introduced. We had been waiting for it, as had those who had expected to be lifted, many of whom got away to safety in time. It was a bright summer's day, and people were excited and on the street, talking about what was happening. Wild rumours were being passed round. Someone said St Peter's Pro Cathedral was on fire. We had a sense of being cut off. Was it safe to go out of the area? There were distant sounds of shooting and there was a smell of smoke in the air.

My own self-protective inclination was to stay clear of trouble, not to seek it and certainly not to generate it. I watched with horror when local republicans built a barricade and brought petrol bombs in a van to the young men posted behind it. Two men living on our street were to be generals for a day. They were saying that the British army was preparing for another raid, so we had to be ready. They didn't make me feel any safer. I didn't trust the army, but I thought I would have a safer, easier day by staying out of their way. The two men who were to be generals for a day clearly thought the same, for once they had armed the kids for battle, they drove off.

An army patrol came up Finaghy Road North and stopped at the barricade. The boys with the petrol bombs took on the soldiers. I ran into our house. Moments later I heard two rifle shots. The soldiers were gone when I went out, and Frank McGuinness lay bleeding on the road. Those who were on the street said that he had not been one of the rioters. The army had served no practical objective in shooting him. They hadn't stuck around to arrest anyone. They did not attempt to enter the estate. They seemed simply to have accepted the invitation to fight and the opportunity to shoot someone, and gone their way.

The IRA, equally, had served no practical defensive or tactical objective by building the barricade or providing the boys with petrol bombs. The fighting was not for defensive purposes. Certainly   83 it was not for the defence of civilians. They fought to demonstrate the futility of internment. That was a political rather than a military opportunity. So long as gunfire could be heard over Belfast after the internment raids, the IRA had established its survival and humiliated the government of Brian Faulkner.

Another political consideration for republicans was that they should be able to implicate constitutional nationalists in their strategy. Both nationalist groupings would be equally horrified by internment. Constitutionalists, after all, had been massing on the streets just two years earlier to demand local government reform; they were hardly likely to accede to a far greater erosion of civil rights now. Constitutional nationalists and republicans were drawn together in common cause by internment. They could disagree on means, but both would share the determination to end internment and remove the Unionist government that had imposed it.

M.L.R. Smith describes the introduction of internment as 'botched' from the British army's point of view: 'The introduction of internment instantaneously united all shades of Catholic opinion against the authorities. Far from stemming the violence, internment provided PIRA with an enormous propaganda victory which boosted recruitment.' A question here is whether the IRA, which thrived under internment, could fairly have regarded the policy as a disaster to itself. That depends again on whether the movement is regarded as an army fighting a confrontational war, as implied by the language it uses itself, or whether the application of violence has a different purpose. If the IRA could gain political advantages from engagements that, in normal military terms, it lost, then the balance of advantage would have to be measured differently. In fact, it most often gains politically where it loses militarily, a fact of their experience that is recorded in the slogan that it is not those who inflict the most but those who endure the most who prevail.

J.J. Lee, in *Ireland: 1912–1985*, regards internment as the worst option that Faulkner could have chosen in a nearly impossible situation. 'Internment merely offered a high profile set-piece for which he could be denounced.' Support for the IRA increased in the Republic, and the Irish government now found it more difficult to persuade its people not to help them. Had the IRA not responded to the internment raids, they might have given the impression that they had no heart for engaging the army. Yet, by withdrawing they could have demonstrated the tactical ability to choose the timing of their clashes with the army according to their own considerations. That way, they could have shown that they were concerned to minimise Catholic casualties; but they had more important things on their minds.

Adams has himself shown that he understands the dangers of bringing weapons into a clash with superior force. In his autobiography he says that he argued against the issue of guns to IRA volunteers in August 1969 on the Falls Road: 'I disagreed, feeling that any attempt to militarise the situation, to bring the IRA into it and to engage the RUC on their own terms would take it out of the hands of the people and bring the entire situation down to a gunfight, which the RUC would surely win.' I am not saying that I believe his account, only demonstrating that he claims some early sense that gunfire can worsen a situation. Things changed, he says, when the police opened fire first. Similarly, in Ballymurphy, during the internment raids, he says that the IRA only returned fire on loyalists and British soldiers who were firing at them. It seems almost as if the moral right to fire back was more significant than the tactical contribution that firing would make. The defence of Ballymurphy against internment raids was organised through young men supplied with petrol bombs. It is questionable whether these improved the prospects of Catholics surviving attack. The British army was employed to restore order. They were not going to be dissuaded from doing that by greater disorder.

From Adams's perspective, army snipers were united with the loyalists in an assault on Ballymurphy. The rationale for maintaining fire against the army was that the army was attacking the population, and if the IRA stopped shooting at them they would overwhelm the area. Since the legitimacy of the army was rejected from a republican viewpoint, they were to be regarded as criminal gunmen bringing only havoc and death. Not to resist them, and to concede to them the right to enter the area and arrest people would   85 have amounted to acknowledging a legitimacy that the republican movement existed to deny. This is not to say that the IRA didn't see things accurately when it judged the army to be an actual physical threat to civilians. On occasions it clearly was. Nor were there any reasons why republican convictions would rule out an occasional tactical withdrawal. But Adams seems to imply that any situation in which someone is firing at you is always improved by your firing back, and there seems to me to be no sensible basis for that kind of thinking, either in republican ideology or in military strategy.

Firing back advertised the power of the IRA as the dominant force on the streets. It made a powerful impression on those who lived there but who were not members or close supporters. Firing back established the IRA gunmen as people who could demand obedience and respect. A man who was seen by his neighbours crouching behind a wall for hours with a rifle, firing at soldiers, was going to be transformed in their eyes. The impression created on the support community by these exchanges of fire was to change the pecking order within that community. Firing back also rallied a support community around the republican project. It wrong-footed the state into fulfilling the prediction that it would oppress the Catholics. It brought people into direct conflict with the state, and each confrontation would set the basis for another, as grievances multiplied and rage was compounded.

The riots during the curfew on the Falls Road the year before had rallied the potential support base of the IRA around a vision of the British army as an invader. In that sense it was a propaganda effort that was directed inwards towards the community. There was a strong element of this, too, in the response to the internment raids, but, more important, there was the humiliation of the Stormont government, and the demonstration that its emergency measures had failed. It was the most productive political deployment of violence yet. The government was now in a position where it had to question its own ability to function. The damage the calamitous introduction of internment had done to Catholic toleration of Stormont struck at the very legitimacy of that government.

It makes no sense to postulate that the IRA gained credibility among working-class Catholics by providing them with defence because it did not actually do this in any meaningful military way. The IRA articulated the hurt and defiance of Catholics rather than defence. It also helped to put Catholics in a position where they had no sure moral foundations or dependable allegiances. The greater number of nationalists who wanted the IRA campaign to stop none the less rationalised it in terms of the damage done to the Catholic community. They didn't want it, but they felt they could identify with the hurt and anger that was generating it.

Those who opposed the IRA also opposed internment and tended to explain IRA anger in terms of the stupidity and brutishness of the measures deployed against them. Six months after the first internment raids, on what came to be known as Bloody Sunday, paratroopers shot dead fourteen people participating in an anti-internment demonstration in Derry. Bloody Sunday's impact on Catholics was profound. Many joined the IRA who would not otherwise have done so – not to defend their community against a recurrence, but to avenge. They felt that the British had put their own legitimacy on the line through the transparency of the Widgery report's subsequent cover-up.

The more difficult position to argue was that the government was benign. Having vaunted the merits of democracy and a fair and independent judiciary as an alternative to terrorism, it was content to provide legal cover through a senior law lord for the murderous rampage of its own soldiers. The moral balance between the IRA and the British government was thereby made easier for republicans to negotiate.

Similarly, in the 1990s the weight of the British establishment was thrown behind Private Lee Clegg, a soldier who had been convicted of murdering a west Belfast joyrider, and the man became a national hero. These events created the impression that the British government had neither the simple good sense nor the ordinary compassion to present itself as impartial before the Irish. They qualified the moral outrage that Catholics felt against the IRA. Dirty as the IRA's methods were, it was rarely entirely clear that they were alone in the moral space they occupied, distanced from a principled state. Taking sides against them could not always be a morally uncluttered decision.

It was exasperation within communities that tended to legitimise violence, not dependence on the IRA as a protector. There was one occasion on which the IRA distinguished itself in its demonstration of its power to use tactical manoeuvres to save lives. This was when the army took the no-go areas in July 1972. (Eight people did die in an atrocious car bomb explosion in Claudy on the same morning, but the bombing was not part of the IRA's defensive measures, just part of the routine violence of the period.) The Secretary of State, William Whitelaw, announced on television the night before that the barricades in all areas would be removed. The IRA declined the opportunity to oppose the British forces coming into the housing estates of west Belfast and Derry. No significant resistance was offered. Simply by acting as if it did not even exist, the IRA did more to save life than it had done during the curfew or internment, or perhaps on any other occasion. Its one and only impressive act of defence was a retreat.

The two incidents detailed above concern the IRA's war, or mock war, with the British army, and the argument is that republicans provided no tenable defence of Catholic areas against these forces. The people of those areas have been constantly under threat from another source: loyalist paramilitary groups. The first attacks from loyalists in the current period occurred in 1966, and these included an excursion into the Falls Road area by an armed gang to kill a drunken man making his way home through Beechmount. The idea that he might have been shot was so remote from the thinking of medical staff at the time that the man, who survived for two weeks, was treated for stab wounds and only diagnosed as shot after his body was exhumed for the murder trial.

The question over loyalist violence is whether it was reactive against the IRA or an overspill of sectarian anger that would have occurred even if the IRA campaign had not existed. Those who say it is not reactive point to the killings in 1966 as reacting to nothing more than the prospect of greater respect for Catholics within the Northern Ireland state and the celebration of the fiftieth anniversary of the 1916 Easter Rising. The loyalists themselves made the best case for their violence being reactive when they called their ceasefire in 1994, after the IRA ceasefire of August that year. That, however, was regarded as the first sign of a political maturing within loyalism and is not something their earlier actions and motivations can be judged by. It was also tactically deft. It put the Provisionals in the position of having to regard the danger of a loyalist resumption as the cost of any future attack.

It may well be that the IRA ceasefire had simply cleared the table and enabled the loyalists to suspend an aimless and murderous campaign and impart some meaning to the use of threat. The fresh start given to the killing contest between loyalists and republicans by the resumption of the IRA campaign in February 1996 created conditions for a more orderly tit-for-tat based on a republican first strike. It enabled loyalists to present themselves as reactive more plausibly than ever before. It may be that the potential to use violence reactively and economically only arrived for loyalists after the IRA ceasefire, and that what preceded it was a much more untidy indulgence of sectarian anger. There were, however, several phases to the loyalist campaign, but throughout there was a coincidence of psychopathic sectarianism and strategic pragmatism. Murdering Catholics at random made a certain amount of cynical good sense, if your objective was to keep reminding all Catholics that there was a price to be paid for some of them supporting the IRA.

It has been a crucial part of republican theology to deny that loyalist violence was reactive. The arguments are that loyalist violence came first, that it responded to the threat of political change, rather than to the IRA, and that it was effectively an arm of British oppression which republicans fought to resist. There may be degrees of truth in all of these, but the most eccentric view of all would be that loyalists would have been just as active in murdering Catholics if there had been no IRA campaign at all. Nor, it has to be said, is it likely that political change to the advantage of Catholics could ever have come about in Northern Ireland without some measure of violent loyalist protest.

Loyalism's tactic was to try to shatter the relationship between   89 the IRA and its supporters by making all Catholics feel insecure. Attacks on innocent Catholics would prove that the IRA was unable to defend its people. Branding all Catholics as IRA supporters and legitimate targets would reinforce the message that the only way for Catholics to be safe was to turn against the IRA. In a sense, this was answering the IRA's claim to be the defender of the people. Far from taking protection from the IRA, the people should see that association with it put them in jeopardy. Republican violence, which was usually greater than loyalist violence, was tailed by the latter in its rising and falling over the years. One reason for this might simply be the efficiency of the security forces; when they are functioning efficiently they curtail both groups simultaneously; but the matching graphs could also argue for the theory that loyalist violence grows to react to the republican campaign's peaks.

The IRA were not defending but endangering Catholics if they were provoking loyalist attacks. The people in Catholic areas were not turning to the IRA for a greater sense of security against loyalists, or if they were, they were learning very quickly that they were not getting it. The IRA, if it was providing credible defence, would have been helping Catholics to feel safer from loyalists. If they were not doing that, and if they were still gaining support, then the grounds for that support must have been something other than the defence that republicans and other analysts claimed it was.

Loyalist violence probably enhanced Catholic support for the IRA. Republicans pointed to it as legitimising their need to defend Catholics. They exploited every opportunity to claim a linkage between loyalist violence and the security forces. There were times when that linkage seemed obvious. My doubt is over whether those who were inspired by loyalist violence to support the IRA did so in order to feel physically safer. I think the IRA articulated the defiance of angry Catholics. The IRA was their champion, who would lash out on their behalf. But their only actual protection against the next blow from loyalists was to stay at home, keep their heads down and let the police or army catch the roaming gunmen.

Republicans would never give the security forces credit for pro-

tecting them, and many would genuinely believe that the police and army were compromised by their own associations with the loyalists. The evidence for this would pile up over the years and never be wholly discredited. But it would always be the security forces, however compromised, who would do most to protect both communities from the extremists of the other. I remember the night Patsy McVeigh was shot dead at the barricade at the corner of our street. The men arrested and released were British soldiers. There were numerous such incidents. A wholly pure view of the army and police as just and independent and law-abiding seemed unsustainable, but a pure view of them as the allies in arms of the loyalists was equally untenable when they were catching loyalists and imprisoning them.

There is some anecdotal evidence that the pressure of the threat from loyalists was wearing down Catholic people before the 1994 ceasefire. In early 1994, a friend of mine was sitting in a café on the Falls Road when the Sinn Féin councillor Fra McCann and some others took a seat near her. 'The other people at tables near him got up and moved away,' she says. 'They didn't want to be in the line of fire.' Loyalists were killing Sinn Féin members whenever they could, and randomly selected Catholics when they couldn't. If a loyalist gunman came through the door, he would be more likely to want to shoot McCann than anyone else, so people gave him a wide berth, and incidentally made him an easier target.

Other anecdotal evidence suggests that the same threat consolidated communities on sectarian lines rather than fragmented them. The fear of loyalism affected all Catholics because it was directed randomly, and that encouraged most to feel that they were safer in Catholic areas than outside them. The result was the immobility of the population of Catholic west Belfast. Living next door to an IRA man or a Sinn Féin councillor no doubt carries its dangers and embarrassments, but the threat of loyalist violence makes that more desirable than to move into an area where the sectarian geography is more difficult to read.

If a loyalist gunman had gone into that café where Fra McCann and his friends were left sipping coffee alone, going by past form he would probably have sprayed around him while he was there, 91 confident that he wouldn't kill any Protestants. Moving to a different table would have given little real assurance of safety. The only meaningful thing to do in that case would be to leave the café altogether, but a kind of lazy fatalism would probably intervene to prevent most people doing that.

Loyalist violence increased in the 1990s and overtook the IRA's in its killing rate in 1993, the year before the ceasefire was announced. That may not have contributed to the decision of the IRA to call a ceasefire. If anything, the IRA appear in the weeks before the ceasefire to have been trying to provoke a loyalist reaction. It did, however, enhance the relief felt by many when the IRA ceasefire was called and was followed by one from the loyalists. The reactive nature of loyalist violence seemed obvious then, and the Catholics of Belfast felt that they were never as well defended as when the IRA was stood down.

5 WHAT KIND OF WAR IS THIS?

As well as the claim the IRA has made to be a defensive force, it has also claimed to be fighting a war of offence against a British occupation. This war is emphasised in its propagandist imagery and in its press statements. Videotapes and photographs commonly show men in uniform patrolling the fields and back roads of south Armagh with machine guns and rocket launchers in their hands. The impression they wish to create is that they hold territory and patrol it, on the lookout for British patrols to attack. Wall murals depict the same thing, soldiers of the IRA engaged in battle with soldiers of the Crown.

I remember crossing the border near Newry on a bus. As we entered the North a teenage boy sitting near me pointed out an army foot patrol to his friend. 'They're in deep shit,' he said, 'if they run into the Rah down there.' The 'Rah' – the IRA – in fact would have been acting wholly out of character had it risked such a random encounter. The boy believed the message of the murals and he accepted the language of war. In many ways that language is pitched at the young and the thoughtless and the distant.

The language that describes the IRA campaign as a war also pervades much journalism and political discussion. A frequent writer on IRA terrorism is Professor Paul Wilkinson of St Andrews University. When he wrote an article for the *Belfast Telegraph* on the IRA tactic of causing huge traffic disruption in England, in the run-up to the 1997 general election, his analysis was based on a simplistic model drawn from bullying or blackmail: a threat is applied alongside a demand, and if the demand is not fulfilled the threat is 93 maintained. Professor Wilkinson wrote:

> The bomb alerts which hit rail, road and air links in London caused
> chaos and cost millions of pounds. But as a means of achieving a
> political goal, they won't succeed. It amazes me that after twenty-
> seven years of these terrorist tactics, the leaders of the IRA haven't
> learned this lesson. They are trying to sicken the next government
> into relinquishing responsibility for Northern Ireland – but that
> won't happen.

This presumes that the IRA's use of threat is an attempt to barter the
lifting of the threat for a British withdrawal, that force is being used
to support a demand in the way in which a mugger or a rapist uses
it. There is little or no consideration here that force might be used
politically in a more sophisticated way, that the application of violence might have a more complex relationship with the result
sought than a direct two-way exchange.

The language that describes the violence as war by old-fashioned
physical contest pervades even some of the most considered journalism. In *The Fight For Peace*, Eamonn Mallie and David McKittrick
describe a meeting between leaders of Sinn Féin and the SDLP at the
Redemptorist retreat house in 1988. They write of the location: 'Its
elevation helps give visitors a sense of being above the fray, even
though it is only a mile or so from the deadly sectarian battlefields
of north Belfast.' This exaggerates the scale of violence for dramatic
effect, but it also misrepresents the nature of the violence, to present
it as a physical contest between murderous armies, rather than as an
exchange of surreptitious murders.

As the language of war underlies the republican political vision,
republicans are the ones least likely to object to this kind of imagery,
even though it misrepresents the Troubles. The principle underlying the ceasefire was that the IRA would 'withdraw from the field'
and prepare to settle terms. This brave gesture, said republicans,
should be acknowledged by the other parties to the conflict and
responded to with similar courage.

They may themselves believe that they were caught up in something from which only a self-sacrificial act of retreat could extract

them. The implication is that by withholding their forces they were creating a military vacuum in which they were at risk of being overwhelmed. Such a sense of being locked into something from which it was dangerous to withdraw may be a comfort to them, for it explains a necessity to kill and destroy. It warrants an attempt at resolution through negotiation rather than a simple cessation based on an admission of failure.

They say they are caught up in this war. We are to believe that they cannot simply walk away from it. Others saw it in the same way. SDLP members frequently explained the peace process as an effort to let republicans 'off the hook'. The hook was their own pride, surely. The Provos were not compelled by battlefield conditions to go on fighting. Regarding the IRA campaign as an element in a conflict or war implies that there is an equal moral onus to change on those who are attacked by the IRA. The truth is more like a bank robber putting a gun to a cashier's head and saying, 'Now what are we going to do to resolve this conflict between us?'

Even those who recognise that the gun at the head is unwarranted frequently imply in their language that the IRA has been trying to fight a coercive war. Writing in the *Sunday Independent* on 15 September 1996, the deputy leader of the SDLP, Seamus Mallon, aired the view that the function of armed struggle was to bring change through coercion, and he interpreted paramilitary ceasefires as an admission that this could not be done.

> The thesis that violence can deliver a solution is a failed proposition, which has been abandoned even by those who used and advocated the use of violence in the recent past. They may hold onto their guns, but they have shed the conviction that the gun can solve the problem.

The problem for Seamus Mallon is that if the analysis of the IRA's past intentions is wrong, his analysis of their later intentions, extrapolated from it, cannot be relied on either. If the IRA campaign was never a coercive war, in the ordinary sense of attempting to push people into submitting to their will, then how can we know that in relaxing coercion they have really changed their fundamental aspiration and tactic? It's a bit like presuming that a man who has chosen to be faithful to his wife must really love her after all, without considering his own impotence or her inheritance.

War is a complex concept. The notion of war as a battlefield contest of strength is too simple for most discussions of strategy. The Cold War, for instance, was a means of presenting a threat that others would have to skirt round or yield to, without a rocket being launched. The IRA's violence was a bit like that. It did not have the power to overthrow any physical opposition, but it demanded of others that they tread gingerly, lest things get worse.

The IRA could never drive the British out through superior force, but it could potentially force on them a recalculation of Britain's best interests and encourage them to believe that it would be less bother simply to concede what was demanded. That is the project that appears to have failed, but it is not all the IRA were doing; it is not a comprehensive description of their method.

They provided an imitation of war as a form of agitation, in order to sustain political discussion of an issue that might otherwise have gone away, or have been resolved through soft compromise. In this they sought to generate symptomatic proof that Northern Ireland was unstable, and also to make an internal settlement untenable. In this their actions were more like those of a protest group obstructing change than the actions of a guerrilla army seeking to impose change.

The strategist Schelling describes two types of coercion, which he calls *deterrence* and *impellence*. Deterrence is usually passive and sets limits to the advance of an enemy. The obvious examples are the nuclear deterrent employed during the Cold War, or the installation of US forces in Dhahran, close to the Iraq–Kuwait border. Iraq cannot invade Kuwait without clashing with the superior forces of the USA. The IRA campaign also can be regarded as a deterrent campaign. It provides a background routine of violence which reminds Britain that the region is unstable and that political experimentation is dangerous. The campaign does not primarily force the British to leave Ireland through making their presence too costly, but it sets limits to their ability to resolve the conflict internally.

By a combination of party activism with murder and sabotage, the republicans were able to provide a simulation of war and also a machinery for interpreting that simulation to the world as the real thing. That ensured that most discussion of the Troubles abroad would accept the simplification that the IRA was engaged in physical resistance against oppression. The survival of that resistance would even appear to be evidence of a popular foundation for it.

One of the clichéd aphorisms of the Troubles is 'You can't bomb a million Protestants into a united Ireland.' Like Mallon's assessment, this presumes that it was the intention of the IRA to apply force to bend others to their will. Similarly, the IRA is often presumed to be trying to sicken the will of the British public with terrorism so that people will beg their government to get out of Ireland. This is another way of acknowledging the IRA as an offensive force, demanding concessions under the threat of debilitating violence, working for conquest by instalments. There was always an offensive component in the campaign, but it was rarely central to it, though there appears to have been a return to this kind of thinking in the early nineties.

The massive inner-city bombs of the 1990s were a change of tactic to a direct application of debilitating pressure on the British. They were clearly part of an effort to urge the British to negotiate with the IRA, and they appeared to be successful in this. In a sense they indicated a return to the thinking of the early seventies when the IRA did believe that they could bend the British to their will with the use of force.

There have been other occasions when the IRA's intention was to strike a truly crippling blow. The bomb at the Grand Hotel, Brighton, in 1984 was a concerted and feasible effort to kill several members of the British cabinet attending the Conservative Party conference. Ministers were injured and others were killed, but the prime minister escaped harm. An IRA statement said: 'Today we were unlucky, but remember: we only have to be lucky once.' That bomb came to represent the doggedness with which the IRA stalked government. Even as a failed attempt to kill ministers, it spoke of the resolve and imagination of a small working-class movement which had come close to removing the leadership of the country. It proved that the people represented by the IRA had a long arm that could answer any humiliation, real or imagined, by reaching into the bedroom of the prime minister.

There have been occasions on which the degree of damage done to the City of London and threatened against Heathrow airport has been of a scale that was highly damaging and expensive. Many republicans felt it was this damage that prompted the British government to engage in the peace process in 1993. Two years later they were confronted with the refusal of the British government to respond as they had expected and, therefore, with the failure of that line of reasoning. The Canary Wharf bomb of February 1996 is credited by more than republicans with forcing the government to name a date for talks. But it, and the bombs that followed, did not compel the government to relax the demand for a ceasefire before Sinn Féin's entry to the talks. All this says, of course, is that the use of force failed on these occasions, not that it was an untenable tactic, nor that it must have been motivated by something other than the will to push Britain into making a concession. Many believe that the Anglo-Irish Agreement was signed by Margaret Thatcher as a direct result of the pressure of the Brighton bomb.

This coercive use of force was not a general characteristic of the IRA campaign through most of the seventies and eighties. The IRA did not escalate its use of such force to the point where it could be decisive, and did not even try to. Such a massive threat from them was appropriate, probably, only to a period in which political bartering was actually under way. It was never the whole campaign. It was the occasional thunder in a brooding sky.

The president of Sinn Féin, Gerry Adams, who is credited with putting life back into a flagging IRA strategy in the mid-seventies, has written: 'The tactic of armed struggle is of primary importance because it provides a vital cutting edge. Without it, the issue of Ireland would not even be an issue. So, in effect, the armed struggle becomes armed propaganda.' This could be interpreted as meaning that armed struggle keeps the question of the constitution of Northern Ireland open; it reminds people that there is an unresolved problem to be dealt with. When there is political movement to resolve that problem, armed struggle can be used more dramatically to help concentrate the minds of the British. However, Adams has frequently referred to the armed struggle as if it is a military engagement seeking physical advantage over an enemy. Attempts within the republican movement to describe their campaign in terms other than war, such as the attempt by Adams to define it as armed propaganda, have been rare.

The armed struggle of the IRA, as viewed in the literature and imagery of republicanism, has the potential to defeat the British army, or at least to frustrate British army attempts to defeat the IRA. It is a continuation of the war of 1919–21 for independence. The objectives are framed as military and strategic. The prisoners are regarded as prisoners of war. In the war for independence, IRA flying columns attacked British army patrols and engaged in protracted exchanges of fire. The objective was to make Ireland ungovernable, and this was broadly successful. Adams draws parallels between IRA attacks on undercover agents in Belfast in 1972 and the offensive organised by Michael Collins against intelligence agents in Dublin in 1920, implying that he regards the two wars as being similar in character.

At the same time, in republican literature and political discourse there is an admission that there will never be a military solution to the conflict between Britain and the IRA. There is the repeated reminder that Britain itself has conceded this point. The war is therefore a clash of military campaigns, but without any possible military conclusion.

If the IRA campaign is viewed as an offensive war to force concessions from the British, it has a number of anomalies. First, it has so far failed to capitalise on the limited physical pressure it has been able to apply. M.L.R. Smith makes this point in referring to the 1972 meeting between republican leaders and the Secretary of State, William Whitelaw, in London. In military terms the ideological absolutism of the IRA was a handicap. Realistic military strategists look to the limits of the damage they can inflict or threaten, and then settle terms accordingly. The IRA had no intention of doing this, and prolonged the war rather than compromise, even when they hadn't the military muscle to enforce their demands. In normal strategic terms this is a foolish and self-destructive course.

Another anomaly of the IRA war is that it never escalates. For twenty years the IRA merely sustained a consistent output of death and destruction, without increasing the threat against the British. The threat seems never to have been: Get out of Ireland or we will slaughter your people; but Get out of Ireland or we will keep doing this for ever. Even when supplied by Libya with sufficient weaponry and explosives to escalate substantially, the IRA appears only to have been interested in sustaining its activities within limits that fell short of provoking a calamity. It made no sense for the IRA to make Northern Ireland ungovernable. They did not have the resources to bring it under control again. They may have felt for a time that developing the civil administration side of Sinn Féin's work would ultimately create the apparatus that would enable them to take control of large areas, but they must have understood for some years that they were not growing big enough to do that. It is more likely that the campaign they were interested in promoting was one of sustained, consistent irritation rather than the physical defeat of their enemy. Escalation was therefore unnecessary.

In the IRA's war, military action is rarely directed at the erosion of the physical strength of the enemy. Shane Paul O'Doherty, in *The Volunteer*, describes his own realisation that killing soldiers was not actually weakening the British. He felt that soldiers were regarded as expendable, and he justified his own letterbomb campaign against individuals in politics and the military as a means of hurting people who had real responsibility.

The IRA war has not, then, been a classical guerrilla war in that there has been no expansion of the military base. It seems not to be evolving towards a mass confrontation with enemy forces for territorial gains. Adams wrote in *Free Ireland: Towards a Lasting Peace* that there had not *yet* been such a 'classic development from guerrilla action to mass military action registering territorial gains'. His language implied that this was still a goal of the IRA, if one with decreasing tenability. He wrote these words for a book that was revised and reissued during the ceasefire of 1995. In fact, we can discount the prospects of the IRA raising a guerrilla army with the competence to defeat Britain by force.

Look at the weaponry of the IRA, and at their skills base. These suggest a profile of the war they have been fighting, and of the war their experience would enable them to fight in the future. The IRA is believed to have access to sufficient weapons to arm over a thousand men with assault rifles. This assessment is based on British and Irish security force figures for the weapons imported from Libya in 1985 and with allowance made for the quantities captured. The Libyan weapons landed off the Arklow coast in 1985–86 included 1,270 AK47 assault rifles and 4 tons of Semtex plastic explosive, 60 light machine guns and 25 heavy machine guns. There have been reported claims by the security services in Britain and Ireland that between one third and one half of this has been captured, but a count of the main arms finds suggests that the proportion recovered is smaller. Ten bunkers uncovered in the Irish Republic up to the end of 1996 yielded 275 AK47 rifles and 5 heavy machine guns. The IRA retains 18 heavy machine guns from the Libyan imports and, even by the most optimistic security force estimates, about 600 Kalashnikovs, and explosives for thousands of very large bombs or grenades. The Ulster Unionist security spokesman, Ken Maginnis, likes to cite figures claiming that the IRA could detonate an Oklahoma-type bomb every day for thirty years.

The supplies of Semtex explosive available to the IRA remain large. Semtex explosive is normally used in very small quantities, either at the heart of a larger bomb or in grenades. A bomb that failed to explode on Hammersmith Bridge in 1996 contained 15 pounds of Semtex and was estimated to have been capable of generating the largest explosion to date in the IRA campaign. That is to say that 15 pounds of Semtex were reckoned to be potentially more devastating than 1 ton of the fertiliser and fuel mix that devastated Canary Wharf in February of the same year. The 4 tons of Semtex imported from Libya would equip the IRA for 600 such bombs.

It would appear that they are using the Semtex frugally, for they prefer to employ cumbersome quantities of fertiliser–fuel mix. The Canary Wharf bomb was transported several hundred miles, and across the Irish Sea, when a much smaller, and therefore more easily transportable, quantity of Semtex would have caused just as much damage. The Semtex is used to boost the power of the fertiliser-mix bombs. It is compressed inside lengths of surgical tubing which is then wound through the fertiliser mix. The discovery that this was possible is what gave the IRA the potential to detonate very large bombs like those that destroyed Canary Wharf and the centre of Manchester in 1996. This discovery allowed them to use their limited stocks of Semtex sparingly and yet to create far greater damage than they could have done before. Conceivably, it could also be that they are preserving large quantities of Semtex for a major offensive in the future, but if their work to date is an indicator of the type of experience they have accumulated – and it must be – then their experience does not prepare them for sustained military confrontation.

It is difficult to assess whether the IRA has trained sufficient numbers of men to use the hundreds of AK47 assault rifles available to them, but the organisation is presumed to have a membership of several hundred. At a critical time, it could also presumably draw on several hundred former members and ex-prisoners. Between 1987 and 1995, four hundred people convicted of murder were released from prison. These may not have returned to the movement, but some may plausibly be available to it in extreme circumstances. However, most of the released lifers were convicted before the IRA acquired its AK47s, when its weapons stocks were much more varied and the organisation depended largely on Thompson submachine guns, Lee Enfield .303 breach-loading rifles, M1 carbines and a diverse range of pistols.

The released prisoners cannot necessarily be regarded as a resource that is currently available to the IRA should it wish to launch a major offensive. Many more of them would be inclined to join with the IRA if Catholic communities were under attack than would simply volunteer to lend their weight to the continuing armed struggle. But their numbers and experience suggest that if there is a civil war in the future, the IRA may be able to enlarge its numbers very quickly to deal with it, and to arm over one thousand fighters. Whether they are actually preparing to instigate such a war is another matter.

The question of whether the IRA should prepare itself for a future civil war has rarely been addressed by republicans. Sinn Féin's Danny Morrison spoke on the subject in 1985 (*Ireland after Britain*, edited by Martin Collins). He was assessing the reaction of loyalists to a future announcement from the British of an intent to withdraw from Ireland, an announcement that he was working to force them to make.

> One side will adopt a pragmatic approach and break from Loyal-ism ... The other side will fight, pushing for a civil war, or some kind of repartition and driving Catholics from the Loyalist strong-holds ... How much blood will be shed will depend on the British ... The Loyalists will only fight in proportion to the amount of hope Britain can give them for being able to hold on to sectarian privilege.

The strategy Morrison had in mind at that time for minimising the danger of civil war was to build up a base south of the border, in the Irish Republic, that would be strong enough to influence the Irish government. In particular, he wanted to keep the Republic neutral and out of NATO, so that Ireland would not, through NATO, be implicated into helping Britain.

A decade later, when the ceasefire was called, it was clear that no mass base in the Republic had been achieved. Already, since 1990, it was no longer possible to argue that Britain was only holding onto Northern Ireland because of NATO interests in the Cold War. None the less, apprehensions about a future sectarian civil war appear to have survived among a number of former Provisionals I have spoken to. Many who are outside the IRA at present, and who may even be sceptical of the intentions of the political leadership, still regard it as possible or likely that Northern Ireland will approach a doomsday crisis. In such an event, some said they would have the 103 skills to use weaponry and the will to do so.

All my five interviewees were men. They were asked to consider the prospects of a future civil war in Northern Ireland, triggered by the fulfilment of republican demands, that is, by an announcement of a British intention to withdraw, and they were asked to speculate on the likely course of that war. These interviews were conducted in the back room of a bar on the Whiterock Road in July 1995, during the first ceasefire.

All the men indicated that they had previously thought seriously about a possible doomsday crisis in Northern Ireland, though they attributed the likely responsibility for this to loyalists. They did not envisage that the IRA would initiate a large war for the sake of advancing their political demands, or that the IRA would attempt to mobilise former members on such a scale unless there was an external threat to Catholics. Most of the interviewees expressed the view that the loyalists had no stomach for a prolonged fight, and they would realise, once Britain had decided to leave, that they had no option but to settle terms with the rest of Ireland. This is the point that Morrison made, if put more crudely. Their own assessment of the difference between the IRA and the loyalist para-militaries is that the IRA have fought confrontationally against the British army, while the loyalists have preferred to attack unarmed civilians, often in their homes. This is a questionable assertion.

Most believed that the IRA had sufficient resources to contend with a major uprising by loyalists, even if, as seemed likely to them, the loyalists would be supported by mutineers within the RUC and the Royal Irish Regiment (RIR). Some believed that Britain would engineer things so that the resources of the army would be reduced before they made the announcement that would trigger the war.

Sean, as I'll call him, said: 'The republican movement would have enough gear now to equip their own people. And hundreds of people who have been republicans for a time could now use that experience. Must be ten thousand guns now. In addition to that, the IRA have been developing their own weapons.' Sean's guess at the number of guns available to the IRA produces a figure ten times that offered by the security forces, but even the smaller number is clearly sufficient to arm a large guerrilla force. 'Denis' said: 'A lot of people have been in the IRA. They could mobilise thousands among the men who have been in Long Kesh over twenty-five years.' 'Joe' said: 'The Rah would be big enough to stop the loyalists. Ex-prisoners and all would come into it. It wouldn't be a question of them facing the Rah as it is now.'

Some of the interviewees saw west Belfast as being easy to protect and supply, surrounded as it is by the Peaceline, and with access from the South along the M1 motorway. There was disagreement between them on whether the Irish army would come to their aid, but most believed that in an extreme situation there would be a compatibility of interest between the IRA and the Irish army. Others believed that the European Union or NATO would come to the aid of Catholics in the North of Ireland.

None of the former Provisionals expressed the view that their movement would instigate a major territorial war as a means of coercing Britain to withdraw. They could only foresee such a war after that concession had been made. Their vision of such a war depended on others taking the initiative.

These thoughts of five former Provisionals cannot be judged to be the considered view of the IRA leadership, but they can be regarded as the core of a discussion among former members. The Sinn Féin Ard Chomhairle member Mitchel McLaughlin, whose view might be closer to the reasoned policy of the IRA, or at least the official Sinn Féin understanding of IRA policy, has claimed that in the event of a clear announcement of a British intent to withdraw, even if the projected withdrawal date was twenty years into the future, the IRA's job would be regarded as complete and it would cease all operations. It would then be the job of other external forces to defend Catholics. He envisaged that a European force would do this. This contradicts the view of former IRA members that they would have a military role to play in such a situation.

The interviewees' conviction that the resources of the IRA in a doomsday situation would be much larger than those deployed to maintain the campaign of armed struggle in normal times assuages any fears they might have now that armed struggle could trigger a widespread conflagration. This may be wishful thinking on their part or a delusion cultivated within republican ranks by their own leadership, or it may be an informed assessment, albeit potentially an inaccurate one.

These former members believe that external forces would come to the aid of Catholics in the North. So long as they were able to protect themselves until those other forces got into position, Catholics would be safe and the republican agenda would prevail. None of this confirms that the IRA has a plan for such a doomsday, but it does show that republicans have discussed such an event among themselves and that they do not see the need for the IRA to expand into a mass army for its goals to be attained.

The development of the IRA from a small number of committed activists into a numerically strong army may not be necessary to fulfil this vision. The IRA has perhaps simply to continue to exist and train people, using only small numbers of volunteers in armed struggle, and preserving its wider membership against arrest or physical danger. If it recycled large numbers, to provide them with experience, it would accumulate a dormant army of guerrillas who might be called upon in crisis. However, the IRA has never conducted such a mass mobilisation and it has never attempted to throw Northern Ireland into the sort of crisis in which it could deploy this army. It has, if anything, avoided civil war by limiting its operations. At periods of extreme anxiety in Northern Ireland about the danger of civil war breaking out, the IRA has never taken the extra destabilising steps that might have generated the doomsday crisis, and it has had twenty-five years of campaigning within which to engineer such a crisis. It must be presumed that it has never had the will to.

On the other hand, the men I spoke to all anticipated that such a crisis would arise from the British making an announcement of intent to withdraw from Northern Ireland and this being resisted by loyalists. The demand for such an announcement from the British is still the formal policy of the IRA and Sinn Féin, so it would be prudent within an expectation of success in achieving this for republicans to prepare for civil war. If they don't expect to win, they shouldn't be pushing on; if they do expect to win, they should be preparing, according to their own logic, for civil war. The question then is whether the experience that membership of the IRA provides would be appropriate to a confrontational war with Protestants over territory.

The average annual murder rate of the IRA in the five years before the ceasefire of 1994 was forty-three and falling. Many of those killings were probably carried out by the same small groups of people. That workload does not suggest that the IRA has a large number of experienced killers at its disposal. It is also true, and remarkable, that the IRA has been able to renew its stock of killers over and over again in the last twenty-five years. It may well have accumulated much more experience than it actually draws on. It either has a small number of people with extensive experience, or a large number with relatively little experience, many of whom may not have killed anyone for years.

Most active members of the IRA are allocated jobs as vigilantes in nationalist areas. They are set to gathering information on criminals and delinquents, arresting them, interrogating them and punishing them, usually by breaking their arms and legs, either with gunshots or clubs. The charade of policing, sometimes called the 'war on the hoods', might keep many of these people fit and alert and closely connected to the IRA. It might help them keep their sensitivities hardened against the suffering of others, and provide them with the opportunity to use guns and other weapons. I suspect that the kneecappers and bone breakers are the pool from which the killers and saboteurs are recruited, rather than that they are a separate department or body of people who might later be added on to the army if needed.

The men I spoke to like to imagine that the difference between the IRA and the loyalists is that the IRA fights confrontationally. This isn't true. You can get an impression of what the military experience of the IRA is by counting up the different ways in which they kill people. Attacks on military installations are usually intended to cause maximum casualties, and therefore the numbers killed might be a reasonable measure of success in such operations. (That leaves out of consideration those bombings of property where the intention was not to kill, and punishment shootings, which were equally intended not to be lethal.) A profile of killings by the IRA over a five-year period, 1988–92, shows that 81 people were shot dead at close range with handguns, 131 were killed in explosions, and 33 were killed by rifles or submachine guns. This suggests a skill base profile of activists that is appropriate not to confrontational combat, but to surreptitious sabotage and murder. The IRA at full stretch could damage huge amounts of property and kill by surprise, but nothing in its experience to date suggests that it has acquired the ability to regroup and repeat a first wave of attacks.

An examination of all incidents in which IRA men were killed in action by the British army or RUC over the ten years up to the 1994 ceasefire – 1983–93 – shows that most were killed not in exchanges of fire, but by undercover soldiers ambushing them on their way to, or just after, an operation. Forty-three IRA members were killed by the British army and the RUC in that period. Only three of these were gunmen killed by return fire. The style of the IRA has been always to avoid extended engagements with their target. Some of those killed were preparing large-scale ambushes on security-force installations, as at Loughgall on 8 May 1987, when eight IRA men and a civilian were killed, and in Coalisland, on 16 February 1992 when four IRA men were killed. These men died, however, at the hands of undercover agents taking them by surprise, not in competitive exchanges with the people thay had gone out to attack. These ambushes by the army against the IRA have raised intense suspicions about the legality of army actions, because men appear to have been killed where it might have been possible to arrest them. Ironically, perhaps, this argument – and it may well be a valid one – reinforces the perception of the IRA as a noncombative army. It was because it did not risk exchanges of fire that it would have been possible to arrest their gunmen rather than wipe them out. Most of the members of the RUC and the British army killed by the IRA were killed also in surreptitious attacks. These facts suggest, not armies competing for physical advantage over each other, but armies at pains to avoid exchanges of fire. A difference between undercover army and RUC ambushes, and ambushes by the IRA, is that the army and the RUC have been able to take control of the target area and hold it; the IRA has always sought to attack surreptitiously and quickly and to withdraw. This strongly argues against any tenable plan by the IRA to lay the foundations of a large military engagement capable of capturing or retaining territory. The actual numbers of people who have used assault rifles must be quite small, even though the number of assault rifles available is high.

The other possible doomsday scenario, of a defensive war against a loyalist uprising, would depend on a different range of skills, maintaining an administrative system within the defended areas, and defending barricades at interfaces. The IRA has shown little indication, however, that it wishes to instigate such a war or that it is preparing an army with the skills to fight it. However, there is still a living lore in republican areas that regards a future civil war as a real danger. Entailed in this lore is a culture of derision towards those who have left the ghetto to live in mixed middle-class areas, and a belief that they will have to recognise who they really belong to when that crisis comes.

War is for the future, however; it is not the actual reality of armed struggle. The language that describes the IRA campaign as war is a propagandist garnish on a form of violent agitation. When he describes the IRA campaign as 'armed propaganda', Gerry Adams is making explicit, briefly, that he understands that well.

The IRA probably learned in the mid-seventies that they could not fight a simple battlefield war. It did not have the resources or membership to direct physically coercive force against the British state. That meant it would have to find means of exerting political influence aided by low levels of violence. It would have to find means of getting returns from a type of violence that is normally called terrorism. M.L.R. Smith looks back on the IRA campaign and argues that there was a time when they thought in terms of a real prospect of ejecting the British from Ireland by force. He demarcates one clear change of direction, away from the piling on of maximum damage to a long-term war of sapping British morale. In the first phase, republicans had studied the numbers of soldiers killed in Aden and Cyprus before the British had withdrawn and calculated that similar numbers of deaths would force them to leave Northern Ireland. In the second phase, republicans realised that the war would be much more protracted. They would have to weaken the will of the British over a long period, by demonstrating their own determination and ability to survive. To achieve this they would have to develop a strong community support base. This support base would help the IRA in practical ways. It would be a field of political action for Sinn Féin, and it would be a propaganda asset in itself, as an advertisement for the public support for armed protest.

This strategy, termed the 'long war' strategy by republicans and the 'total strategy' by Smith, was predicated on the understanding that the British would not withdraw, except after a long campaign. It expanded republican action beyond the military.

This doesn't mean that a strategy of killing more and more soldiers had been abandoned, just that a strategy of low-level irritation, sustained over a long period, had been acknowledged to have more potential than a frantic charge of destruction such as was tried in the early 1970s. Danny Morrison reaffirmed the value of piling up the murders as late as 1989, twelve years after the development of the 'long war' strategy. Morrison said then, 'When it is politically costly for the British to remain in Ireland, they'll go . . . it won't be triggered until a large number of British soldiers are killed and that's what's going to happen.'

On another occasion, talking to Robert White (*Provisional Irish Republicans: An Oral and Interpretive History*), Morrison made it clear that he viewed republican strategy more as an effort to sap the will of the British than to incapacitate them. 'It isn't a question of driving the British army into the sea. It's a question of breaking the political will of the British government to remain. And that's why ten years ago [in 1977] the IRA stated the theory of the Long War.' Morrison regarded the killing of soldiers as an integral part of the sickening of the British will. He could no longer imagine a limit to the number of such killings the British would endure, but he anticipated that when they realised that maintaining government in Northern Ireland would always cost army lives, their will to continue would be deflated.

110

In the year he said this, only 3 British soldiers were killed by the IRA, out of 56 people killed by them in total, so it seems implausible that Danny Morrison was attempting an honest description of IRA intentions and methodology. If he was, then he would have had to admit that the effort was failing badly. In the two previous years the scores had been similarly low. The following year the Provisionals killed 23 soldiers out of a total of 67 people killed by them, and 24 out of 52 the year after that. This sudden peaking of British army deaths resulted from the success of a small number of bomb attacks, and the deaths subsided to more routine levels in the following year. British soldiers usually accounted for less than one quarter of IRA killings.

Certainly a huge effort was being put into killing soldiers through the development of mortars and attacks on army bases, but the low casualty rate shows how unproductive this was. The real effect of mortar attacks was to impose on government the expense of defending soldiers and property against attacks through the reinforcement of buildings. New bases were built with thick walls and small windows, with heavy, spring-loaded bombproof doors. The cost of building these was increased by the need to protect civilian workers who were listed by the IRA as legitimate targets for attack.

The 'long war' strategy was a method for sustaining the IRA campaign, aligned to a theory that British morale would be eroded by the durability of the campaign, rather than by the actual physical damage caused. The threat was now no longer one that said: Get out of Ireland or we will kill a lot of people. The threat said: You may as well get out of Ireland now, because one day you will be so sick of this incessant bombing that you will go anyway.

The 'war' has been a campaign of protest. The missile fired at Downing Street has more in common with the dead rat in a shoe box sent by another disgruntled citizen than with, say, the shell fired into Sarajevo.

6 A LONG WAR

Most writers attribute the 'long war' strategy to Gerry Adams, and trace its emergence to the letters he wrote in the late seventies from prison to the republican newspaper *An Phoblacht*. Under the pseudonym Brownie, Adams wrote of the need to lay the groundwork for a long campaign, and he devised a strategy for this. It was like the Maoist idea of the guerrilla fish swimming in the water of the community. In Mao's vision it was the basis for gradualist expansion. In republican terms it seems to have been a means to consolidating a base that would survive rather than grow.

A document captured by the Garda Síochána from IRA member Seamus Twomey in December 1977 outlines the transformation planned for the IRA and its methods of operation, but the emphasis here was on preserving the movement against British efforts to break it. The transformation entailed the establishment of a cell structure, and the training of members in how to resist interrogation. It wasn't clear at this stage how the 'long war' strategy was going to bring the British to a realisation that they would have to leave Ireland.

There is a question over whether the reorganisation of the IRA into a cell structure was ever completed. Bishop and Mallie express doubts about this, saying that in some areas the cell structure never developed beyond wishful thinking. What did emerge from that period of reorganisation was the creation of a Northern Command. This was a military rather than a political asset. The political development of Sinn Féin really didn't get its fillip until the hunger strikes campaign of 1981.

As we have seen, the 'long war' strategy, as understood by Smith, acknowledged that the final goal of bringing about a British withdrawal might not be achieved by military means, and that political tactics also had a part to play. The maximum possible pressure would have to be brought to bear on the British by this strategy, which was articulated in the 1980 Easter message of the IRA leadership as an effort to 'tier together all aspects of nationalism and socialism and all strands of rural and urban discontent into a surging wave of republicanism'. This, Smith reasons, was a means to the maximising of coercive pressure on the British. Certainly this line of thought had echoes of the earlier republican socialists of the 1930s. But what was it about the 'long war' strategy that was actually going to eject the British from Ireland?

Smith's view is that the IRA felt that a combination of armed struggle and political development at community level would serve to make the British presence untenable and provide clear evidence of mass support for the killers and saboteurs. The total strategy would have the advantage of allowing republican activists to present themselves before their supporters in legal activities. This would allow them also to develop relationships with the media. As explainers and justifiers of the IRA they would retain an immunity to actual responsibility for IRA actions. In his book, Smith lists the coercive elements of the strategy as: international pressure; armed struggle designed to undermine the morale of British forces and to provide a tangible expression of the rejection of British rule; political mobilisation which would generate support for the armed struggle and prevent an internal accommodation in Northern Ireland; and British public opinion, which would come to feel that Northern Ireland was too costly and expendable. In combination, these elements of a total strategy would, the IRA thought, drive Britain out of Ireland. The 'total strategy' would also enable Sinn Féin to build up a base that would allow it to supersede the SDLP as the main representatives of nationalists in Northern Ireland and to undermine the positions they were taking by branding them as collaborationist. It was in the early eighties, as Sinn Féin's political growth accelerated, according to Sean O'Callaghan and Suzanne

Breen, that the IRA contemplated killing John Hume. They might well have wished, at that time, that Hume would disappear, while there remained a plausible prospect that Sinn Féin's political growth would continue.

The change in emphasis, after the introduction of the 'long war' strategy, was towards irritation rather than coercion. The IRA could scare off foreign investment, and reap the propaganda advantage of demonstrating their 'determination and coordination'. The point was not now to make Northern Ireland an unbearable financial burden, however, but over a protracted period to erode the will of the British through the incessant nagging of drip-feed violence, none of it with the potential to force the issue, but all of it accumulating into profound irritation.

The paradox at the heart of the 'long war' strategy was that it had significant political drawbacks, yet it sought to consolidate a political programme. It was trying to support the growth of Sinn Féin, and yet its violence was costing the party votes. At a later phase, it may be that the party realised that the political programme could only advance if the support base was spared the danger of the armed campaign and the trials of reactive military pressure from the loyalists and the British. The question remains, however, which element of the 'total strategy' was so valuable, through the 1980s, that it was worth sacrificing votes for.

One objective of the 'total strategy', according to Smith, was the prevention of a settlement within Northern Ireland. Any settlement reached between constitutional nationalism and unionism would cramp the claim of republicans that an outstanding constitutional problem remained to be solved. For republicans, however, blocking an internal settlement was not just a means to clearing the space for agitation for British withdrawal; it was an intrinsic part of their agitation in itself. The denial of the opportunity for other parties to come to agreement internally was a means to force them to consider, in time, a united Ireland. The IRA campaign frustrated all political endeavours to reach a settlement, not with a view to creating a stalemate, but with a view to forcing unthinkable options on the British. Republicans saw their campaign as narrowing the options of the British to the point where they would have to consider withdrawal. If settlements were attempted as a means of bringing peace to Northern Ireland, then they were vulnerable to the demonstration by the IRA that they had failed.

Violence, as armed propaganda, would demonstrate the instability of Northern Ireland. If Northern Ireland was unstable, then those who had worked to create peace and stability had failed and would have to try again. Once the government was thinking in terms of political experimentation to assuage the IRA, it was in the hands of the IRA to let them know whether they had succeeded or not. Every bomb said, Try again.

It was equally in the hands of other paramilitary groups to do the same, but this would have been no problem for the IRA, where the settlement offered was anything short of British withdrawal. Any resistance from any source would contribute to that narrowing of British options and advance the republican project. The clearest example of that was the Ulster Workers' Council strike of 1974, which wrecked the prospects of the powersharing Assembly. It did the IRA's work for it.

The paradox of loyalist violence is that it simply contributes to the impression, which republicans work to foster, that Northern Ireland is an unresolved constitutional problem. All political violence weighs in the same side of the scales, against assertions that the state can work or be made workable.

The blocking of an internal settlement in Northern Ireland appears to be a central republican strategy, but Gerry Adams himself has declared it a failure. He said in his autobiography that he thought Sinn Féin was 'short-sighted' in choosing not to contest the elections to the 1974 powersharing Assembly, even on an abstentionist basis. He has questioned, in *Free Ireland: Towards a Lasting Peace*, the tenability of a strategy of using violence as a veto on political settlement, saying that the armed campaign of the IRA had arrived at 'a situation of deadlock in which Oglaigh na hEireann were able to block the imposition of a British solution, but were unable to force the British to withdraw'. This 'produced a sense of war-weariness'. This was his rationale for the peace process: that such a strategy of veto had been employed but had produced fatigue and deadlock.

In Adams's earlier writings there had been clear suggestions that he had thought through the means by which violence would function as a veto on an internal settlement. In 1985 he wrote in *Ireland After Britain* that, at the end of the day, the British would have to withdraw because the problem of the instability of Northern Ireland would not be removed. 'Every British attempt so far has failed, and as each option is tried, knocked back, or falls of its own accord, they will have to consider the option of withdrawal.' In essence, violence or instability would prompt the British to attempt political compromises in Northern Ireland, and violence would prove that these in turn had failed. If the violence persisted long enough, the British would be forced to acknowledge that all their efforts had failed and they would then have to consider, as a last resort, an option for withdrawal. In fact, the British evaded the question of how to devise a peaceful settlement by maintaining direct rule. They understood the nature of the problem they faced and devised the best means of coping with it. Direct rule was their own 'long war' strategy.

For a long period, no proposals for settlement were offered by the British. After the Anglo-Irish Agreement in 1985, no initiative was taken by the British to set up a devolved assembly or any form of constitutional arrangement. They offered nothing for the IRA to veto, and the IRA campaign became a routine part of life in Northern Ireland. As direct rule was already in place and functioning, a proactive campaign of removing Britain by force would have been required to change it. This is the sort of campaign that the IRA is not equipped to fight. Direct rule was presented by the British with no pretensions anyway to being a solution, a formula for peace.

In 1988, in *A Pathway to Peace*, Adams suggested again that the republican strategy was to restrict the political freedom of the British government to achieve an internal settlement in Northern Ireland. 'National self-determination is also the democratic option which the British government refuse at present to contemplate.

They will only concede it when their room to manoeuvre is narrowed down to that democratic option.'

Objections to the peace process were voiced in a debate at the Sinn Féin *ard-fheis* in 1995. Dublin delegate Seán Mac Brádaigh said: 'No one believed that the armed struggle was going to bring about the perfect society in Ireland, but what it was going to achieve was the prevention of any settlement on British terms.' This view concurs with the aim described by Adams of narrowing down British options until they had no choice but to concede 'national self-determination'. By this understanding of republican strategy, their favoured term 'resistance' suggests not physical resistance of British armed forces, as is implied in their propaganda, but the resistance of political endeavours to settle peace on Northern Ireland by means unacceptable to republicans.

Clearly, Mac Brádaigh thought that, by 1995, this strategy had been abandoned. He thought that the IRA was no longer committed to using violence to veto settlements, but was working through Sinn Féin to promote negotiations on an inevitable compromise. It seems logical that it couldn't have been doing both. The problem for republicans had been that a campaign committed to vetoing proffered settlements had no political work to do other than to maintain its operations as a reminder to Britain that, should they attempt any settlement, they would have to take the threat of violence into account. With the peace initiative promoted by Gerry Adams and John Hume, things were moving again, and though Mac Brádaigh appeared not to see it when he spoke in early 1995, this new programme for finding a settlement may have provided just the sort of context in which threats of violence might be productive again.

A yet more cynical reading would say that the scepticism of the peace process voiced by some republicans and their allies served more than anything else to make the supposed peace initiative plausible. How could we say that Adams was playing tricks on us when his own friends and comrades were publicly rebuking him? Seán Mac Brádaigh's criticism of the peace process sent journalists home from that *ard-fheis* convinced they had seen clear evidence that the peace maker, Gerry Adams, had converted most of his movement and had yet to convert all of it.

The question is whether the peace initiative that included the ceasefire of 1994 was consistent with the 'long war' strategy or a divergence from it. Through the ceasefire, republicans held to the principle that violence was not of their own volitional making but was a product of circumstances that the IRA alone had no power to change. Only demilitarisation could ensure peace, and this required that the police and army should accept that the onus on illegal para-military groups to disarm extended to them as well. A history of injustice had brought us to this. If that injustice could be dealt with, the causes of violence would disappear.

The violence, essentially, had come to be seen as evidence of the need for political change. The political wing, Sinn Féin, would now work for that change, while the violence provided a reminder to others that they had not yet succeeded in making the vital compromise that could bring peace. The power to endorse any settlement as productive of peace would now lie with those who made war, that is, with the IRA.

The project would be made more tenable by people accepting the vocabulary with which republicans and their allies dressed it. The IRA would not be described as terrorists trying to impose their will on a resistant society, but would be caught up in a conflict with society, a conflict that demanded mediation and, inevitably, some concessions to the demands that were enforced by violence. If after all efforts at mediation and political compromise, the IRA continued with its murder and sabotage, that would prove, according to the new language, that the conciliation effort had failed to achieve the peace it was designed to create. Northern Ireland would still be an 'untenable political entity'. All parties to the conflict would have to go away and try yet again to create the conditions in which the IRA no longer felt the need to produce violence. If this is what was going on, then it was the tactics of the protection racketeer. The message of the peace initiative was: Hey, we've got a problem here: maybe you better do something or a lot of people could get hurt.

The more that political initiatives failed, the closer the

government would be brought to realising they could do nothing but try the one last thing that until then was unthinkable, and prepare for withdrawal. Another explanation might be that the strategy of blocking change through violence requires that the protester should cease violence every once in a while to see how much the government is ready to concede.

The formula that regards violence as following directly from political circumstances has huge political advantages. It challenges everyone to rethink their political position for the sake of assuaging violence. It also allows the initiators of the violence to wait and see whether they like what others come up with before they make a political move of their own. There are also military advantages to this.

The IRA skirts all prospects of its resolve being tested by divorcing the violence from the decisions of the political leaders of Sinn Féin. This was demonstrated several times. In June 1997, three days after the British government made it clear that it was conceding several Sinn Féin demands, for a time frame for talks and for a procedure for entry into talks, the IRA sent killers out to murder two policemen (see Chapter 8). Intrinsically it was an illogical thing to do. It showed that the IRA was not amenable to any concessions to Sinn Féin. The logic of this was that the IRA wanted to emphasise its distinction from Sinn Féin. That would have the political advantage for Sinn Féin of making its demand to be regarded as a separate entity more plausible, and it would also send a military message to the government that it need never feel safe from attack, even with things going well politically. The IRA, this message says, has to be regarded as a force of nature, which is not amenable to political assuaging short of a declaration of intent to withdraw.

While the government was making contact with Martin McGuinness in the early 1990s, the IRA was bombing Warrington and Bishopsgate. The government asked for a cessation of IRA operations to make dialogue possible. Sinn Féin responded as if the bombings were wholly outside their control. Their tactic was not going to be one of bartering bombs for concessions. The more valuable tactic was to reinforce their analysis that violence followed automatically from the political conditions and to offer help to other parties in assuaging those conditions. Sinn Féin politicians would exercise their strategy of whittling away at British commitments, but they would insulate the IRA against having its own commitment similarly eroded in return by British negotiation efforts. Republicans had inched their way into the British resistance to their conditions, effectively slicing it away like salami. There would be one integral package to trade with, the principle of the right of the IRA to use force, kept intact until the very end. That is how deterrence works. It has to be as credible as a law of nature. Northern Ireland was to be like an ancient minefield that Britain had stepped onto; and on which she had discovered no possible alternative but to withdraw.

Violence is all the more effective if it is presented as unreasoning. A child can stop a tank if a tank has a driver. A famous picture from Tienanmen Square illustrates that. A man in a white shirt blocks the way of a line of tanks and they attempt to veer round him. A tank with no driver makes no such calculations. The IRA violence was to be presented as like a tank out of control, unstoppable other than by those who knew how to access and work the controls. Sinn Féin would have the access codes. If government followed the formula prescribed by Sinn Féin then the violence could stop. All other means of trying to stop it would fail.

So, the long war would narrow the options the British government had for settling the problem of violence. All the IRA had to do was maintain the violence, and Sinn Féin would offer the formula for assuaging it. Any attempts to assuage it by other means would be proved by continuing violence to have failed, and the British would simply have to go away and try again.

A strategy of vetoing an internal settlement through the narrowing of options would also insulate republicans against the emphatic assertions of the British that they were not going to withdraw. It was already understood within the rationale of the strategy that the British would continue to resist the option of withdrawal until all alternatives had been tried and proved not to have brought peace. Experiments like powersharing and joint sovereignty would be stepping stones along the way.

A period of creative political endeavour on the part of other parties to establish a powersharing executive would not be looked on by republicans as a threat to their hopes of a united Ireland. On the contrary, it would be seen as another experiment doomed to failure. The sooner all the options were used up, the sooner Britain would arrive at the conclusion that the problem was unsolvable without their withdrawal. To see Britain trying yet again to cement the middle ground in Northern Ireland could only give republicans heart that the collapse of another option was imminent.

By this reading, the peace process dovetails with Mac Brádaigh's 1995 vision of IRA intentions, even though he did not appear to see this himself. The peace initiative gave the 'long war' strategy new conditions to respond to. It put republicans back in the game of inviting responses to its violence as a means to create a settlement, and then of invalidating them with more violence.

Whether this could work in the new conditions of the 1990s, and against a background in which the people had clearly decided that they wanted peace, was another question. Many believed, as did John Hume, for instance, that the IRA campaign may have run its course in terms of its acceptability among Catholics, but that is different from it having exhausted its strategic potential.

It is possible that republicans genuinely thought in 1994 that their strategy had run its course and been defeated. The entanglements in the way of getting into talks, however, presented them with a new game to play, and new prospects of rallying support around interim positions. During the first ceasefire, support for the republican movement actually increased because republicans were able to pass themselves off plausibly as making genuine efforts to find peace in the face of British intransigence. After that ceasefire ended, support continued to increase, because a section of the electorate believed that republicans were more serious than anyone else about wanting peace, and that their formula for it was a reasonable one. People who would not normally have voted for Sinn Féin saw some merit in their argument that the British demand for decommissioning of weapons was a demand for a surrender that the British had not earned. That republicans had simultaneously been demanding the abolition of the police force and the disarming of state forces seemed not to enter their considerations. These could be dismissed, perhaps, as rhetoric that would vanish if talks got under way.

The 'long war' strategy was not wholly directed against the British. A veto on a settlement, founded on the principle that violence arose from circumstances that only the British could alter, had the power to narrow the political options of other political parties in Ireland too. The SDLP accepted this principle that violence was a product of injustice and lack of democracy, and though the party was the main political rival of Sinn Féin, it set about working for a settlement that would remove the causes of violence, presuming these to be historical rather than conspiratorial. This is clearly implied by the first paragraph of a declaration drafted by John Hume and Gerry Adams, and popularly known as the Hume–Adams Accord. (It was in fact a statement that they hoped the British and Irish governments would make jointly, and it had an input into the final drafting of the Joint Declaration which they did in fact make in December 1993.)

> The Taoiseach and the Prime Minister acknowledge that the most urgent and important issue facing the people of Ireland, North and South, and the British and Irish governments together, is to remove the causes of conflict, to overcome the legacy of history and to heal the divisions which have resulted, recognising that past failures to settle relationships between the people of both islands satisfactorily has led to continuing tragedy and suffering. (*Sunday Tribune*, 27 August 1995)

History is thereby to be blamed for bombs, and the onus is on the British and Irish governments to stop the bombing by resolving the problems in relations between the two countries. Eschewing violence themselves, the SDLP saw it as a product of 'Unionist intransigence' and worked against that intransigence as a means of removing the compulsion on republicans to fight. This effectively endorsed the republican vision of their campaign as a war driven by circumstances rather than as protest violence. In that sense, the violence of the IRA acted as a leverage on the SDLP, spurring them to work harder for a settlement that republicans and unionists could agree on – effectively, to get the best possible deal for republicans in the face of unionist resistance.

No amount of violence from the IRA would discourage the SDLP from seeking such an agreement. IRA attacks like the Shankill bomb of October 1993 and the Canary Wharf bomb of February 1996 would only reaffirm the need to work harder for such a settlement. All violence came to validate the argument that violence was a product of circumstances, and that the only way to end it was to change the political context in which it arose. In this sense every bomb added urgency to the SDLP's pursuit of a settlement. Their political agenda was being set for them by the IRA.

The central argument of the SDLP was that the lack of political progress towards change created a vacuum which was inevitably filled by violence. This was presented as the rationale for taking the initiative away from paramilitaries, but was arguably doing the opposite, providing the rationale by which their threats were translated into efforts at political experimentation. Effectively, the SDLP served to remind the British and Irish governments of the need to try another initiative, while republicans positioned themselves again to demonstrate that it wouldn't work.

The 1994 ceasefire was frequently explained as a product of the campaign of the IRA having exhausted itself. The SDLP leader, John Hume, said privately that he believed republicans needed to be 'let off the hook'. Many regarded the campaign as having reached a stalemate in which both sides had to acknowledge that there could be no military victory. In terms of violent protest, however, the prospect of military victory is not real anyway. The war, if it is to be called a war at all, is not a contest of strength. For the insurgent group to concede that it cannot defeat its enemy by physical means is simply to describe the conditions under which it has always operated. For the state to make such a concession is much more significant. It is to acknowledge that the methods of the insurgent are successfully challenging its political imagination to find some tenable palliative constitutional measures. For both sides to concede stalemate is in fact for both to acknowledge that the violent protester has the advantage. It is the state's aspirations that have been curtailed, not the terrorist's, for the terrorist never had military victory as an option in the first place.

The strategy of narrowing British government options through a veto of violence was successful in preventing an internal settlement and instrumental in prolonging the conflict. It was a tenable means of serving the republican objective. The IRA were not after all pursuing a discredited strategy, just a very tiresome one.

7 THE FISH
IN THE WATERS

There are those who see the republican movement as a conscientious political conspiracy which plans all its moves to get its way; there are others who take their bearings from what they regard as the mood of the community. They see republicans as reflecting the responses of working-class Catholics to political changes. At its most naïve, this view sees, say, a car bomb in Poleglass not so much as the work of a few activists, but as a coalescence of communal tremors set in motion by Tony Blair's commitment to the Union or John Major's alleged 'binning' of the Mitchell report. The other view, that small groups make decisions on who and how to kill without reference to the community, has its weaknesses too, but seemed most plausible after the Canary Wharf bomb that ended the 1994 ceasefire.

The commentator Conor Cruise O'Brien attributes all republican decisions to conspiratorial planning. Another critic, Eoghan Harris, whose name is often linked to O'Brien's, tends to trace republican motivation to a sickly romanticism rather than to political pragmatism. Contesting such explanations, Ed Vulliamy, reviewing John Conroy's book *War as a Way of Life* for the *New Statesman*, says:

> Conroy's book teaches a lesson that writers on Northern Ireland seem to find hard to learn; that it is keen eyes and ears, not a big mouth, that help to explain a battle like this, and that breezy political pedantry will fail where an interest in real people will succeed. Thus he [Conroy] produces the best book to date on Northern Ireland.

125

The implication is that this is a war that grows out of the hearts of ordinary people, out of their hurts and frustrations. In January 1997, the political journal *Fortnight* criticised the IRA defector Sean O'Callaghan for an appraisal of the movement as monolithic. The magazine argued that he was overlooking the fact that any organisation must operate as a system that incorporates diverse opinions and responds to the interaction between other parts of the play. Writers who concentrate on the community or social aspect of the republican movement tend to credit republicans with little tactical good sense. Violence on the streets is seen as a product of community outrage or a long hot summer, rather than the orchestration and planning that the security forces might see behind it. *Fortnight*'s criticism of Sean O'Callaghan is that he shows little sense of the systemic factors; that he doesn't understand that republicans are confined to a sort of grammar of circumstances. So republicans should be seen as trapped by circumstance? The danger facing those who see republicans as confined to a game in which others play is that they overlook the possibility that republicans might be just as clever in their playing of the game and in their deployment of the political grammar as those they play against – or more clever.

There is a conviction among some journalists that you cannot really understand republicanism unless you understand the social forces underneath it, and that to regard it simply as a cynical conspiracy is to miss the crucial underpinning, the truth that the republicans reflect the stresses within their communities. This, however, is to take republicans entirely on their own terms, and to skirt the question that they would want you to skirt, which is, what are they up to? Those who promote a view that republican energies are driven by disturbances within their support community could be blamed for crediting the IRA with being the one political movement that doesn't plan ahead.

After the Canary Wharf bomb of February 1996, many critics, even within the nationalist tradition, condemned it as a decision taken by an army council of seven people, without reference to the desires of a support community, let alone the Irish people as a whole. In ordinary party politics the tendency of parties to move away from the support base and act almost autonomously is well understood. No one believes that the British Labour Party is much moved by its annual conference, let alone the feelings of ordinary people in working men's drinking clubs. The SDLP, under the leadership of John Hume, was regarded pretty much as a one-man band, with the party morally obliged to back the leader. But when it comes to Sinn Féin and the IRA, there is a presumption of a need to explain their actions in terms of an organic relationship with the community.

A corollary of this idea, that the community is the seedbed of feeling to which the IRA responds, is the conviction held by the peace movements and others that the people are to blame for the Troubles, that it is popular sectarian attitudes that translate into violence. The Peaceline is regarded almost as a symbol of the inability of Protestants and Catholics to live together, whereas it would be more charitable, and more realistic, to see it as a product of the fear of the many of the violence of the few. Many analyses of the Northern Ireland violence malign the communities from which the violence stems. In part, this is a failure to see that conflict is sustained more by fear than by hatred; it also endorses unthinkingly the programmes offered by violent political minorities.

Northern Ireland is often spoken of as a 'sick society' which produces grotesque violence out of the hearts of us all, through the hands of the few. Another myth is that the violence is the product of the evil few, the terrorists. Often, unthinkingly, the same models are lumped together in a single trite, incoherent vision. The 'sick society' model tends to prescribe constitutional change as the solution, though, also arguing from this model, evangelicals will argue for a return to Jesus as the only possible solution. The 'evil men' model tends to prescribe a security-based solution. Take out the bad men, and everything will be all right.

Paramilitaries prefer the 'sick society' model. Both loyalists and republicans will argue, for instance, that their prisoners were decent people whose turning to murder and destruction was a response to the circumstances they found themselves in. This argument has been used to absolve even the most brutal killers. But for the political problems of the time, it is argued, Basher Bates would never

127

have taken a meat hook to a Catholic. Politics alone drove him to it. Basher woke each day into the light of an intolerable political problem, and could not assuage the hurt of a compromised British identity without drawing blood. Similarly, the most callous and destructive of republicans were born into the horror of house searches and pogroms and discrimination. Who could blame them for what the integrity of their aversion to these things drove them to?

Both loyalists and republicans grew up in communities that affirmed the course they chose. On a day in the early seventies that two policemen were killed by a bomb in Belfast, a neighbour called me over to her door. 'Did you hear the news?' she said. 'They got another two of the bastards.' There was no clear consistency to the feelings of many: they would rarely approve a killing, but they would feel better about some than others. People who offered no support to the IRA would still occasionally admit to feeling uplifted by the cleverness or appropriateness of a single violent action. People tended to discuss the campaign in its details rather than in its principles. 'That was awful; they shouldn't have done that' was a remark that carried the implication: 'I could understand it better if they had killed so and so instead.'

In this chapter I want to explore the relationship between the IRA and its host community. That community is represented by republicans as one of their core validations. Out of the hurt community comes the urge to violence; out of the community's allegiance to its suffering prisoners comes the sustained loyalty to the republican cause; and out of the community's love for the peacemaker comes the vote for Sinn Féin – that is how they would have it. This supposed organic link between the community and the killer is under stress at times when the IRA's actions appear wholly unilateral and inconsistent with the expectations of peace engendered within the community, so other validations are needed. These come from within the republican theology, but it is when standing on that theology alone that republicans seem most eccentric and inept. The touchstone of community is vital to them.

The responsibility for violence can be displaced onto the community, and the community comes to validate the integrity of republican claims. For instance, those who argued for better policing could be told that they were out of touch with the community which, it is said, wholly – not partially – rejects the police. Those who are shocked by the anger and singlemindedness of this can be told simply that they don't understand.

The vociferous political activist easily appropriates the right to speak for the whole community, because the dissenters from that opinion tend simply to withdraw. I watched this during the planning of protests against Orange parades passing through the lower Ormeau Road in 1995. An agreement had been drawn up between the Lower Ormeau Concerned Community Group (LOCC) and the local Ballynafeigh Orange Lodge. It would concede to the residents of the lower Ormeau area the right to veto all parades past their homes in coming years. The condition was that for that one year, two more parades could be allowed through without protest. This agreement had been witnessed by an auxiliary bishop of the Catholic diocese and by the then Deputy Chief Constable of the RUC, Ronnie Flanagan. These people thought it was a good deal that would prevent a sensitive issue turning into a long series of potentially violent confrontations; if that is what the organisers wanted.

On 11 July, the Lower Ormeau Concerned Community Group called a meeting to re-examine the agreement. This was the night before the big Twelfth parade in Belfast. The LOCC said it was angered by the participation of the Ballynafeigh lodge in a massive protest at Drumcree. They wanted to think over the agreement again. About two hundred people turned up. I went into the hall too and watched, though the media was banned. I watched Bishop Dallat commend the agreement. Gerard Rice, a former republican prisoner and regular spokesman for the group, chaired the meeting and called for speakers. I noted that when some of the speakers called for the following day's parade to be allowed through without protest, about one third of the people in the hall applauded. When others called for the parade to be stopped, the other two thirds cheered and clapped. A group of men at the back of the hall stamped their feet and whistled. The impression created for the rest of the media outside was that a single ardent opinion was declaring itself robustly.

Gerard Rice then said that there was no need for a vote to be taken, and he declared that the protest against the parades would resume the following morning. He went out to the press and told them that a unanimous consensus had been reached against the parades. The people who had gone to call for an end to the protests might as well not have gone at all. Just by going to the meeting they had added weight to the position they had sought to oppose. You could imagine why those people would have very little inclination to go back to another meeting like that.

As I walked out of the hall I saw women standing at their doorways in the neighbouring streets and wondered why they hadn't come to the meeting to say what they wanted. A television journalist asked me how the meeting had gone. I said 'No comment', and walked on. An hour later I appeared on the television news as one of those who had gone to the meeting and contributed to the supposed unanimous consensus on blocking Orange parades. If Rice said the vote was unanimous, he was saying that all those people seen leaving the meeting were part of his campaign against the Orange Order. Orangemen watching the news would see those people's faces and remember them as their enemies. The next day at the parade I was spotted by women who had seen the news. They pointed me out to their friends as one of the agitators. They huddled close and whispered about me.

All the people who had gone to the meeting to try to soften the resistance to the parades had taken the risk that they would be publicly exposed as supporting the very position they contested, and once exposed they would be at risk of a beating or worse from supporters of the Orange Order. Why would they bother again? Vociferous machine politics like that simply leaves such people behind, or it uses them to swell numbers. It ropes them into a notion of a consistent community, beleaguered and at odds with the rest of the world, or it shuts them up.

In the mid-seventies, Gerry Adams had described how the relationship with the community was to be consolidated. The problem before that, for the IRA, had not been that no such relationship existed, but that it was too informal. Too many people could see republicans in action; too many members drank with nonmembers in clubs and bars and talked too much. There was not enough discipline. What Adams wanted was a semblance of Mao's guerrilla fish swimming in the water of the people. The community would protect the movement and the movement would be integrated into the community. The community would be the validation of the IRA, the opportunity for them to say that they were responding to the demands of their people.

A number of areas are regarded as heartland communities of the republican movement. There are characteristic differences between them, which can be interpreted as suggesting an internal homogeneity. There is west Belfast, which itself divides into parts of different character; there is north Belfast; there is Derry's Bogside and Creggan, and there are the rural areas of south Armagh and mid-Tyrone.

Alex Maskey, who comes from the New Lodge, has said that the people of the Falls did not really understand sectarianism the way the people of the New Lodge did, who lived close to a Protestant area. Father Denis Faul, describing his mid-Tyrone area for me, said, 'Here it is about land. People still talk about the Protestants having taken their field, even though it happened three hundred years ago. They still feel a sense of belonging to that bit of land and of being entitled to have it back.'

In south Armagh, people feel simply that they are Irish people invaded by British forces. Talking to the Carragher family, noted republicans in the area, I often heard the remark, 'There are no Protestants here. Why do we need the army in to keep people apart. There is no peace for them to keep that's better than the peace there would be if they left.' Crossmaglen has no easy affinity with the rest of the North. It is a southern town that suffered the misfortune of the border being laid down on the wrong side of it. It was always a centre of rebellion though. In the 1850s, this area was home to the Ribbonmen, whose secret trials and organisational framework were similar to those of the Provisionals today. It would not be at all surprising if the very grandparents of local republicans had been

Fenians and their grandparents had been Ribbonmen.

Derry had the deepest grievance at the start of the civil rights campaign and suffered the greatest aggravation of it in the massacre of Bloody Sunday, but it settled down under direct rule into a Catholic city that doesn't agonise about its identity. The low level of violence in Derry in the 1980s and 1990s suggests that even though the most senior members of the IRA lived there, they could not mould a local annoyance into sympathy for frequent acts of murder. Republicans blamed their failings on informers. Many local people said simply that the nationalists of Derry loved their town and would not tolerate further attacks on it.

You can get a quick insight into the character of the largest republican area, west Belfast, just by reading the local newspaper, the *Andersonstown News*; this is the paper published outside the republican movement that gives most space to its issues and most respect to its arguments. The letters page may carry intense criticism of the IRA, alongside very supportive comments. For instance, there will be an occasional run of letters complaining about joyriders and demanding action from the IRA, and those opposing IRA policing will write in with their views. Sometimes there is a transparent lack of criticism of the IRA, as when a representative of the Falls Taxi Association wrote to complain of disruptive police checkpoints in the management of bomb hoaxes. No blame at all, apparently, attached to those who had stolen the cars in the first place, and put imitation bombs in them, on main roads at rush hour.

The entertainment pages of the *Andersonstown News* give an idea of the social preoccupations of the area. Space is given to drinking clubs like the Felons and the Rossa's, but the larger, more colourful ads are for the big bar lounges with their discos and bands. The Felons club, the favourite drinking club of republicans, advertises every week. For example:

> A meal for two is up for grabs for whoever answers the Felons brainstormer and free pints are on the go for questions answered correctly. Mother's Day Fayre and cabaret, choice of four menus and a vegetarian special.

The clubs themselves differ in character. Many people who would not want to drink in an overtly republican club will be happy to drink in a sports club, where the band might sing rebel songs and there will be a collection for the Green Cross to support the republican prisoners, but where the mix of people will include those who are openly sceptical of Sinn Féin.

The bands that do the rounds of the clubs know the old republican favourites. Some bands come out with more raucous and blood-thirsty songs, celebrating specific IRA achievements. In recent years, these seem to have lost their popularity. I tried to get copies of the tapes of one of these bands through the Sinn Féin shop on the Falls Road. They didn't stock that band's music, but I could get tapes of the Wolfe Tones and the Flying Column. The music of the Wolfe Tones is luridly sentimental.

The *Andersonstown News* reflects the character of west Belfast perhaps more accurately in the incidentals, like advertising and the letters column, than in the news features. Columnists like Des Wilson and Squinter suffer from the limitations of all columnists: their individual preoccupations may appear more representative of a broad swathe of opinion than they can really be. Father Des argues every week that Irish 'democrats' will have to leave the unionists and the British behind, since both are newcomers to the notion of democracy. Squinter writes to slag off the police and the black-taxi drivers and to point up the foibles of the people of west Belfast. Occasionally he is angry, as in a description he wrote of events he witnessed around the shooting of two men in a bar and the police handling of the incident.

The newspaper carries dense pages of ads for joiners, plasterers, plumbers and photographers, indicating large numbers of self-employed people, perhaps on low income, servicing homeowners in the area. You can have plans drawn for your new conservatory and your freezer repaired without turning the page. A wide range of small, home-based businesses exists now to cater for people living in the same area who own their houses and furnish them with satellite dishes and computers. This is no longer an area in which neighbours expect to have roughly the same income as each other. This

133

describes a different Andersonstown to the one in which I grew up, and in which the Provisional IRA grew up. It is more diverse and more prosperous. I sometimes try to flashback in my memory to a time when there were fewer cars, roads were narrower, and clothes were darker. It is not an easy leap, and there is a thriving interest in nostalgic journalism feeding, presumably, a widespread enthusiasm for trying to make it.

The most revealing part of the *Andersonstown News* are the deaths and memorial notices. The In Memoriam column begins almost every week with: 'In Proud and Loving Memory of the Volunteers, Belfast Brigade IRA, killed on Active Service'. Often the names of two or three people follow. With decades of dying to pick through, the paper will usually have a peppering of notices remembering dead republicans, dead Catholics killed by loyalists or the police or army, and dead Catholics killed by the IRA, though never dead soldiers or policemen. Sometimes the dead IRA volunteers will be remembered further down the column by their families. Sometimes the families will adorn the notice with the same military language, often not.

Some of the dead are remembered decades after they died.

> HERDMAN: Loving memories of Terry, who died 5th June 1973, RIP. Sweet are the memories, silent they stay, no passing of time can take them away. Always remembered by Libby, loving daughter Lisa, grandson wee Terry.

I cut that one out in 1997, twenty-four years after Terry Herdman's death. Terry was shot dead as an informer by the IRA when he was seventeen years old, and the memorial notices now extend into a third generation, like a quiet protest against his killers in the same space in which they too remember their dead. So much for the notion of a uniformly supportive republican community.

Some of the republican leaders are remembered with the same devotion down the decades, but with less coyness within their families.

> HANNAWAY, Liam. 16th Anniversary. In proud and loving memory of our dear father Volunteer Liam Hannaway, Belfast

Brigade Oglaigh na hEireann, who died on the 2nd February 1981. Mary Queen of Ireland pray for him. Always remembered and loved by his sons Terry, Kevin and Diarmuid, his daughter Josephine and families.

STONE, John. 22nd Anniversary. In proud and loving memory of my uncle John, died 21st January 1975. Vol. B. Coy, 2nd Batt. Belfast Brigade. St Martin pray for him. To me you were someone special, in my eyes you will always shine, of all the uncles in the world, I am glad that you were mine. Always remembered by his niece Bridgeen, boyfriend Patrick, son Padraic Pearse xoxo.

Over the page of the same edition, another IRA man, Jim McGrillen, gets nine tributes to mark the twenty-first anniversary of his death. There were almost four full columns of tributes to the INLA leader Gino Gallagher on the first anniversary of his murder.

The verses that accompany these tributes support the argument that the republican tradition is deeply romantic, though the practice of publishing them undifferentiated from prose damages the effect they might have. Usually the tributes to the dead are adorned with familiar verses that recur in the newspaper's columns week after week.

Lay him away on the hillside along with the brave and the bold, write his name on the roll of honour in letters of finest Gold. Soft be the soil that covers your grave for proud are the people who bore you and green is the memory of your soul gone to join the fallen before you.

As common as this nostalgia is a sort of gruff, affectionate humour.

GALLAGER, Gino. RIP. Ireland unfree shall never be at peace. Loved and respected by all who knew you, one big gentle man. Your smile tells it all.

Occasionally someone makes a novel choice, like these lines from Walt Whitman, chosen by Danny Morrison and published in the republican newspaper *An Phoblacht*:

FOX, Paul (21st Ann.). In proud and loving memory of my friend and comrade, Paul and Cumann na mBan Volunteer Laura Crawford, killed on IRA active service on 1 December 1975. Nor

135

do I forget you Departed, Nor in winter or summer my lost ones,
But most in the open air as now when my soul is rapt and at peace,
like pleasing phantoms, your memories rising glide silently by me.
Never forgotten by Danny Morrison.

Paul Fox and Laura Crawford died when the bomb they were transporting exploded prematurely in a car park in King Street.

Though republicans loyally remember their dead and pay tribute to them as fallen soldiers, there are clearly divisions within the families of the IRA dead on just how militaristic the tribute should be. Often the notice coming from close family members will make no mention of the IRA connection. Of twelve tributes to the bomber Frankie Ryan published five years after his death, eight recall him as a volunteer who died on active service. They include separate tributes from his brother and sister. None of the tributes from his parents and uncles and aunts make mention of his having been in the IRA. Patricia Black, who died beside him in a doorway in St Albans, got nine tributes that year. Eight of them honour her as an IRA volunteer who died on active service. Only one, to 'our aunt Tricia', does not.

There must be disagreement within some families over whether it is a point of honour to them that their deceased were in the IRA, that they were trying to kill other people when they died. Do they suppress those quarrels? Do they decide that all are entitled to their own opinion, even when the opinion they disagree on is whether the memory of a son or daughter is to be cherished with greater pride because of a part played in a war that the one abhors and the other supports? In a place like west Belfast, the question of support or disdain for the IRA may arise at the most profound moment in a family's experience. The greater question may be whether they are to fall out over that or to support each other.

The parents of Patrick Kane, who was jailed over the murder of the two corporals, Robert Howes and Derek Wood, on the Andersonstown Road in March 1988, fought for years to have him cleared, and were finally successful in June 1997. They watched him develop physically and emotionally in prison, however, and form friendships with members of the IRA. Into their home they brought items of prison craft, the paintings and Celtic crosses and harps, made by men who were serving justly imposed sentences for real crimes. The contact with the IRA prisoners through their son brought them to consider whether any of them should really be in jail at all, whether the tragedy of the Troubles was not something that fell unbidden on hundreds of men and women whose lives would otherwise have been blameless.

It is when there is this kind of personal bridge to the IRA within the family that absolute condemnation becomes almost impossible. The rationalisation that people adopt is that paramilitaries were caught up in events over which they had no control. As we have seen, a similar notion still rests at the heart of the Sinn Féin analysis of the Troubles.

Many of those who were killed by the IRA are remembered in the same In Memoriam columns in the *Andersonstown News* as are members of the IRA. The killer and the victim could even be honoured on the same page. Who knows? Terry Herdman's notice that I quoted on page 134 is one of the most discreet. Others refer blatantly to the murder of a loved one, though they won't identify the killer. Readers who don't know may just presume that the notice is a tribute to someone who was killed by loyalists.

CAMPBELL. 13th anniversary of my dear daddy, murdered by cowards, 9th June 1984.

Jimmy Campbell was shot dead by the IRA in a drinking club. Of nine notices published together by members of his family, seven make their protest against the Provisionals with that phrase 'murdered by cowards'.

The death of someone murdered by the IRA is often remembered without any mention of how the person died.

MULHERN, Joseph. 3rd anniversary. Died 23rd June 1993. In proud and loving memory. Our hearts still ache with sadness, the silent tears still flow, for what it meant to lose you son, no one will ever know. Sadly missed and always remembered by Dad, brothers and sisters.

Joe Mulhern was a member of an IRA punishment squad in

Twinbrook, and he was killed by the IRA because they blamed him for passing information to the police and loyalist paramilitaries about a shop store where explosives were kept. A teenage boy was murdered by loyalists when they attacked that shop and the explosives were discovered by police investigating the attack. It is noteworthy that within republican culture an explanation that relied on loyalists and the police being regarded as allies was credible enough to allow for a man being murdered. Christopher Harte also was shot dead as an informer. He was held responsible for the capture and killing of Pearse Jordan in 1992 on the Falls Road. The RUC intercepted Jordan's car and shot him in the back as he tried to run from them. Christopher Harte had been an IRA colleague of Jordan's and attended the wake in the Jordan family home. Seven memorial tributes were published for Christopher Harte in the fourth year after he was murdered. Only one refers to him being 'killed'. The casual reader would not know that he had not died in a car crash.

The friends and family of the disgraced man, expunged as anathema from the republican community, repeatedly emphasise that they loved him, love him still and will never forget him. It is almost as if they are trying to cope with the danger that he will be forgotten, trying through the wording of the tribute to resist the weight of a republican culture that would erase his memory, or regard him only as an embarrassment to the community.

> HARTE, Chris, 4th anniversary. 12th February. Padre Pio pray for him. Your name we often mention, our thoughts are with you still, you haven't been forgotten, Chris, and you never will.

Though some notices reflect tragedy, others are a vehicle for a native humour and reflect the fact that this is a culture in which there is no shame attached to being in prison.

> To My Little Gravy Train in the Grease Pit. You know that I love you and always will, so make this man of yours so happy by marrying him. All my love always. From your wee honey bun, H7 Long Kesh.

138   That was one of several Valentine's Day greetings from a republican

prisoner. Other greetings were from family members to prisoners:

McANOY, Brendan, H7. Happy Valentine's Day Buster love. You're my Valentine each and every day of my life and I'm loving you and missing you with every beat of my heart, darling.

WEIR, Bow (H7). Best wishes for Valentine's Day Bow. Love you millions. Your wee wife Ann Marie.

WEIR, Bow (H7). Happy Valentine's Day, daddy. Love you. Your wee princess Caitriona.

Brendan McAnoy is serving a twenty-five-year sentence. Albert Weir is serving an eighteen-year sentence.

The notices in the *Andersonstown News* are windows into the relationship between a paramilitary organisation like the Provisional IRA and the community within which it operates. They illustrate the fact that the republican movement is a coherent community in itself, linked to the wider working-class Catholic community around it by ties of family and fear, but distinct from it too. You can see that clearly in the way in which the republican movement remembers its own dead.

Martin Doherty was shot dead by loyalists in an attack on the Widow Scallan's pub in Dublin during a Sinn Féin fundraising event. His obituary in the prisoners' magazine *The Captive Voice* was written by a prisoner in Portlaoise jail, in the South, who knew him well. He writes:

It was virtually inevitable that Doco, if present in the Widow Scallan's, would have been the first to react and the first to wade into the death squad . . . it was hard to believe that the big man with the big smile, who had knocked a million laughs out of life, was dead.

Doco is remembered as 'the dedicated soldier, who seemed to thrive on danger'. His political motivation is admired:

He was aware of the part he was playing in keeping alive the spirit of unrepentant Fenianism in Dublin, and he was proud of it. As a member of that class which, in Connolly's words, has never betrayed Ireland, Doco was adamant that partition and British occupation had to be ended.

Doco had been betrayed and served a sentence in Portlaoise, and on his release he 'demanded, rather than volunteered for active service in England'. His engaging smile enabled him to 'waltz unchallenged through supposedly secure military installations. And to their misfortune, some of the Brits discovered the steel behind Doco's smile.' Now Doco is dead and in Valhalla, writes his comrade:

> As he gannets down tankards of celestial gargle there are bound to be some who lack his stamina and perhaps some gnarled Gaelic chieftain, or maybe even Tone himself, will slurringly plead, 'Jaze, Doco, take it easy.' And Doco will pause, give a great grin and reply: 'That's the sort of me', and carry on as before, forever.

Going by this tribute to Martin Doherty, the valued attributes of an IRA volunteer are that he is cheerful and tough. He excels his mates by drinking harder than them, and by taking greater risks than he would expect of them. He kills and never doubts that he is right when he kills. His politics are his deepest conviction. They are rooted in history. His fight is driven by a personal yearning to put things right for the people of his oppressed country. Therefore he is heroically generous.

The personal qualities of admired republicans are always subservient to the political principles. The integrity of the cause is never compromised, not even in humour. Instead the good nature and intelligence and generosity of republicans are always described as if they rest on the bedrock of political conviction. I would love to know if republicans laugh about their politics among themselves; they certainly don't take well to being chided about them by outsiders. Attempts at teasing them are usually met with a stiff rebuke.

Chrissie McAuley's tribute to Maire Drumm, written for the twentieth anniversary of her death (*Republican News*, 31 October 1996), emphasises the debt to the dead and the sobering need to stick to the principles laid down by them. Maire Drumm, a Sinn Féin leader in Belfast, was murdered by loyalists while a patient in the Mater hospital in October 1976. The tribute written by

Ms McAuley, a former republican prisoner, begins with a quote from Maire Drumm: 'We will not take any steps backwards, our steps will be onward; for if we don't, the ghosts of the martyrs who died for you, for me, for this country will haunt us for eternity.' That in itself is an indication that the debt to the dead is an important bind on republicans. To admit at any time that those who died for Ireland had been wrong, after all, would be to acknowledge as true the criticism of their enemies and rivals, that they were murderers. For an organisation that was born out of a contempt for those who compromised republican principles, this leaves very little room for manoeuvre.

Ms McAuley writes: 'Twenty years have not dulled the memory ... [of] Maire Drumm.' The memory must have dulled, of course, as memory does. I remember Maire Drumm as the mother of one of my schoolfriends. I remember visiting her home and forming the impression that she was more amenable to intruding children than my own mother was. I remember her vaguely, noting that she was a republican then, and her making some brash remark that in my own family would have been considered tactless. I remember seeing her later on a platform in Andersonstown, excoriating the Women Together group with a wrath that raised goosepimples on me. And I remember the last time I saw her, having a joke with her in the dark of a black taxi going up the Falls Road at the end of 1972. She was going home from a night out, and she was full of laughter.

Her husband Jimmy was remarkably soft-natured for one of the most ardent and active of republicans. I was with him in a car touring Andersonstown during a crisis, when refugees were taking shelter in a school hall, and I overheard him whisper his disgust at the stupidity of someone who had posted two armed men at the school gates. Looking back, Maire Drumm seems almost to have been the woman imagined by the songwriters of 'Four Green Fields' or 'The Broad Black Brimmer', who gave us the myth of the Irish mother passing on to the next generation the responsibility of fighting to free Ireland. Nevertheless, she would have known by the last time we met that I was taking no black brimmer onto my head for the Provisionals or anybody; she probably thought I was a shallow and feckless wee man compared to the brave boys with the guns.

Chrissie McAuley writes of her first meeting with the hero of her youth:

> ... when her eyes met mine she smiled, told me to keep my chin up, that the struggle would continue. There was a calmness about those strong yet kindly features of hers that I shall never forget.

Maire Drumm's gift was for dispelling doubt about the correctness and the inevitability of the struggle.

> ... she was ... like our dear departed comrade Pat McGeown, a key link with the loyalist community, trying to dispel the myths and forge genuine understanding about the nature of the new Ireland republicans were striving for, to the benefit of all: Protestant, Catholic and Dissenter.

But surely, even Maire Drumm didn't think she could convert loyalists to regarding the campaign of the Provisional IRA as good for them. The virtue that is most admired in republican culture is the tenacity of one who never doubts, and who deals with the doubts of others. The dead are honoured for keeping faith with a tradition and passing it on.

The same elements are clear in the oration given by Sinn Féin chairperson Mitchel McLaughlin in tribute to Sean Sabhat (South) and Fergal O'Hanlon on 5 January 1997 in Limerick. They had died on New Year's Eve 1957, while attacking Brookeborough police station.

> Like so many of this generation, Sean and Fergal gave their lives in pursuit of their ideals and in so doing, sowed the seed of freedom in a new generation of republicans. Today's republicans are determined that we will see that seed bear fruit, we are determined to win a negotiated settlement based on freedom and democratic principles.

I remember an attitude in my childhood that it was good to sing rebel songs like 'Kevin Barry' but that singing 'Sean South of Garryowen' had a different meaning. Kevin Barry was a legitimate hero of the war for independence, but South was a skitter and a criminal. Now he has the vintage that Barry had then, but would he have understood in his own day the modern Sinn Féin vocabulary of Mitchel McLaughlin, any more than Kevin Barry would have understood the republicanism of the 1950s?

'Sean Sabhat, like so many Irishmen and women before and since, decided to strike for Irish freedom in an attempt to force Britain to negotiate a withdrawal from the occupied Six-Counties,' said McLaughlin. But the notion that a British withdrawal should be a negotiated withdrawal is a creation of the 1990s.

The nobility and human decency of people who plant bombs in cities is perhaps overemphasised in republican tributes to counter the fact that it is so little noticed outside republican circles. It is a mythology that helps republicans to cope with their own experience of vilification, or 'demonisation', as they would call it. Anyone reading the writings of prisoners, particularly about the period of the hunger strikes, must be struck by the mix of affection and adulation that republicans had for the ones who died. What republican culture provides is a space within which people who have been appallingly violent will be remembered only for having been brave and good and true. Whatever doubts they might have had in their own lives about whether it was right to kill and destroy for politics, the continuity of the culture determines that there will always be people who will think well of them for what they did.

Perhaps they need to have that tradition survive, lest their own latter years be plagued with solitary and painful reflections on the carnage they created. Perhaps the old soldiers of all armies need the same support, and perhaps all active soldiers in all armies know that they will one day need the comfort of like-minded people close at hand, to validate their past bloodletting and keep the doubts at bay.

Republicans' descriptions of their social life together depict a boisterous and wholesome lifestyle. For all of Doco Doherty's 'gannet'-like drinking, he is essentially depicted as a loveable, matey character, a bit of a showman, who relaxed from the important business of killing into playfulness. Danny Morrison's tribute to Gerry Adams in his review of Adams's autobiography reprises the memory of past suffering, claiming that the 1981 hunger strike 'was handled with love and loyalty, comradeship and care, the very qualities developed at the Adams hearth and home by parents who knew deprivation and discrimination and who knew – without feeding it to their children – that republicanism provided an explanation and an answer, but at great personal cost to the adherent'. Morrison seems aware that the Doco lifestyle is open to criticism.

> [Gerry's] references to dancing and drinking are scant. Understandably so. He's woeful. Worse than Bryan Ferry, though he thinks he can ceilidh – which is a real scream. And his failure to develop as a great drinker has been of major disappointment – to some of us. David Trimble would drink him under the table before the dawn. And, God, his conscientious attitude to work (there are 36 hours in his day) indeed drove some of us to Trimble's table.

In summary, Gerry Adams was an ordinary boy who had greatness imposed on him by the trying circumstances he inherited.

The republican culture, then, is strongly self-affirming. It is set within a larger culture which contains a mix of support, ambivalence and disdain. The interaction between these is often described by republicans and others as symbiotic: the republican is the fish in the water of the community, and without the community the republican fish cannot survive. Certainly the IRA has found a role for itself within the communities in which it operates. The Sinn Féin offices are often called 'advice centres'. They are the contact points for councillors who do much the same kind of work as councillors from other parties, usually more energetically. In addition to that, Sinn Féin tries to enact a usurpation of the state, by replacing state functions.

The link that exists between the community and the republican movement in personal contacts and family connections means that republicans are not outsiders who have been grafted onto the community, but a section of the community whose members have absorbed a political ideology which unites them with each other more closely than with those who are not part of the movement. The dividing line between the community and the movement can run through the middle of a family, making claims to consideration from those who are wholly opposed to what the movement does.

One of the crossover points between the IRA and the people is through the policing that Sinn Féin provides. The person who does not necessarily support Sinn Féin or the IRA may be driven by exasperation to ask for the movement's help against burglars or car thieves or drug dealers. A Sinn Féin councillor says, 'Sometimes I ask these people if they would like me to go and shoot the person that's annoying them in the legs, but they don't want to know about that side of it. They are content to initiate something that ends up like that, but they don't want to feel that they are responsible for how it ends.' The old argument of Sinn Féin is that it wants nothing to do with community policing, for it has a political programme to get on with, but it is confronted by the demands of the community for protection, at a time when the RUC provides none. It is an elegant juxtaposition of excuses, for it affirms community support and damns the RUC at the same time. Just by going out and breaking a joyrider's legs, a republican carries out an act of propaganda that airs two of the movement's most cherished issues.

Sinn Féin can't actually provide a full policing service. Most people who own cars or videos that are stolen have these insured and have to report thefts to the police so that they can make their insurance claims. For this reason alone, Sinn Féin cannot hope to woo people away from the police completely. When confronted with pederasty in Catholic areas, Sinn Féin leaders had to advise people to go to 'the appropriate authorities'.

Republicans resent the imputation that they intimidate their communities into supporting them, and those who think that manipulation is always done through intimidation overlook the potential of political action at community level to wrong-foot critics and implicate support from rivals and even state institutions. At times, however, the intimidation is nakedly obvious and the garnish of moralistic justification is gauche and transparent.

An example of this was the kneecapping of Damien McCartan. McCartan was a taxi driver in the Markets area of Belfast. The IRA attempted to hijack his taxi for 'an operation'. He resisted and was taken hostage by them. He escaped and rallied friends who then confronted the IRA and retrieved the car. In the IRA's statement in *An Phoblacht*, 1 April 1993, explaining why he was kneecapped, the IRA said that he had 'risked the capture of our materials' and 'endangered the lives of our Volunteers'. The Volunteers were wholly in the right, by this view, and McCartan was wholly in the wrong, though they had attacked him first, with weapons, and he had retaliated to save his own property.

The IRA routinely adopts the language of legitimate authority. A leaflet distributed in Twinbrook, for example, in May 1992, stated: 'The IRA reserves the right to punish those people who won't desist from their Anti Social Behaviour.'

The shooting of joyriders is presented as an act of generosity not just to the community but to the young people, for whom the IRA wants only 'the best', according to the same leaflet. The IRA frequently employs the formal language of the state penal system and social services. They talk about people 'reforming', about 'monitoring behaviour' for 'good conduct.' They patronise youth, and they expect parents to come to them and discuss their parenting and the progress of their children.

People have to plead with them, and they present themselves back to these people as reasoned and patient but firm. Intermediaries are seen to get results. Promises of good behaviour are often accepted. The IRA appears not to want to be thought of as intimidating the whole community for support.

The basic reason why the IRA is obeyed may be fear of punishment, but it will often be described in other terms. An illustration of the distinction expected by the IRA between fear and discretion is the case of Derry man Michael Williams, who called police to the house next door to him in Creggan in March 1990, when that house had been taken over by the IRA. Afterwards he said he didn't know the IRA was in the house – he had heard screaming and thought the woman there, Mrs Garnon, was in danger. The police arrested one man at the Garnon house and captured a rifle and an RPG7 rocket launcher. In the view of the IRA, Mr Williams had acted without discretion and deserved to be punished, yet, as they argue it, it is not the inevitability of punishment that should have restrained him but his own good sense and trust in them. If he was concerned for Mrs Garnon's safety, said Sinn Féin councillor Hugh Brady, he should have gone into the house and checked for himself. 'People know that the IRA is not there to attack the community. A neighbour could go into the house and talk to the men there. That's been done before.' A few days after the incident, Williams left Derry, ahead of an IRA raid on his home.

The compliance in the work of the IRA by the Creggan people was rationalised by republicans as passive cooperation. It was rationalised by the people themselves as street wisdom. No one calls it fear. A Derry journalist says, 'Nine out of ten people in the Creggan knew they could be shot for doing what Michael Williams did, so they wouldn't have done it.' It is within this confusion of threat and consideration that the IRA relates to those it calls the community. Those who fall foul of the IRA are unfortunates who must suffer for their naïveté, vulnerability or indiscipline. The IRA of itself is never to blame; it is the one responsible agency which acts always as it must, however distastefully.

Sinn Féin offices have a 'civil administration' section. This is in line with republican practice going back at least as far as the war for independence, when the IRA fouled up the workings of the British administration and set up its alternative system, arbitrating on civil disputes and imprisoning thieves. The civil administration section today conducts itself with the confidence of a statutory agency, and it seeks to extend its legitimacy by implicating real statutory bodies and voluntary agencies. The man who led the civil administration of Sinn Féin through the 1980s, and who supervised all the kneecappings, is well known to many community workers in Belfast. His nickname is Chico. Chico had an office in Connolly House. There he would speak with parents of the joyriders whom he monitored. Social workers connected with NIACRO and other organisations would visit him there for guidance on the level of threat against people they were working with, perhaps to ask for an extension on an order to leave the country, so that social workers would have time with the boy in question.

The probation service, which also worked closely with joyriders, 147 was familiar through its clients with the workings of the IRA. The probation service funds Lynx, a community project in Twinbrook for weaning boys away from joyriding. The director of Lynx is the Sinn Féin councillor Annie Armstrong, who has led pickets against the homes of drug dealers and conveyed to them what she says is the community's insistence that they leave the estate. The probation service advises Lynx on who in their area may benefit from Lynx's help, using lists provided by the police. So there is no strict separation between a Sinn Féin councillor and community organisations and even statutory bodies. Each inevitably becomes implicated in the work of the other. Many of the community workers who deal directly with the IRA say they believe the IRA is not using the policing of hoods for political ends, though the IRA's political advantage may be precisely the legitimation these groups give it by dealing with it.

One community worker spoke highly of Chico. He regards him as a conscientious member of his community who wants to restore order. He contrasted Chico with another member of a punishment squad, nicknamed by the joyriders Joe Shootem, who has since been shot dead by the IRA as an informer. Joe Shootem, he says, was a sadist. Once, after a punishment beating in Poleglass, when the squad had dispersed, Joe Shootem returned to the injured man lying bleeding on the grass and gave him another kick in the face for his own gratification. This distinction between good IRA men and bad IRA men is one that recurs frequently when you talk to people who have dealings with them. The same people who will tell you that their local vigilante leader is a sadistic thug will also often have faith in another member of the IRA who deals with them more sympathetically.

Brendan in Ardoyne had two teenage sons who had been joyriding. He was worried that they would be punished by the IRA. His friendly local Sinn Féin councillor, Joe Austin, suggested a solution to his problem. He advised Brendan to apply for a Place of Safety order for his sons. He should report them to Social Services as being in danger to themselves through joyriding and at risk of being shot or maimed by paramilitaries. Brendan saw this as a thoughtful intervention by Joe Austin, a strategy for ensuring that his sons would not be kneecapped or ordered out of the country.

The boys were installed in St Patrick's Training School by the juvenile court and a Place of Safety order valid for one year was ultimately issued. After some months, Joe Austin visited the boys in St Patrick's, judged them to be fully repentant and told Brendan that he had reported the change in the boys 'to the community' and that it was now agreed that the boys could be released and that they would be safe. On Brendan's assurances to Social Services that he now believed his sons were safe from threat, they were allowed home, even though the Place of Safety order had not expired.

Joe Austin said afterwards: 'This is a way of saving boys from beatings; you should commend it. That would be good politics.' It would certainly be good politics for Sinn Féin to wrong-foot the state into providing custody for boys whom Sinn Féin judged to deserve it.

A huge amount of IRA energy has gone into policing joyriders in west Belfast. Throughout the 1980s and into the 1990s, the primary use of pistols by the IRA was in the kneecapping of 'hoods'. More bullets were expended on young Catholic males than against any other category of target. This policing is the most visible part of paramilitary activity. The victims usually live to tell the tale, if not to the police, then at least to their families and friends. Shootings have been known to be carried out by appointment, like a thrashing from a Christian Brothers headmaster who has ordered a boy to attend his office after school.

The parents of joyriders have close and difficult relations with the IRA. IRA men come to their homes to monitor the behaviour of their children, and parents have often been called to Sinn Féin offices to hear complaints against them. Many of these parents supported the IRA in the early days of the Troubles. One man said, 'We backed the Rah. We stole cars for them and cheered when people were killed and let them tell us what was right and wrong. The kids won't do that. They won't be pushed around. You might think I am stupid, but that's the conclusion I have come to, that the kids are giving two fingers to the Rah. That's what it is all about.'

There is a feeling among parents of joyriders that the IRA should recognise that what the mother of a joyrider suffers is not all that different from what the mother of an IRA man suffers, though the one expects to be honoured and accords only contempt to the other. One woman said, 'I know Chico's parents and they are the nicest people you could meet. People don't blame them for what he is, so why do they blame us for what our boys are?'

Some of the joyriders, like Jimmy, are themselves sympathetic to the republican cause but contemptuous of the IRA. 'They're going to be looking for support from the people they've shot. Mind you, I have nothing against the Rah, I think they are right to try and push the British government out of here. From I have been a child I have hated the Rah, for bombing innocent people. They say it's a war, but where's the war? They say civilians have to die. But at the end of the day they're right. We're under British rule.'

Jimmy clashed with the IRA and his family was ostracised. 'I was pulled in, beat a few times, told that if I done anymore I'd be in trouble. My father was put out of a club by the Rah. They said if you can't control your son you're not welcome here. He came into the house and went buck mad.'

Young Jimmy's father passed on the same treatment to him that he was getting in the drinking club on his son's behalf. He shunned Jimmy, and he blamed him and not the Provies for his not being able to go into his local bar. Eventually, Jimmy was kneecapped, an injury he saw as a part of an ongoing personal war he was waging against the IRA. 'Any Rah man I knew I tortured, never let them sleep at night. They used to move us on from street corners. I tortured them. That was because they were coming where we were drinking and saying 'We're the Provisional Irish Republican Army, move on. They more or less provoke you into cars. I move on and get a car and then I'm back.'

The joyriders are at war with the IRA. Pip says he skidded stolen cars in front of the homes of IRA men to annoy them. Another, Looper, attacked a van used by the IRA and broke its windows. S— painted the windows of the home of a leading member of a punishment squad.

As the republican movement censures families like Jimmy's for the actions of their children, and brands them as unfit for full membership of the community, so other families also acquire the power to intimidate the disgraced families. One father says that most parents of joyriders have paid money to neighbours who have complained to them about damage to their property. 'A man calls at the door and says, Your son dented my car last night, I want a hundred pounds or I'm going to Connolly House. People pay. They don't know if their son was to blame or not, because they never know when they can believe him. And even so, if you know he was in the house, who are the chucks [the IRA] going to believe?'

It is that sense of disgrace within a community that aggrieves the joyriders and their families. They are branded. Jimmy says: 'I have no hatred for the man who shot me . . . He was in an organisation and he has to do what he's told. I've talked to him about it. If I passed him on the street I would say All right to him. It wasn't him. It was people putting in complaints who got me shot.' He has no respect for those people. 'There's a lot of sleekit oul dolls putting in complaints, and they want to see results if they're going to support them. But little do they know that their sons are doing it too.'

By this view of things, the IRA is manipulated by people outside it, who challenge it to show its strength against the local hoods. The man who shoots you has to be absolved of blame if you are to stay in the community. You will meet him in bars and you will have to control your anger against him. He may be a friend of your father's. As far as he is concerned, he did a job, and if you are no longer running around stealing cars, then he did his job well.

Perhaps the most striking examples of the division between republicans and their opponents occur within families: cases where the sons of men who have been in the IRA have been kneecapped by the IRA. Pip grew up without his father. As he remembers it, the man was always away, interned or in jail, or 'fucking about, I don't know'; but he would turn up to punish him when he got into trouble, as when he was caught shoplifting at the age of thirteen. 'My Da was going to break my fingers. He came to my granny's house, see. I think he would have done it only for my granny. She stopped him. He just gave me a wee slap. You know, don't do it again.' Later, when he started stealing cars, he was conscious that choosing to go with the hoods put him at odds with the IRA.

Threats from the IRA and beatings from his father had no effect on Pip. One beating occurred after he had stayed at his mate's drinking all night. 'My da came round. I think he was only out of Castlereagh. He brought me into the room and gave me a kicking and broke my nose. He was physically just getting into me. He jumped all over my head. And that didn't stop me. The next week I was out again.'

Pip's thrashings from his father were effectively IRA punishment beatings. Pip's father says that the republican movement's first preference, when they discovered that Pip was joyriding, was to put the onus on him as the father to stop him. Other fathers, not republicans, describe a similar process of increasing disillusionment with their sons, leading them finally to concede that the IRA might as well take over.

A joyrider parent says that the appeal to the father to do something about the son challenges the father to be a real man, like the republicans themselves who will have to take over responsibility for the boy if the father fails. The IRA is therefore preserving the myth of manhood as a status that has power to control others. The father invariably fails every time he tries to coax his son away from joyriding, and the family is damaged by his increasingly vehement efforts. In the end the father says, Well I can't do a thing with him. So the powerlessness of the father legitimates the IRA's actions. The father is ultimately exasperated and sees no alternative to kneecapping. He may have started out with the greatest concern for his son. He is defeated not by the IRA, but by the joyriding syndrome.

The father of a Poleglass joyrider described the process of attempting to woo the son back into the family, and that final helpless surrender. 'You say, OK, you're going out there and getting pissed and getting into cars. If you stay home with us, we'll buy you a drink and you can get pissed in front of the telly. That works for one week, and then all that happens is that he stops hiding from

152

you when he's drunk. Then you start trying to keep him in. You lock him in his room and he gets out the window. His social worker comes and tells you to take the new locks off the window because you can't do that to him.

'Then you take him out into the garden and lay about him with a hurley bat, just to give him a taste of what the Provies will do to him. Then you crack, and you say, Well let them have him.'

What is horrific about the kneecappings and beatings is that a young man and his family and most of his friends would know for weeks what was going to happen, and would be helpless to prevent it. They would often simply allow the procedures to take their course, as if they were as implacable as those of the ordinary law.

Pip says: 'My uncle came down and said, The Rah kicked your ma's door in looking you. They're going to shoot you. Come on up to the house. So I went up to his house and got a change of clothes. I never thought I would have got shot, because they said it that many times, You'll get shot; you'll get your legs broken. It never really fucking registered. So I was running about and got a carryout with my mates and all.

'On the Sunday, I was walking round to my aunt's, my other aunt's for my dinner. It was a cracker day, and I was walking and a car pulled up behind me. I never even looked round. Next thing I was just grabbed, and there was three or four men and they said they was from the republican movement. They said, You're going to get a punishment shooting . . .

'So they dragged me up and they laid me down and they shot me. I think it was the left knee first and then it was the right knee. I can't remember. I was shot anyway. It was just the nerves, you know. Waiting for them to pull the trigger. The gun actually jammed. It felt like hours waiting for it. It jammed three times. The fourth time it worked.'

Pip's kneecapping was not a neat efficient one. One leg was severely damaged and the toes had to be amputated. His father says: 'Knowing the attitude of my son, if he'd just got a clean one, he'd have gone back to car thieving, and he could have ended up dead as well. He could be shot by the army. In turn, he could have killed

153

somebody himself.' Pip's joyriding lifestyle changed after that. Occasionally he was confronted by IRA vigilante groups, but he realised from the way that they responded to him, when they knew his name, that he was no longer under their suspicion. 'Basically, they must have just started to trust me. They knew I wasn't fuckin' about.'

Pip's father bears no resentment at all against the men who crippled his son. He says simply: 'My own capacities as a father didn't work with [Pip] and I believed that I needed more muscle to attempt to frighten him out of the position which he adopted within the community. The republican movement provided that muscle.'

It makes sense, if only in terms of heredity, that the son of an IRA man will be as wild and dangerous as his father. It is understandable that the father will be outraged by the son. The father risks his life, but insists that there is some point to it. The son shows the same daring, but for nothing other than the thrill. This questions the integrity of the father's dangerous life. Maybe he is just the same as the son. That thought must occur to him.

It is not possible to say how many of the joyriders are children of republicans, but several are. Wurzle, who killed a pregnant woman while driving a stolen car, was the son of an IRA man killed in a feud with the Official IRA in the mid-seventies. His mother later married an IRA lifer in prison. Wurzle's family connections with the IRA did not protect him; he was kneecapped twice, and his mother and her second husband were later ordered out of their home in Twinbrook by the IRA. A girl joyrider in Poleglass is the daughter of a republican. She has been punished by having her head shaved and her body thumped. J.B.'s father was a member of the Official IRA The father himself was kneecapped and the Official IRA retaliated by shooting another man of about the same age.

The IRA presents itself as guardians of conscience, representatives of the real decent community as distinct from the antisocial elements who live among them and who are defined as not really being part of the community at all. Even those who live among them, and know the community too, but don't see things in their way, may be dismissed as not properly part of the community, as not understanding the depth of feeling on issues like policing or house searches. The bluntness with which you are ready to dismiss the legitimacy of the police may become the marker of whether you really belong in the community or not. Say anything against the trend of republican policy and you may be dismissed simply as not understanding how the people of the community think.

Through policing and political activism, republicans are able to generate an impression of a coherent republican community in an area like west Belfast. It is not easy for someone who rejects the beatings to declare that openly. It is not a small thing to disagree on. If you oppose the beatings then you oppose the notion that the RUC are a rejected force in west Belfast. If you want the RUC to police the area, that implies that you want them to arrest republicans. You are coming dangerously close to declaring yourself a potential informer. What meaning does your support for the RUC have if you are not prepared to help them?

Better to keep your mouth shut in company than to declare such ideas. The person you are talking to may have a son or a brother who would end up in jail if you had things your way.

8 THE TROUBLE WITH GUNS

The trouble with guns is that there is such a limited number of things you can do with them. In choosing to employ the same tools for their campaign as their predecessors had used, republicans from 1970 onward confined themselves to a political methodology that had only a narrow potential. The challenge for them was to extend that potential. They were creative and successful in this. They discovered that armed protest can provide a lot more than a physical shove against an enemy, and that it can actually be used to close off the options of your enemy – and even those of your political neighbours. It can challenge them to apply their minds to a problem that you want resolved, even when that problem has no similar urgency for them.

By such devices, military weaponry becomes a political tool, but its use brings a huge political cost. Republicans say they have been demonised, though they could not have reasonably expected to be loved when they were killing people and destroying property. They were able, at times, to present a charming facade, to win friends in the media and abroad, to inspire an astonishing sufferance, at times, of their brutality, so that severe critics would accept the proposition that they had little choice; but through the 1980s they reached the limit of their potential to convert voters to their cause, and change insisted itself upon them.

Ultimately, violence was damaging. Once the organisation started pouring energy into extending the influence of Sinn Féin, there emerged a conflict between the method and the aspiration. Killing people would cost votes. That was never more clearly admitted than in April 1997, when the IRA called a *de facto* local

156

ceasefire to facilitate Sinn Féin's election campaign. In doing that the IRA risked abandoning two valued principles. The first of these was automaticity – to take a word from the American writer on military strategy Schelling – meaning the presentation of violence as a virtual force of nature, uncontrollable in the end by anyone other than those who create the conditions that – you say – create it, in this case the British. The second principle sacrificed by the April 1997 ceasefire was distinction, meaning the contrived distinction between the IRA as the makers of violence and Sinn Féin as the explainers of it.

Strategically, automaticity is the principle that your forces cannot be controlled or bartered with. This makes them much more dangerous. A human force is made as unthinking as a landmine. Its violence has the inevitability of the workings of a machine or the spontaneity of a force of nature. Just as the Russians, during the Cold War, were to be persuaded that all-out nuclear war would inevitably follow any advance of their tanks into West Germany, IRA violence was presented as an inevitable product of political circumstances, which could not be curtailed or reasoned with. Automaticity is something that your enemy has to believe in, even when you don't wholly believe in it yourself. Essentially it is a form of deterrence, though in the case of the IRA campaign, the thing to be deterred has already happened, the British are here, and the violence has to be presented as an inevitable consequence.

Another modern example of automaticity, as a strategically valuable conceit, is the conviction that you die if you mess with the SAS, because they shoot first and ask questions later. That widespread belief, whether true or not, is an asset to the SAS. To waive it, by insisting that the SAS will always observe the strictures of the civil law, would be to limit their effectiveness. The three IRA members shot dead by the SAS in Gibraltar in 1988 were to be regarded as having been killed as if by a natural law as implacable as electricity. The knowledge that the SAS were so ruthless, and would be excused their excesses, would deter further IRA missions a lot more effectively than any suggestion that the SAS were thinking, considerate people who would tailor each ambush to the conditions of the time.

The erosion of limits set by the United States in Iraq since the 157

Gulf War shows up the strategic danger of surrendering automaticity. Your limits can be tested and stretched. Similarly the IRA, in showing itself ready in April 1997 to curtail its own threat for political advantage, was taking such a strategic risk; it was showing that it was potentially amenable to bartering in changed political conditions. It was also compromising the political argument of Sinn Féin, that violence arises from political conditions that it alone has no power to change. The sacrifices in principle made to enable that ceasefire can be taken as indications of the importance of it to the IRA. The latter was not going to risk jeopardising the credibility of its implacable resolve if it was not going to get some advantage in return. Success in the elections was clearly such a valued goal that the IRA was prepared to make costly sacrifices to help achieve it.

Sinn Féin argues that the violence of the IRA is a product of circumstances, and that only the correction of those circumstances can end it. The importance of this principle, strategically, is that it focuses the minds of others on creating political measures to assuage that violence. If the violence can in fact be switched on and off to suit electoral purposes, it clearly isn't generated by political conditions, it clearly isn't the passion of the aggrieved in action; rather, it is the tool of a thinking movement.

The distinction between Sinn Féin and the IRA that is insisted upon by Sinn Féin is compromised because the violence is stopped as a favour to Sinn Féin, presumably at the request of Sinn Féin, and probably with terms and time limits agreed with Sinn Féin. This distinction has been of vital importance to Sinn Féin because throughout the 1990s the position of the US, British and Irish governments has been that there could be no question of Sinn Féin entering negotiations to secure a political settlement to the conflict without an IRA ceasefire. The Sinn Féin response to this was to insist on its distinction from the IRA and to claim the right to be involved in negotiations purely on the strength of the party's electoral mandate. But if that mandate was won with the help of the IRA, then the plausibility of the distinction between the two movements was lost, and the very mandate that Sinn Féin said won them the right to enter talks was shown to be contaminated.

The election of 1997 showed that the Provisionals had overcome some of the contradictions of the 'long war' strategy, that they really had a new game to play, and that they were playing this new game well. Sinn Féin's share of the vote in Northern Ireland rose from 10 per cent to 16 per cent. Their electoral standing increased dramatically, reflecting the fact that the party had won international respect for its efforts at peace making. Behind this was the real prospect that Sinn Féin would overtake the SDLP, now a party of ageing men. Seamus Mallon had had heart problems, Hume was clearly exhausted and overwrought. The party's only two other MPs, Joe Hendron and Eddie McGrady, were sceptical about the whole peace process anyway.

Hume's endorsement of Adams as a committed peacemaker, as a collaborator in a shared project and as a man who could be trusted and respected could not be withdrawn in time to prevent Adams increasing his vote against Hendron in West Belfast on the back of it. Had the 1997 election resulted, as it might well have done, in Sinn Féin being the leading nationalist party in Northern Ireland, all prospects of a partitionist devolved settlement would have died. Politics would have been reduced to a simple, uncluttered argument over whether the region was British or Irish. This has to be regarded as such a prize for republicans that the entire peace effort may plausibly be assumed to have been directed at achieving it.

The year of elections showed the strongest signs yet of demographic change affecting the balance between parties in Northern Ireland. The academic Brendan O'Leary interpreted this in the *Irish Times* of 2 July 1997, arguing that unionism had forever lost the prospect of once again dominating Northern Ireland, that the Alliance Party would hold the balance of power in the coming decades, and that the IRA campaign was now immoral and unnecessary because nationalists were being removed from the danger of being dominated by a unionist bloc.

In articles and speeches after the 1994 ceasefire, Tim Pat Coogan had also argued from demographic trends that the war for nationalists was effectively over. This entailed some assumptions that few republicans would be happy with. They know that not all nationalists, as voting cultural Catholics are usually called, actually want a united Ireland. The Derry journalist Frank Curran spoke of this in a 1996 interview with me for the UTV series *No Offence*. He thinks that Catholics will bide their time and make their decision when they see what the options are. A republican might derive sectarian satisfaction from the humiliation of unionism, but would not see any prospect of a united Ireland while there remained a chance that the middle ground might knit into an allegiance against republicanism.

Garret FitzGerald returned to the demography arguments in the *Irish Times* in August 1997, concluding that the likely outcome was not nationalist supremacy but realisation of the need for mutual respect between evenly balanced communities. Like O'Leary, FitzGerald saw the demographic trend as pointing towards the politics of reconciliation rather than victory for either ethnic bloc.

In the 1997 elections, constitutional nationalism nearly lost out to republicanism. Through the peace initiative, it had appeared to validate republicanism as a junior partner that was deluded only about means. If republicanism was the youthful energetic wing of nationalism, thought many Catholics, what good reason was there not to vote for it and contribute thereby to the project that John Hume had started? Constitutional nationalism appeared to have no coherent project of its own, other than to put manners on Sinn Féin. John Hume was seen as a heroic, self-sacrificing man who had obviously worked himself to exhaustion for peace. Those who had procrastinated long enough almost to destroy his health – Sinn Féin – were paradoxically regarded as allies of Hume, frustrated only by British intransigence and the unionist veto.

Sinn Féin's standing was further helped by the issue of electoral pacts, which surfaced once more in the run-up to the election. The essential unity of nationalism could be demonstrated by electoral pacts, and those who refused such pacts could be presented as traitors to their tribe. But if nationalism was to be a unified ethnic force, then the lesser part of it was under moral pressure to take the leadership of the larger. Sinn Féin slipped through that challenge by wrong-footing the SDLP into appearing to be the side that was least interested in a pact. Had the IRA not resumed its campaign in February 1996, Sinn Féin would have entered the election of spring 1997 as junior partners in a coherent nationalist ethnic political coalition. But without a ceasefire, the SDLP could not make a pact with them. That turned out to be to Sinn Féin's advantage, for the SDLP could then be presented as the party which had betrayed northern Catholics. The SDLP, it could be argued, would rather let the DUP's Willie McCrea win Mid-Ulster than let Sinn Féin's Martin McGuinness have a free run.

Catholics in Northern Ireland asked unreflectively: If unionists can unite against nationalists, then why can't nationalists unite against unionists? No one had explained to them why politics should not be simply an interethnic contest, least of all John Hume, who had already defined it as such. Ironically, if the day ever comes when constitutional nationalism makes a deal with unionism in the middle ground, it will be the republicans, if they are still in the minority, who will be diverging from the tribe if they reject it.

For two decades up to the 1994 ceasefire, the IRA maintained a level rate of murder and sabotage, as a form of political protest against an internal settlement in Northern Ireland. This may have been driven by simple political absolutism, in which nothing but the whole goal would suffice. It may have been a means of raising the ceiling on compromise, so that, though ultimately republicans might have to do a deal, the final compromise for which they would be able to trade an end to violence would be one that was much closer to their ultimate goal. In the meantime they successfully invalidated the prospects of powersharing or any other internal arrangements. Until they reached the point at which they were ready to trade, the violence served to remind anyone tempted to consider working for such a settlement that there was little point in their trying. Even a political agreement that was endorsed by 80 per cent of the population, if such were possible, would not bring an end to violence.

Republicans would talk us all into a clear linkage between two things that were not necessarily part of each other: constitutional agreement and peace. What satisfied most people in both communities might not be enough to satisfy republicans. Linking agreement and peace together would put all parties under a moral onus to find, not the best compromise between their different positions, but an agreement that could include Sinn Féin. Like children at a party organising games, it would make little difference what most people wanted if the huffy brat who owned the ball couldn't be happy too.

For two decades the veto of violence operated. Experimentation with political initiatives designed to assuage the wounded sense of Irish identity that lay behind the violence stopped with the Anglo-Irish Agreement of 1985. That agreement had been open to three-yearly review, but the reviews did not come. The British government had worked out that the best counter to the republican veto on settlements was to be sparing with initiatives. Then the IRA's violent protest would have nothing to connect with. The production of murder and sabotage would continue with little variation, but would seem increasingly pointless.

There were moments, as on Remembrance Day 1987, when eleven people were slaughtered by a bomb explosion at the cenotaph in Enniskillen, when the campaign seemed blindly barbarous and wholly untenable. It continued, however. What would happen, I once asked Alex Maskey, leader of Sinn Féin in Belfast City Council, if the IRA stopped? 'We would go back to Stormont,' he said. 'It would just be Orange rule again.' But even in a devolved government, I said, the whole balance of parties would be different now. It would be nothing like it was.

'We would see no difference.'

Things might have changed enough for many. They had not changed enough for him, and it was his allies alone who would decide when the line had been crossed at which it was safe to relax the veto. That would be when they were sure there would be no internal settlement at all, of any kind. What prospect was there, then, for a middle-ground settlement appeasing republicans and bringing them on board? Logically, very little.

The consent principle, which had been coined within the Joint Declaration of the British and Irish governments in December

1993, guaranteed the constitution of Northern Ireland against change that was not approved by the greater number of the people there. Republicans called this 'the Unionist veto'. Gerry Adams had said to me in an interview:

> I don't think it is up to the British to define self-determination for the Irish people, that's the first thing. I think we can then define it as a whole in any way we want, we can exercise it in any way that we want. I think one of the problems with the declaration is that from the British point of view it addresses the issue which is significant and welcome but then it appears to say 'you have the right to self-determination but . . .' and it goes on to qualify it, and my view is that you can't have half a right or a third of a right. You either have the right or not. We of course have that right, that's denied us by external impediment, by British interference; how we exercise that right without internal or external impediment is just a matter of common sense.

The flaw in Adams's logic was that the consent principle had not simply been bestowed on the Northern Irish, by the British, as a qualification of the right of the Irish people as a whole to self-determination. It had been declared also by the Irish government and endorsed by all other nationalist parties in Ireland, north and south. It was itself a form of self-determination by the people of the island of Ireland.

The acceptance of the Joint Declaration by the SDLP and the Ulster Unionists was the first major step towards the creation of a middle-ground consensus. In that sense it was a huge problem for republicans. Republicans were getting suggestions from the government, from John Hume, and from David Trimble in small hints, that a political deal was possible. It could, however, only be a deal that knitted together the middle ground in Northern Ireland. Hume and Trimble were also having meetings to discuss the looming crisis at Drumcree through the spring of 1997. Republicans must have understood that talks that proceeded on the basis of the consent principle would have no chance of producing a united Ireland. They had known that since 1993, and rejected the consent principle because it blocked the way to a united Ireland. The fact that in 1994 they called a ceasefire, then, even with the consent principle in place, seemed to hint that they had decided they could in fact live with that principle. It implied that they had recognised and accepted that the only tenable settlement was one in which Hume and Trimble created powersharing between them.

But that is what the armed campaign of the IRA had sought continually to prevent. They were seriously tested on whether this apparent change was real, because the greater stumbling block had been the demand that they decommission, that is, give up, weapons. That demand was endorsed by the report of the international body chaired by Senator George Mitchell, who was later to chair the talks process itself.

In the mid-1990s, people believed in the good intentions of Sinn Féin because they chose to be optimistic. For two decades pessimism had been the unerring guide to Northern Ireland politics. People now wanted to believe in something good happening. Many were overwhelmed by the personal charm and evident conviction of Gerry Adams. Though he often came across as ill-tempered, fumbling and unfocused in media interviews, and always evaded the core questions about the relationship between Sinn Féin and the IRA, at a personal level he won sceptics over. Suddenly they could see why he had to be cagey. Hadn't he to move slowly and bring the whole movement with him? How could he move from a negotiating position before negotiations started and tell us frankly what he would settle for? Wasn't he at risk personally from the hard men of the IRA if we drew him out too far? Excuses were made for Adams on the basis of hopeful conjecture.

The commitment of Gerry Adams to finding peace was endorsed by John Hume, but many others were impressed by Adams too and took him to mean something by his words which he never actually said, which was that the IRA were ready to settle for less than a British withdrawal, so long as it was agreed by the Irish people as a whole, their view expressed through the contrivance of simultaneous referenda North and South.

What is striking about much of what has been written already on the peace initiative of the republicans is that though that initiative is open to very different subjective readings, many writers have chosen to make optimistic readings from the information available. Mallie and McKittrick, for example, point to a number of negative signs in 1994 which shook the faith of many who believed that a ceasefire was coming. They included Father Alex Reid, who had been a channel of communication for republicans, and who began to doubt whether republicans were serious. The spate of attacks on loyalists in the summer of 1994 is cited as one of the negative indicators, and Mallie and McKittrick record a suggestion that the attacks were a stratagem to wrong-foot the loyalists into continuing their violence after an IRA ceasefire. The security forces would then turn on the loyalists and the world would see them as the real evil. That is one plausible reading, but there are others. Might not the attacks just have been an attempt to provoke increased sectarian violence so that a ceasefire option could be waived? On what basis does an observer opt for one reading of events over another?

Similarly the massive attacks on London are treated as possible evidence that the IRA had begun to think it might drive the British out of Ireland by inflicting untenable damage on the British capital, but Mallie and McKittrick simply conclude that the IRA must have dismissed this idea. Why did these writers not consider seriously that the big new bombs were an integral part of the new strategy? They made a choice to believe in the ceasefire in the face of serious evidence against the sincerity of the IRA. In the end their choice presumably came down to subjective impression.

The tendency to interpret the vague language of republicans optimistically was evident again in the days before the IRA's restoration of its ceasefire on 21 July 1997. It can be seen in much of the *Irish News*'s coverage of Sinn Féin statements. For example, a front-page story on 17 July 1997 claimed that Sinn Féin had relaxed its demand for Irish unity. Reporter Michael O'Toole wrote: 'Sinn Féin has given the broadest indication yet that it would be prepared to accept a political agreement which fell short of a united Ireland.' Already, O'Toole is acknowledging that Sinn Féin only ever hints at accommodation, but never makes its position explicit. The hint in this case is a line from a long statement from Gerry Adams,   165 published in an inside page, in which he says that Sinn Féin would press for a 'renegotiation of the union', which O'Toole interprets for us, on his own initiative, as meaning that Sinn Féin will not be insisting on an abandonment of the Union. In fact, the statement by Gerry Adams focuses mostly on nonnegotiable concessions that Sinn Féin is demanding of the British government, concessions that it believes should be granted regardless of the talks process. Only in the final paragraphs does Adams allude to the talks themselves. There he says that Sinn Féin will urge the Irish government to press for Irish unity, and that the party itself will work for 'political, economic and democratic transformation of this island'.

Hyped as a 'marked departure' from 'thirty-two-county' rhetoric, the statement itself is equally amenable to being read as an entrenchment of the Sinn Féin position, as an insistence on major political change outside the context of the talks process, including the disarming of the RUC, progress towards improving conditions for and releasing of political prisoners, and equality of status for the Irish language. (Later, republicans claimed that these optimistic readings of their position amounted to a dirty tricks campaign against them.) The SDLP, by contrast, had been arguing that reform of the RUC would come after a political settlement.

Another example is worth citing of the remarkable optimism of observers of the peace process. Part of the lore of the 1994 peace-making is that it hinged at the end on whether or not veteran republican Joe Cahill would be given a visa to enter the United States. (The panic to persuade Bill Clinton to issue the visa is outlined by McKittrick and Mallie.) This seems incomprehensible. Would the IRA at the point of decision in August 1994 really have carried on over such a thing? Imagine telling a policeman's wife that her husband had to be shot because Nancy Soderberg opposed giving Joe Cahill a visa. Yet, that is what Jean Kennedy Smith told Soderberg, what Alex Reid told Albert Reynolds, what most observers of the peace process accept. These people believe simultaneously that republicans are peacemakers and also that they would kill for the right of Joe Cahill to a US visa. They appear not to notice the paradox.

166

One of the problems for those who produce violence but seek to negotiate an end to it is, perhaps, that the focus of the violence shifts from the big aspiration of a united Ireland to the lesser aspirations of steps in their peace process. So republicans have threatened to maintain violence simply to insist on the right not to decommission weapons; but the implied threat that they would continue to kill and risk the lives even of their own members, just to get Joe Cahill a visa, seems implausible.

Those writers who accept such an implausible idea are perhaps going further than they ought in attempting to understand the problems of the republican movement.

The problem, of course, is trying to interpret republican intentions when indications point almost simultaneously in contrary directions. This dual-purpose character to the political agenda of republicans is routine, but was rarely as distinct and puzzling as in July 1997. Then, republican politics seemed to be moving towards war on behalf of the community and also towards political talks with unionism on a compromise settlement. What was amazing about that month was the speed of events, and the fact that the prevailing spirit of the beginning was so comprehensively superseded at the end. Many writers, primarily Conor Cruise O'Brien, had predicted that the republican movement would use street protest to bring about warfare on the streets, to seek out a renewed legitimisation for their campaign. By the end of the first week of July 1997, that assessment seemed well validated, and the calamity of unprecedented civil unrest seemed imminent. Two weeks later, the calamity having been averted, the IRA declared a new ceasefire, on precisely the terms it had previously said it would. Its preconditions had been met, and it kept its word.

Two incompatible tendencies worked themselves out over the same period. The one tended towards chaos, the other towards a ceasefire. The stage at which communal warfare seemed inevitable was when republicans and others were preparing to oppose Orange parades planned for routes that passed through Catholic areas of Belfast, Derry and several small towns. The previous year, the whole of Northern Ireland had been engulfed in protest and riot, after the police blocked the way of an Orange parade from Drumcree towards the Catholic Garvaghy Road. The Orangemen had mustered so much disorder that the police simply had to back down and turn their batons on the Catholic residents of Garvaghy to clear a way for the parade. At the beginning of July 1997 no apparent means existed for averting a repeat. Whatever the decision taken by the government, it seemed inevitable that huge disorder would follow. If the RUC barred the way of the Drumcree parade, as they had in 1996, a similar muster of Orangemen all over Northern Ireland was likely; if it did not, then rioting by Catholics would follow. The Catholics would resist the second contentious parade of the week, through the Ormeau Road and, once humiliated at Garvaghy, would prepare greater resistance. What was most dangerous was that tens of thousands of Orangemen would be marching in Belfast on the same day. There could be a riot on an unprecedented scale.

The question of the contending rights of Orangemen to march through Catholic areas and of residents' groups to stop them was one that had the power to create a renewed validation for the republican cause. Had the scale of trouble predicted actually occurred, then such a validation might have followed. Republicans, however, played the game less ambitiously, apparently simply to prove that a nationalist community veto operated effectively. Just as Protestants mustering in numbers had the power to block change, as demonstrated so many times before, Catholics now showed they had the same power. That is to say, republicans seem to have been content not to push Northern Ireland over the edge for a regeneration of armed struggle, but instead to use street protest to contend civil rights issues. The question is whether that implied an overall lowering of their sights, or a complementary strategy. Would republicans direct their energies into street protest for intermediate goals as an alternative to working for a united Ireland, or would the intermediate struggles simply be a way of inching forward towards the primary goal?

The armed struggle had become tedious over the years, through the eighties and into the nineties, and blocking an internal settlement in itself did not give republicans any tangible achievement to show their followers. Street protest did. And it offered the anomalous image of Gerry Adams on the Andersonstown Road recovering hijacked vehicles and personally returning them to their owners. Whether Adams could have prevented chaos, had the contest over parades run its course with neither side backing down, is very doubtful. He must then be credited with supporting a massive gamble by the residents' groups and their republican supporters, and presumably with having ideas on how to manage the calamity if it occurred.

The potential value of a confrontation over parades was that it could serve the regeneration of republicanism and the legitimation of armed struggle, as similar calamities had done in the past. Republicanism received its fillips from events that appeared to confirm its analysis, or events that raised such emotion among Catholics that the inconsistencies in the republican analysis could be overlooked. Undoubtedly, the early trouble was exacerbated by social and political factors. Frank Curran has pointed to the six months mandatory sentence for rioting as an important one. Hundreds of young men were sent to prison on the basis of evidence from soldiers that had little or no local credibility. This familiarised law-abiding families with the insides of prisons and drew them into an allegiance with other families, including republicans, for whom imprisonment was no disgrace.

There were often such fillips available to republicans. The very frequency of them argues for the unviability of Northern Ireland. The republicans did not always have to rely on their own energies and imagination to produce such crises, though often they did. The chief example was the hunger strikes campaign, another was the peace process itself. Both had the power to project the British and unsympathetic Irish nationalists as the real obstacles to progress. In the same way that the Easter Rising was a revolt against Redmond, and the Hamas campaign is a revolt against Arafat and the PLO, the IRA campaign is a revolt against John Hume. At the end of the hunger strikes, the IRA dismissed the SDLP as 'imperialist lickspittles'.

These upheavals also have the power to call home to the tribe those Catholics who normally back the SDLP. After the RUC forced

169

an Orange parade down the Garvaghy Road in Portadown in July 1997, the SDLP swung round to the radical position of demanding the rerouting of and even a moratorium on parades, whereas before they had wanted negotiation and compromise. The moral tug of an issue like parades radicalises the whole of nationalism, and it is Sinn Féin that benefits. In the quieter times that follow, the SDLP softens its position and is seen to have sold out.

Part of the explanation of the SDLP's change of position over Orange marches lies in the confrontations that took place over the 1996 parade. When the RUC gave way before Orange protest at Drumcree in that summer of 1996 and reversed a decision to halt the Orange parade along the Garvaghy Road, it seemed to many Catholics to have thrown away whatever credibility it had established as an impartial, nonsectarian force. The Orange Order had refused the instruction from the police that they should stay off the Garvaghy Road, where their insistence on marching was leading to increasing disruption of public order by both sides. The Orange Order got its way by force of numbers. Republicans argued that this showed that the police force had not changed fundamentally since 1969. It would still do what the Ulster Unionist Party or the Orange Order told it to do.

The credibility of this argument in the face of the facts was a serious embarrassment to middle-class Catholics who wanted to participate in the Northern Ireland state and live at peace with Protestants. Now it seemed that everything their cousins and siblings in Andersonstown and Ardoyne had said about the police was true after all.

The next round of the quarrel between the Orange Order and the residents of the Garvaghy Road was due in the first week of July 1997. This was anticipated a full year in advance, and the expectation was that the police would either confront the Orange Order once again but this time not give way before protest, however great, or once again they would clear the Garvaghy Road for an Orange parade, in which case the disaffection of Catholics from the police would be complete and irreversible. Suddenly it seemed as if the entire problem of Northern Ireland had coalesced into a single issue of territorial rights on a stretch of road less than a mile long. Republicanism and Orangeism cling to anachronistic mythologies, the one that Ireland must fulfil its destiny as a single jurisdiction, the other that democracy can only be assured by a British Protestant monarch forestalling the encroachment of Vatican authority. Both are evident nonsense when phrased so simply, but the contention was between people of the different traditions insisting on rights, and the matter was serious enough to threaten violence over the whole region.

The Secretary of State for Northern Ireland Mo Mowlam said that the government would work to find agreement between the residents of the Garvaghy Road and the Orange Order. It failed to do this, and its integrity in the project came under scrutiny when a document leaked after the 1997 parade was allowed through showed that the British government had been seeking all along to find some way of getting 'Orange feet onto the Garvaghy Road'. What had not been clear was that the government would actually decline to make a decision on the merits of the contending claims of the Orange Order and the residents' group. That was to be the job of a parades commission which had not yet been legally authorised to make such rulings. In the meantime, the decision would fall to the police, and they would make it on the basis of public order considerations. If opposing the Orangemen was likely to produce greater violence than clearing the protesters off the road, then the Orangemen would not be opposed. Put simply, the police were given the freedom to choose the easier of the two contenders to deal with, without having to consider the rights and wrongs of the dispute.

So they assembled behind riot shields on the Garvaghy Road in the early hours of Sunday, 6 July 1997, ploughed the protesters off the road, and sealed the residents into side streets to make way for a thick phalanx of trudging Orangemen. The RUC came in new riot gear that included balaclavas worn behind visors. They moved along the road, shoving protesters forward. As angry men from the area lunged themselves at the police shields, some were batoned about the head.

171

The immediate result of this was a consolidation of Catholic opinion against the decision. John Hume, who had worked for compromise on previous contested parades, and on this one, now argued that the right of Orangemen to march a contested road was not equivalent to the right of residents not to be imposed upon, because the greater physical inconvenience was the one facing the residents. Orangemen compelled to walk a road parallel to the one of their choice were hardly suffering the same inconvenience as residents forbidden access to the main road past the end of their street and forced to hold mass in a side street for want of being free to cross the road to church.

The case for compromise had been based on a model of the opposing groups' rights as competing and equal. It failed when it became clear that the demands of the residents and the Orangemen were wholly exclusive of each other and not equally balanced. The residents seemed to have a greater right, because they suffered the greater imposition for the sake of the rights of the Orangemen.

The government's decision not to adjudicate on the points of principle separating the Garvaghy Road residents and the Orange Order left open the question of which party had the greater right in the issue. A problem with the 1997 decision to let the Orangemen through is that it could only work once. If the default from making an agreement was always going to be public order, then each side could make its own calculation on which way things would go if they declined to agree. The one most likely to get its way would have no incentive to make an agreement. The one least likely to get its way could prepare itself to reap what political advantages were available.

The Orangemen knew after Garvaghy Road 1997 that they had no incentive to negotiate over the Ormeau Road because, for want of agreement, the public order consideration prevailed, and since they posed the greater threat, they would get their way, if they insisted on it. Mowlam's insistence that a decision on the Ormeau Road Twelfth march be made either by agreement or on public order grounds seemed very risky. With the Twelfth approaching and the danger of the whole Belfast parade mustering at the lower

Ormeau in support of the local parade if it was stopped, there was a real danger of unprecedented street violence. Faced with that prospect, the Orange Order withdrew its Ormeau Road parade and three others in contended areas. Northern Ireland had been saved from its greatest threat not by government but by the Orange Order, which had realised that the cost of standing its ground might be a calamity for Northern Ireland.

The government had chosen to work for agreement, and for want of it to fall back on the public order principle. If the competing rights of Orangemen and nationalists weren't equal, however, this fall-back principle produced the risk of inherent injustice. If the state was unjust, then protest against the state was warranted, and arguably, force against the state was legitimate. That had been the inference drawn by republicans, and thousands who flocked to join them, in 1969. The graffiti and placards that followed Drumcree 1996 had said, 'Back to '69'. The argument from republicans was that nothing had changed since then. With such a vivid demonstration of the division in society, it was more plausible than ever that the violence of the IRA was a symptom of a fundamental malaise. Perhaps we had even been distracted from that malaise by the horror of the campaign. Perhaps we had concentrated too much after all on condemning that campaign and had overlooked the gravity of the underlying problem. What seemed implied by the confrontations over parades was that Northern Ireland was a society that would be tearing itself apart anyway, even if the bombers and gunmen stayed at home. It wasn't the intransigence of the IRA that threatened to take us all into a civil war, but old-fashioned territorial sectarianism.

There were some who argued that the issues were the same, that it was the IRA who directed the residents' groups. I had seen an indication of that myself at a residents' meeting in the lower Ormeau area in 1995, when a rousing mob of men at the back of the hall cheered for every speaker in favour of confrontation and held silence after every speaker against it. Gerard Rice, who chaired the meeting, refused to allow a vote and went out to tell the media that there had been a unanimous consensus in favour of blocking the next day's Orange parade. Two years later, in areas where compromise was reached with Orangemen, the local nationalists and clergy were often clear that the deciding factor was the low level of involvement of Sinn Féin. These were areas where the marching lodge was made up of people who lived in or close to the streets they wished to march through, who shopped in the same shops that the Catholics of those streets shopped in. Charles Kenwell is a storekeeper in Dromore, County Tyrone. In 1997 he met with a group of residents convened by the Church of Ireland and Catholic clergy of the town. The group was representative of all political parties and several other organisations. The Sinn Féin presence at the meeting was low, but proportionate. Its objections to the parade passing through Church Street on the Twelfth were overruled by the other Catholics present.

The emergence of the parades issue in the mid-1990s was fired by a number of things. Orangemen marching down the Ormeau Road in Belfast in July 1992 had horrified local residents by taunting them with five-finger salutes while walking past the local bookmaker's. Five Catholics had been shot dead there by loyalist paramilitaries in February 1992. In Portadown, where the parades were frequently accompanied by rioting, local Jesuits had organised protests that stopped short of blocking the road. Every year through the mid-eighties and into the nineties, protesters would have a tea party in the middle of the road before the parade came along, and they would consent to being carried prone to the footpath by policemen.

At the Ormeau Road, in Portadown and in Derry as well, and in other areas too, protesters changed tactics and organised to block roads and force a choice on the police between redirecting the parades or clearing the roads by force. There are several indications that this was a strategy devised by Sinn Féin. The three residents' groups involved were all led by former republican prisoners. Yet, Sinn Féin had not always had a strong party line on parades. A Social Attitudes survey in 1990 had asked people if they thought that Protestant parades were too closely or too loosely policed. There was sufficient diversity of opinion among Sinn Féin voters to suggest that they were free to make up their own minds on the issue. Twenty-seven per cent of Sinn Féin voters canvassed said that controls on Protestant parades were used too little, while eighteen per cent said they were used too much. There was clearly no party line on the question at that time. It seems reasonable, therefore, to speculate that a policy decision was made within the party some time after 1990.

The argument that protest groups were directed by Sinn Féin was discounted for practical purposes by the Secretary of State, Mo Mowlam. She chose to deal with the residents' groups as if they were wholly representative of the areas from which they came. Sinn Féin now represented more than 16 per cent of the electorate and had very substantial majorities in some areas. The Orange decision not to negotiate with people who were members of Sinn Féin or former prisoners could not hold up against democratic standards when this amounted, as it did in some areas, to refusing to deal with anyone but representatives of minorities. It also seemed inconsistent with the fact that unionists had to deal with Sinn Féin councillors in local government.

Yet the suspicion of the Orangemen was that they were being forced to deal with Sinn Féin directly, working to its own agenda, and not just with people who happened to be members of it. They suspected that those members of Sinn Féin who were leading residents' groups were taking their guidance not from the other members and their communities but from the party itself. The Orange Order and other sceptics were sure that the opposition to parades was part of a larger conspiracy. The focus of accusations of conspiracy at Garvaghy Road was Breandán Mac Cionnaith, who was seen as a republican with a record of violence. He had aligned himself with similar protests in Derry and Belfast. His partner in the coalition at Garvaghy Road was the Jesuit priest Father Eamon Stack. Father Stack defined the role of the protest not as a challenge to the Orange Order, but as a challenge to the state to treat Protestants and Catholics with equal respect. He believed that if he could hold the coalition together, in the face of criticism, that would create the best chance of a peaceful end to the crisis. He said that the coalition had decided to offer such slight resistance to the parade from Drumcree church that, should the police choose to force the march through, they would be able to sweep the coalition's resistance aside. The point would then have been illustrated dramatically that the police favoured the Orangemen, but no one would have been hurt.

Gerry Adams appears to have endorsed the conspiracy theory of parades protest himself in words attributed to him in an edition of the RTÉ current affairs programme *Prime Time* broadcast in spring 1997. Adams had been addressing a meeting of republicans in a closed session in Athboy, in the Republic, the previous autumn and had challenged those present, 'Do you think Drumcree happened by accident?' Adams said that three years of hard work by activists had produced the massive stand-off at Drumcree in 1996, which had resulted in the reversal of a decision by the RUC, from confronting the Orangemen to beating Catholics off the road to escort them through. Adams said that these were the sort of 'scene changes' (whatever that means) that the party had to exploit. Privately some members of the Garvaghy Road residents' coalition were furious. 'That's just Adams shooting his mouth off,' said one. In fact, Adams's words do suggest someone asserting an implausible point, speaking to people inclined not to believe him, as if he was trying to persuade them that the peace process and street politics were producing results.

However conspiratorial the origins of some of the residents' groups, the issue they raised attracted greater support as the tensions between the two sides increased and as the policing of the disputes became more violent. This echoed the period of the civil rights protests in the late sixties and the increasing disaffection of Catholics with the police at that time. The simple law such events followed seemed to be: the worse things get the worse they get. Violence simply produced more violence in an irresistible spiral. Heavy-handed policing, however necessary in terms of the conditions of the day, would always annoy people sufficiently to ensure that the next confrontation would be harder to deal with.

The insistence of Orangemen on marching through Catholic areas despite the opposition of residents made it appear as if it was the right to annoy those residents that was most important to them. When police action to remove protesters led to people being injured by plastic bullets and batons, the simple impression made was that the state would deploy force to preserve the rights of Orangemen over the rights of Catholics. It wasn't that simple. In fact, the police stopped nearly all parades going through the lower Ormeau Road. They took their guidance, however, from public order legislation, which required them to make their decision on a parade on the basis of which course would lead to least violence. That meant that the larger parades along the Ormeau, on the Twelfth of July each year, were forced through. The message of that to Catholics was that when Orangemen mustered or threatened to muster, they got their way.

This process was familiar to any observer of the Northern Ireland Troubles. An issue acquired legitimacy and support as it was repressed. The anger that an issue can mobilise at first may be very little, but once heads have been cracked on the streets the same issue can rally much stronger commitment. Right to the end, there would be Catholics who would not go along with this plan to block roads against Orange parades. On RTE radio, on the Friday morning before the 1997 Drumcree parade, Catholics interviewed in the centre of Portadown said that they thought that the parade should go ahead, and that the people of the road should simply go into their houses and ignore it. Others could see that if the issue was brought to the point of confrontation, attitudes would harden on both sides, and forces on both sides would then be easier to rally and harder to deal with.

The government was in a genuine double bind which it genuinely wanted out of, but neither the Garvaghy Road residents' coalition nor the Orange Order would concede significant ground. A long delay in announcing a decision on the parade allowed both sides a chance to relax their positions, right up to the very end, and neither took it. This was foreseeable. They had made their contrary positions clear well in advance. Equally foreseeable were the ways in which the images of the day would be read. To Catholics the sight of police in riot gear with shields shoving protesters off the road would mean simply that the Orange Order still had the power to summon the full weight of the state to its aid. Mowlam said the decision was dictated by circumstances, and in the interests of public safety. Ronnie Flanagan, the police chief constable, said it was clear that violence would have been directed against Catholics if the parade had not been allowed to go ahead.

One of the Jesuits at Garvaghy Road said that the inevitable result of the decision to let the parade go through would be the humiliation and disillusionment of the people of the area. It would be much harder now to persuade them that a peaceful way forward was possible. The miscalculation of the Jesuits had been that a peaceful way of stopping Orange parades through their area was possible. It wasn't.

A conspiratorial reading of events would say that republicans inspired this confrontation and reaped an affirmation from it of their assessment that peaceful politics would not bring justice for Catholics. A more sympathetic reading would say that republicans had been trying to prove that peaceful protest could bring change, or at least that they were conducting an experiment to see if it would. Either way, the conclusion would have been the same, that peaceful protest had failed and that Catholics' rights were expendable for a bit of peace and quiet. In which case the republican response would inevitably be: Well, we'll see about that.

The republicans did not invent the division between Catholics and the Orange Order, and they had stayed out of this quarrel for decades. Catholics had learned to live with Orange parades. That may have entailed a denial of their own sense of intimidation. They always knew, under their skin, that too much trouble would follow the disrupting of these parades for it to be worthwhile. They sensed that the Orange Order was too big and too strong. I remember as a child watching an Orange parade through Belfast city centre. Two young soldiers stood near me, unarmed but in uniform. A man in a black suit broke from the parade to reprimand the soldiers. He ordered them to stand to attention, and they did. The Orange Order had seemed to be in charge of more than its own members.

178   According to IRA defector Sean O'Callaghan, the strategy of the

IRA was to bring loyalists into confrontation with the state, or at least to wrong-foot them into being the greater offenders, and perhaps to demolish the legitimacy of the demand that republicans sign up to the Mitchell Principles committing them to peaceful negotiation (by showing that unionists flouted them too, but were kept in the talks because of their numbers). If that's what republicans were up to, then that strategy was effectively countered by the decision to let the Drumcree parade go ahead: paradoxically, the effect of favouring the Orange Order was to put an onus on unionists to behave themselves and to accept later restraints. By winning, the Orange Order was losing. As soon as the members of the Orange Order set one foot on the Garvaghy Road it owed Mo Mowlam a very big favour.

The Orangemen got their parade down the Garvaghy Road in 1997. They decided days later to waive four other parades which till then had been just as important to them, including their parade down the Ormeau Road on 12 July. They took great credit for that decision, though many complained that they had taken it only because they were threatened by the mustering Catholics on the other side of the Ormeau Bridge. The police had told them that they could not provide enough protection for the parades. The Orange Order had had one very strong hand to play, but only one, and the trouble was that it was too strong. It could redirect the main Belfast parade of nearly thirty thousand people to the Ormeau Road, to demand the right to walk through. There were strong hints that this is precisely what it intended to do. The police advised Orange leaders that loss of life on a large scale would be unavoidable if they did that.

In holding firm to its insistence on marching the Garvaghy Road and winning the government's cooperation, the Orange Order had thrown away a potential moral advantage. Afterwards, it could be said against it that it had accepted a victory won by a massive threat against the state and that it had given nationalists an excuse for violence. At the same time it had discarded the opportunity to set an example of tolerance. This was not a good starting point for unionist entry into talks on the future of Northern Ireland. A conspiracy against the Orange Order might have just failed, but the real untenability of the Orange position remained clear, perhaps clearer. Furthermore, it was not the Orange Order that had confronted the supposed republican conspiracy to foment disorder and defeated it, but government and the RUC. This was a bit like a rich father bailing out a delinquent son; he would be seen abroad as the brat's chief ally, but when the boy was safely home, the real price of saving his hide would be made clear.

The strategic way for republicans to have responded to circumstances in which the Orange Order had discarded a moral point would have been to restrain all violence from their own side. A government in disapproving form with the Orange Order, and owed a favour, would have perhaps have had more time for peaceful republicans. Adams addressed a crowd on the Falls Road on the afternoon that the Garvaghy Road march was forced through. He said that, as someone who had lived all his life on the Falls Road, he saw no reason why the people of the area should suffer in the protest, that there should be no violence that wasn't 'consistent with a coherent strategy'. Republicans had clearly anticipated well how things would go and had prepared their response. It appears to have depended to the end on the Orangemen being foolish enough to try to enforce their demands, for when the Orangemen instead backed down, the republicans seemed wrong-footed and unready to articulate a response.

The lessons of the Garvaghy Road crisis were revolutionary. The Orange Order found that its only weapon when threatened was too big to be usable. It had a nuclear option, in that it could mobilise the whole Belfast parade against the lower Ormeau, or it could rally thousands at Drumcree if obstructed there. The potential of either move was too calamitous for the tactic to be permissible. It was faced with a strategic problem that the United States would understand; it can obliterate all life on the planet, if it chooses to, but it couldn't restore order in Somalia.

Republicans had been demanding parity of esteem as the central plank of the new republican politics, but they seemed ill-equipped to recognise it when they won it. The republican complaint was that the unionists operated a veto on change, but the stand-down of the Orange Order indicated that a nationalist veto functioned too. The point had already been made by Mowlam (and the Conservative Secretary of State Sir Patrick Mayhew before her) that political change would require the consent of both communities. The contention over parades had provided a practical illustration that when Protestants insisted on having their way they inevitably set limits to their own freedom.

There was another sense in which the dispute illustrated the potential of republican protest. The implications of this were horrific, but arose directly from the nature of the decision taken over the Garvaghy Road parade. The RUC chief constable, Ronnie Flanagan, said that he made his decision on the basis of the relative threats from each side. That meant that if nationalists could provide a counter-threat greater than that of Orangeism they would, logically, get their way. The terms on which the decision was taken presented the IRA with the first opportunity for it to meaningfully provide tactical defence for a Catholic community. Drumcree presented the IRA with a possible new way of understanding Catholic defence; it need no longer be strictly the mythical defence of Catholic lives against attack, but the defence of Catholic interest by threat. There was now a practical means of deploying the threat of violence in the interests of the Catholic community. A new legacy was available to them to replace the legacy and lessons of August 1969 if that was what they wanted to make of it. The implied message of Flanagan's decision was that the IRA or others in the nationalist community could avert the danger of future impositions by presenting an even greater threat than that posed by Orangeism. The very criteria deployed by the police were an invitation to both sides to compete to provide the greater threat. It hardly seems creditable that a modern government would give insurgents such a message, but the implications of the decision taken at Garvaghy Road in 1997 were as simple and obvious as that.

In 1996 the threat posed by nationalists, and weighed in the balance against the Orange Order, was that the IRA campaign, already resumed in England, would extend to Northern Ireland. By 1997

Gerry Adams was saying that prospects of a ceasefire might hinge on the Garvaghy Road decision. To observers, this seemed to have little plausibility, because it was the sort of thing that was routinely said. The IRA was not going to change its plans over a parade, any more than it had been willing to over, say, the release of Lee Clegg, the paratrooper convicted of the murder of Belfast joyrider Karen Reilly. Outrage would produce riots and destruction, but there would always be a clear distinction between the IRA's agenda and the enactment of community anger through rioting on the streets. The threat of a resumption of violence by the IRA was far greater than the threat from Orangeism, because it offered years of violence against a week of it. By 1997 the IRA was assumed to have committed itself to a resumed campaign, and few believed that it might be persuaded to change its ways by a decision in favour of nationalists on the Garvaghy Road. Those who understood the background machinations for a ceasefire, and how close they were to success, understood the IRA well enough to know that they would make their decision on the basis of the demands they had already made, and not in response to passing crises.

The potential was clear for the IRA to use its violence to enforce occasional demands in the Catholic interest rather than as a sustained campaign against constitutional compromise. If it wanted to bully the government into interim concessions, it could do that. A campaign of violence in defence of Catholic interests would be very different from the long war against an internal settlement. It would have to be occasional rather than consistent. It would respond to conditions as they changed, rather than attack randomly like a force of nature. If violence was pegged to a single irresolvable condition like the British presence, it would have to be seen as nonnegotiable on any other terms. If it was to press for Catholic interests, it would have to present itself as negotiable. The threat, outweighing the Orange threat, would have to be seen as dependent on the decision to be taken, so that the state could know that when it favoured the Catholic interest the threat would be withdrawn. If violence was going to follow, whatever the state did, there would be no incentive to bargain with it.

The instrument of Catholic defence of this kind has usually been rioting and destruction, presenting itself as communal outrage. Paradoxically it does more to damage Catholic communities. This is how it has always been. Rioting on the streets followed the release of Lee Clegg, as it followed the Garvaghy Road decision. The core campaign of the IRA seemed not to be responding directly to these things. (An old example of force used creatively by the IRA in the defence of interests was the killing of prison officers during the 1980–81 hunger strikes campaign, which carried the message that if prison officers ceased applying harsh measures inside the prisons they would be spared. Strategically in IRA terms, it was reformist rather than revolutionary.)

Sinn Féin's campaign against Orange parades was arguably part of a new strategy, away from armed struggle towards more constructive campaigning for the Catholic interest through social action. Those who dismissed the parades protests as simply a republican plot were not only overlooking the real groundswell of support gathering round the issue, but were failing to consider what the nature of the plot itself might be. Had Mo Mowlam banned the Drumcree parade at the instigation of nationalists, she would have signalled to them that there was a potential for progress through social action rather than violence. That in itself would not of course have been a satisfactory reason for banning the parade, but it would have been no worse than the reason for which it was allowed to go ahead.

One legacy of the decision to force the parade through the Garvaghy Road was that the republicans found an opportunity to show political maturity. Gerry Adams, who had three weeks before been slithering out of commenting meaningfully on the IRA murder of two policemen in Lurgan, was now calling for restraint. And the SDLP and Sinn Féin were once again sharing a common purpose, only Sinn Féin seemed the party more able to pursue it. Republicans now had a civil rights agenda and were plausible champions of a people that the state was content to walk over when it suited their practical interests. If there was a lesson in all this for republicans it was that they need never fear that the government would deny 183 them for all time the opportunity to present themselves as the vigorous champions of Catholic rights. There would always be something to fight for, and there would always be popular support to mobilise. They would continue to grow as a party while they had such issues to fight.

The experiences of the marching season point to the existence of a nationalist community veto. They showed that whereas the Orange Order had power to dictate its will, that power was cumbersome and unusable, and they showed that republicans, when they campaigned on community issues, could rally increased political support and draw in support from the SDLP. There was little indication at the end of the crisis that republicans were impressed with these discoveries, or that they would rest their future political tactics on them to the exclusion of the campaign for a British withdrawal. Yet a ceasefire was only days away. Just a month before the Twelfth, it had seemed obvious that the Provisionals were intent on war.

It was one of the sunniest days of the year. Two policemen, Roland Graham and David Johnston, walked back towards their station along Church Walk in Lurgan. Two or three men, said to have been wearing women's wigs, ran up behind them and shot them both in the head. They slumped dead together onto the pavement. For six hours their bodies lay where they had fallen, shielded from public view by a furniture van. Forensic staff came and photographed them and gathered evidence. Reporters a few yards away waited for statements from politicians and a senior police officer. Children skited about excitedly and asked anyone who would pay attention to them if they had seen the bodies at all. A hot but ordinary day dragged on.

There is a strange contrast between the atmosphere at a scene like that and the condensed version of it reproduced by the media. You almost don't believe that you were there, when you see it all again on television. That's because it didn't feel so urgent at the time. The woman police officer, who was probably a friend of the dead men, stands with a clipboard at the corner of the street, directing passers-by away from the bodies, taking abuse from some of them for her civility. The reporters are anxious at first to get the details, then relax and wait, then get bored, then begin to exchange jokes with each other. They are to go away and tell the world how significant this moment was, in which two men died, but already it is routine to them.

David McKittrick, writing in the *Independent* the next day (17 June 1997), said: 'the killings have confounded the analysis of almost everyone, including both the opponents of republicans and their sympathisers'. McKittrick was one of the optimists. His analysis, as developed in the book on the peace process, *A Fight for Peace*, that he co-authored with Eamonn Mallie, was built around a belief that the IRA was working out a wholly unarmed political approach. The IRA document outlining the rationale for such a strategy was called the 'TUAS' document. This was being read to mean Totally Unarmed Strategy. Sceptics, after the ending of the first ceasefire of the peace process, in February 1996, were interpreting it to mean Tactical Use of Armed Struggle, which seemed to fit better with both the acronym and the facts. The murders in Lurgan, however, seemed to fit neither notion of what republicans were up to. Certainly this was not unarmed politics, but in what sense was it a tactical deployment of violence? That theory suggested that republicans would work their way into a political process and try to manipulate it in stages. They would use salami strategy, and wear away at the stipulations laid down on their involvement. This double murder seemed more like a reckless act of murderous passion which could only provoke censure and retaliation. The British government was already speaking, through officials, to Sinn Féin, and was already meeting the Sinn Féin terms for a ceasefire. Just three days before the shooting, these officials had told Martin McGuinness that the government had conceded the core Sinn Féin demand for a time frame for talks. The murders didn't seem to fit with any theory that attributed any kind of new refinement of strategy to the IRA. Why hit out at the precise time at which your enemy is giving way to your demands, and make it harder for him to concede further without looking like a weakling?

Constables Graham and Johnston knew, as we all knew, that there was no IRA ceasefire in place. The Provisionals had suspended their violence for the elections but had signalled its resumption when they planted a van bomb on a mountain road near Poleglass two weeks before the Lurgan shooting. Most of the media took up the IRA's own language and called that bomb a land mine, though it was no different from any other booby trap of its kind. The IRA said it had been abandoned because of civilian activity in the area. They would leave it to the police to decommission it. The police stayed away in case the message was simply a ruse to draw them in. Children set alight to the bomb and it flared like a giant roman candle. Sinn Féin condemned the police negligence. The day before, they had been picketing the same stretch of road because of the risk to children from traffic. Now they had no comment to make on the IRA's decision to leave a bomb where children played. In Sinn Féin's eyes, the only people to blame for the danger those children had been subjected to were the people whom the bomb had been designed to kill.

In Derry the previous week, an IRA sniper had opened fire on an army car. The IRA claimed to have hit someone inside it. The police and army said no one had been injured. Rumours said an inexperienced gunman, or gunwoman, had lost balance after a premature first shot and had not recovered in time to take accurate aim. The intention had been clear, however, and constables Graham and Johnston knew well that they were at risk.

There were grounds for optimism, however. Anyone reading the politics of the moment would have thought this an unlikely time for the IRA to strike. It was mid-June. The inter-party talks had resumed at Stormont. Tony Blair was new to government with a massive majority and had declared his commitment to getting a solution to the Northern Ireland problem. The Secretary of State, Mo Mowlam, as well as conceding the republicans' demand for a time frame for talks, had said that the train would leave the station, with or without republicans on board. She had even said that if they were on that train it might leave without unionists, if they couldn't stomach talking with Sinn Féin. Fianna Fáil leader

Bertie Ahern had just secured his place as taoiseach in the new Dáil. Everything was in place, or was close to being in place, for a more sympathetic handling of republicans. It was decision time for the IRA. Most of what their new political allies and their declared strategy had sought for them had been achieved, or been brought within reach.

Republicans had a problem with Blair, but it was one of interpretation. Blair had come over to Belfast and said he did not envisage a united Ireland within the lifetime of anyone in the crowd he addressed. He was declaring his personal reading of the realities of Northern Ireland, and underlining the consent principle contained in the Downing Street Declaration, the joint statement by the British prime minister and the taoiseach in December 1993 which laid down the basic principles of the peace process. Republicans put an ominously negative spin on this, interpreting the remarks as a declaration of British government policy to rule in occupied Ireland for another ninety years. Had they been disposed to giving Blair space to be creative they would not, presumably, have misrepresented his words so eagerly.

The killings of the constables closed down a series of meetings between Sinn Féin leaders and British government officials. Blair read the shootings as a rejection. Like the old sages of the Upanishads rejecting definitions of reality with Not this, Not this, republicans were still spurning the most imaginative efforts of governments and political leaders to contrive a dignified course into negotiations for them. Shooting Roland Graham and David Johnston appeared calculated to abort the whole peace process and to close off the prospects of Sinn Féin getting onto the talks 'train'. It brought into question the commitment of republicans to peace making in any terms at all, other than victory. It appeared to have been just a ham-fisted continuation of the war, with no specific political significance other than to remind the government and everyone else that there was no ceasefire in place yet, perhaps – if the thing was thought out at all – so that it would be all the more valued when it came.

The shootings suggested that armed politics was still being used in the same way it had been used through the 1980s, not to facilitate a settlement but to prevent one. The Lurgan killings seemed to signal not that something had changed, but that, as yet, nothing had changed. The republican explanation was that these things happen when there is a conflict in place, as if by some process of subterranean effervescence that only they understood. The rest of the country might be in shock and the United States support base might be outraged, but this wasn't to be seen as politics, they implied, but as chemistry. When republicans aren't getting their way, these things happen, and there isn't much that can be done about it other than for government and others to go and work harder to find a way of meeting republican needs.

Shock has a limited life span in Northern Ireland. Within two weeks, government officials were taking phone calls from Sinn Féin again and writing position papers for them. Business had resumed.

After the Lurgan shootings, it began to appear as if republicans could not be wooed into talks. In fact, a ceasefire would come immediately after reservations expressed by Sinn Féin had been cleared up to their satisfaction. The outstanding obstacle to talks, so far as the IRA was concerned, was the demand that weapons be decommissioned in advance. The government was still working on ways to assure republicans that this demand would not actually obstruct the course of the talks themselves. Republicans had succeeded in persuading many political figures that the demand for decommissioning of any weaponry at all before a final settlement could not be met. Yet to proceed with an armed campaign, in opposition to this demand for decommissioning, would smack of a bloody-minded insistence on fighting for nothing more than the right to retain those weapons. That is what was happening. Republicans were now being criticised by friends like Bernadette McAliskey and former allies like Ruairí Ó Brádaigh for risking and taking life merely to secure a negotiating position. They didn't want, however, to be sucked into a prolonged talks process that would smother them and get them nothing. Yet it was hard to see how any talks process would get them any more for nationalists than the SDLP could secure alone.

When a ceasefire was called a month after the murders, what was most surprising about it was its integrity. There had been a clear list of demands put to government since the previous October. John Hume had carried them himself to John Major. He said at the time: 'I put peace on the table and they rejected it.' Tony Blair met those demands, and the republicans kept their word.

There were other pressures on them, but these need not be regarded as having been decisive. After the shootings in Lurgan, many, including the US friends of republicans, began to doubt whether republicans were serious or not. Congressman Peter King, a personal friend of Gerry Adams, for the first time called for a unilateral ceasefire by the IRA. Editorials in the New York newspaper the *Irish Voice* declared total bewilderment, and discussions on the republican bulletin boards on the Internet reflected the same confusion and distaste. Republican supporters across the world who normally spent several hours a day by their computers ready to defend the movement against criticism simply disappeared for that week.

The timing of the declaration of a ceasefire, when it came, seemed calculated to damage the Ulster Unionist Party leader David Trimble and the whole unionist family, but it is not like republicans to move so nimbly. The 'long war' is a lumbering process. The talks process was approaching a vote on government proposals for the decommissioning of weapons, which Trimble and others saw as a waiving of the issue. He was threatening to walk out of the talks if the proposals were not firmed up to insist on the actual physical handing over of weapons, as a precondition to Sinn Féin staying in talks. Trimble was not going to get his way, but he was in danger of taking the blame now for scuppering the talks at the very moment at which the IRA had made the process look most hopeful. What argued against the view that the IRA had simply called an opportunistic ceasefire, in order to wind Trimble, however, was that it came within the government's timetable. Any later than the end of July, and Sinn Féin would not qualify for entry into talks. It came soon after the government's final reassurance that the decommissioning question would not hold up those talks, and it allowed Sinn Féin to influence the debate on the decommissioning proposals.

Some commentators, like John Waters in the *Irish Times*, re-marked on the significance of the ceasefire starting 526 days after the Canary Wharf bomb, which had come 526 days after the start of the first ceasefire. The coincidence seemed to be a message from the IRA, perhaps a declaration that they pick their timings with care, a hint that they will be dictated to by symmetry before they'll be dictated to by governments. Who knows? It allows people to believe that the IRA are working to a recondite agenda. Maybe they are.

The fact is that they were getting what they had asked for. Mean-ingful symmetry and the chance to throw unionism into confusion seem simply to have been an added bonus. After the ceasefire declaration, it was possible to scrutinise the documents sent to Sinn Féin before and after the Lurgan killings and to see the development of the government's position. It was after Lurgan that the decision was made by the British government not to let the decommission-ing question hold up talks.

A letter, or *aide-mémoire*, sent three days before the Lurgan mur-ders outlined the time frame and also addressed decommissioning:

> The government has always made it clear that it wants to resolve this rapidly to the satisfaction of the participants so that it does not block the substantive political negotiations. Realistically, this can only be on the basis of implementing all aspects of the Mitchell report.

The report of Senator George Mitchell in January 1996 had sug-gested that the parties to the talks consider that weapons could be decommissioned in parallel with talks, rather than at the start of them or at the end. The report had also set down six principles by which all parties, signing up to them, would commit themselves to nonviolent politics, as a condition of being allowed to participate in the talks.

What was missing from the *aide-mémoire* was a clear promise that the decommissioning issue would not hold up talks. That was what constables Graham and Johnston died for, and it was granted to Sinn Féin in a further letter, from Mo Mowlam to Martin

McGuinness, on 9 July. Dr Mowlam's letter quoted and beefed out assurances that the two governments had made within days after the Lurgan murders: 'Both the British and Irish Governments share the view that "... voluntary and mutual decommissioning can be achieved only in the context of progress in comprehensive and inclusive political negotiations". It is in this context that both governments "... acknowledge a particular responsibility to carry the process forward with energy and determination so as to build confidence without blocking the negotitations".' Clearly if decommissioning could only happen in the context of progress, it could not come at the start of the talks. That was the promise the republicans were waiting for. If unionists were demanding that the IRA surrender weapons, an Independent Commission would take up their complaint and seek a response to it, but the talks would not stop. Republicans might come under serious pressure to begin disarming during the talks, but their absolute refusal to do so would not stall progress towards completion of the talks process.

The point that the question of decommissioning would not hold up talks was reinforced by a reassurance from Mo Mowlam that if the parties failed to agree within a time frame, the two governments would continue to work for agreement anyway. This meant, effectively, that if the unionists wanted to waste the period of the talks by demanding IRA guns, they would simply squander their prospects of influencing the terms of the referendum to be put to the people of Northern Ireland by the government. The crucial words were:

> [The government] cannot give a guarantee of a successful outcome because that will require agreement and consent among both unionists and nationalists, as well as both Governments. There are many difficult issues, any of which if not addressed in good faith and resolved satisfactorily, could hold back overall agreement. But both Governments will be working to overcome obstacles to agreement and, if these negotiations do not succeed despite their best efforts, they will together continue to pursue rapid progress to an overall agreed settlement acceptable to both unionists and nationalists.

The government wasn't going to bail people out of their intransigence.

The irony of the republican position when the prospects of entry into talks arose was that the very guns that had been used to prevent an internal settlement became the main obstacle to it when they were silenced. The guns did not even have to be fired in order to serve the purpose they had served for so long; they had only to exist. In fact, they didn't even have to exist either, so long as sufficient numbers of people believed that they did. Yet at this moment of extraordinary tactical refinement the republicans were saying that they wanted into talks and that they would accept the outcome of those talks. All they required of the other parties was that they should ignore the guns. The trouble with guns is that it isn't easy to ignore them. Unionists argued that the threat implied in the retention of guns would influence the course of negotiations unfairly, would pollute the democratic process. They were taking a possible political advantage in skirting talks on the excuse that they could not negotiate with people who held arms, but they had a point too. The question over the republican refusal to allow for that point is whether they ever expected the other parties to deal with them while they retained their weapons, or if they were really secretly hoping that the unionists would take fright and refuse. Were the silenced guns of the ceasefires effectively doing the same job for republicans as they had been doing before?

Arguments over guns would continue, if that was what the unionists wanted, but that would not harm republicans. They had nothing to lose by the talks failing to address constitutional issues and getting bogged down in trying to produce disarmament. All that would show was that unionists were unwilling to negotiate. In the end the governments would frame the terms for a referendum on a new devolved settlement, and that was likely to be something that would suit nationalists better than it would suit unionists. Further, if it failed, that would remove devolution as a tenable settlement and challenge the governments to start thinking about joint authority.

Unionists had said they would not negotiate with guns 'on the table, under the table or outside the door'. In saying this they were repeating a phrase coined by John Hume, and taunting him with the charge that he had changed his own mind on this. Republicans had persuaded Hume and the two governments that decommissioning would be simply impossible, because it would betoken surrender. It was more complicated than that. Decommissioning would be a symbolic declaration of the unity of the IRA and Sinn Féin. That is something that was worth great efforts by governments to achieve, and by republicans to avert. If the IRA could be persuaded to give up weapons by those who bartered with Sinn Féin, it would have admitted that it was the same movement. It would also have admitted that republican violence was negotiable. Where might that end, but with the whole IRA campaign being talked down? Violence was being presented by Sinn Féin as a virtual force of nature, which they could show others how to assuage, not as a concerted political campaign that was amenable to reason.

The political value of a refusal to decommission was that it locked unionists onto a single issue and made them appear obsessive and unreasonable. How was it, wondered nationalists of all shades, that everyone else could see that decommissioning amounted to surrender and was therefore too much to ask, but unionists could not see this? It was a significant tactical achievement by republicans to win so many people over to thinking in this way, and it worked to their advantage. The demand for weapons to be given up, even as tokens of good faith, was refused not because it is impossible – nothing is impossible – but to make life difficult for others.

There were strong indications that massive quantities of explosive had been decommissioned in the past, for practical reasons. Several large bombs were discarded in Belfast in the run-up to the Downing Street Declaration, and no such bombs were ever detonated in Belfast again. That suggests that the IRA was dumping gear. It made perfect sense for them to do that rather than hold onto it. Why risk someone getting caught with bags of fertiliser mix that were not going to be used?

By refusing, for political reasons, to decommission, the IRA would eventually either bring the unionists into talks on the   193 understanding that the IRA was a legitimate army, or the war would go on. Hume says it is more important to decommission mind-sets, but that is exactly what the unionists were trying to do; they were trying to get a declaration from the IRA that they had no further attachment to weaponry. They knew as well as anyone that there was no serious prospect of the IRA being completely disarmed, or at least most of those who led the Ulster Unionist Party knew this. The fact that the gesture would have been only a token was often cited by nationalists as evidence that it was meaningless, when it was precisely as a token that it would have been valued.

The arguments for and against decommissioning were frequently framed in terms of the physical value of weaponry in war. The IRA, said one side of the argument, could not be expected to give up its weapons when it had not actually lost the war. The British had failed to defeat their enemy, and were in the position of having to settle terms, essentially to sue for peace with an army that had fought them to a standstill. Conor Gearty, writing in the *Guardian*, drew an analogy with the PLO which, far from being disarmed by the Israelis, had been assisted in expanding its weaponry so that it could control its territory and police dissident elements.

This was not war in that sense, however. No one was going to concede territory to the control of the IRA. The British, while interested in finding a settlement to the satisfaction of the majority in Northern Ireland, had not been brought to the table by force to concede a constitutional stand-down. It had the option of continuing to police the disorder in Northern Ireland if it chose to. The actual significance of the weapons was political rather than military. The IRA had chosen to discuss the decommissioning demand only in terms that saw it as an undesirable and unearned surrender. Why would they deplete their fighting potential when the dispute was not yet settled? Why, some argued, would they risk leaving the Catholic population undefended before they had won guarantees of its safety?

But the IRA would not have been depleted as a military force if it had decommissioned the same number of weapons in a year as it actually expended anyway. The political advantage of refusing to decommission those weapons must have been reckoned to be greater than the political advantage of letting them go. That superior political advantage lay in forcing a reduction of the conditions for Sinn Féin's entry into talks and imposing the precondition on others that a tactical ceasefire was an acceptable starting point for negotiations. The IRA was successful in that project.

The IRA effectively defeated the British principle that a ceasefire had to be a clear declaration of an end to violence, and got the British to accept what John Hume articulated once himself, that a tactical ceasefire is better than no ceasefire at all. In this they created more room for themselves to operate. It became possible for republicans to speak more openly about the prospects of the second ceasefire ending if others didn't accede to political change.

Thus, following journalists' reports that the ceasefire was to be reviewed after four months, Sinn Féin's Máirtín Ó Muilleoir wrote thus in the *Andersonstown News* of 26 July 1997:

> As for the shock horror IRA November review of its ceasefire, the reality is that the republicans need to review their ceasefire not every four months but every week. How else is the IRA to protect the peace? How else is it to consider ways in which the ceasefire could be underpinned? Ordinary nationalists, determined to defend the peace, demand consistent monitoring by the IRA of its ceasefire.

The first ceasefire had been received on the understanding that the war was over, bar the freedom of leading republicans to say so clearly. The second one was received with what Gerry Adams called 'more realism'. Instead of people arguing over whether or not it was purely tactical, he appears to have judged that people had accepted that a tactical ceasefire was better than no ceasefire at all. The anomaly in the republican claim on the people's trust was that they were telling them that they were giving up the use of force, while they had retained force to the very moment they were granted their demands. Clearly, they had not been converted to the principle that force had no political merit for them.

The conclusion I am led to by the arguments I have outlined in this book is that republicanism is an inappropriate response to the conditions it claims to have been fostered by, and it is one that exacerbates sectarianism and obstructs compromise. It is a creation of both conspiracy and social and political conditions. There was nothing inevitable about working-class Catholic disaffection framing itself into a republican agenda. There were other movements that might have prevailed, with greater prospects for reconciliation and reform. Some of these were armed groups that actually accepted the Provisional analysis that defence was needed, and these were swept away in the political rivalries of the period, so that a stark distinction emerged between just the SDLP and Sinn Féin.

A community of republican conviction that was unimaginable at the beginning of the Troubles now seems so intractable that it cannot be bartered away. In addition, there is an Irish identity in areas like west Belfast that is stronger than it ever was before. Gerry Adams says he can buy his newspaper and get his hair cut in Irish. Yet one of the most telling things about that first generation of modern republicans is their anglicised names. It was later generations who took the Gaelic form; that would have been simply eccentric in 1970.

The civil rights ambition of that time was that social revolution could happen without reference to the old republican template. It seemed a plausible dream then, but it proved hopeless. Republicanism was sufficiently alive to direct the course of the calamity that followed and also to sustain its hierarchy through the upheaval itself, to establish for many the prevailing version of what had happened. The republicans were strong enough to knit their present into the country's past, and to revive the old problem, of how to get off the hook of republican absolutism. A republican definition of the problem ties you to the problem itself so tightly that you can never solve it.

It produces a community of experience, experience that affirms the original vision. So the hunger strikes had to happen – because republicans insisted on being regarded as legitimate soldiers of a long-defeated government. The British then were the enemy, for

many who were not republicans, not because they would not concede that legitimacy to republicans, but because they would let men
die rather than give them their own clothes.

The point of this book has been to challenge some of the basic
myths about republicanism. I have argued that the IRA campaign
has not been defensive, in the sense of protecting the lives of people
within its support community, and that it has not been offensive, in
the sense of being part of a territorial war. I have argued that the
armed struggle has in fact been a form of political protest, effectively a veto on an internal settlement. It has often been described
as the expression of the hurt of a community, but I think I have
shown also that the community within which the IRA moves has a
diversity of political opinions and that the organic links between
people and the movement, through sympathy with the prisoners
and the dead, do not actually translate into a commitment to republican politics, but often involve an acquiescence in things that are
not approved of at all.

Eamonn McCann has suggested that we are asking too much of
the IRA in demanding that they simply stop their campaign: that
amounts to asking them to stand down as the legitimate army of
the Irish Republic declared by Pearse and validated by the general
election of 1918. That is the problem; that the IRA cannot simply
reverse its motivation. The Provisionals came into existence to be
true to the old principles and in opposition to all who compromised
them. There is nowhere now for them to go that does not compel
them to admit that they were wrong all along. Perhaps John Hume
was willing to at least endorse their past, in rewriting the history of
August 1969, as the price of getting them to stop now, but that
entails a lie that is offensive to both republicans and their critics.

The Provisionals, if they really want to stop, are caught in two
ways. They have to reconcile the new politics with past action
which said that compromise was betrayal. And, ironically, having
long argued that the Irish people had a moral right to take up arms
to enforce a claim for British withdrawal they are left with no
grounds for objecting to other paramilitary groups taking up what
they have put down. The Continuity Army Council and the INLA   197

are doing just that. Unless the Provisionals argue that the exclusive right to fight for Ireland lay with themselves alone, they can have no grounds for complaint about others bombing on.

The peace process has been dominated by a scepticism among most parties that the Provisionals can really be making such a radical transition, not just from purist republicanism enforced by violence to pragmatic negotiation, but from forestalling a compromise to embracing one.

Initially, from the British side, the peace process was organised procrastination. The republicans wanted to be in talks within three months and were, but these were not the constitutional negotiations with the British that they had expected. On the night before the first trip to Stormont in December 1994, Gerry Adams presented the talks team to the media outside the Sinn Féin offices on the Falls Road. These were the negotiators. This was a historic moment, the return to that moment in which Michael Collins had faltered. The striking things about that night were that so few people were there, and that Sinn Féin really appeared to believe that a historic moment had come.

'What's your fallback position, when the British say no?' I asked Gerry Adams.

'Do you think the Union is safe?' he said, as if the very idea was ridiculous.

But nationalist Ireland has endorsed the consent principle that determines that there can be no united Ireland until majorities on both sides of the border want it. That does safeguard the Union.

John Hume's theory demands that the British government must ultimately go back to the mistakes of 1912 and 1974 and confront the unionists, and break their veto over constitutional change. He has repeated this theory several times, particularly in his book *Personal Views*. For Hume, this means a confrontation at the point of constitutional reform. It does not include the idea that Orangemen should be confronted at Drumcree over their right to march. In fact, he has worked for compromise to prevent such confrontation, and spoken of the civil rights of Orangemen. Hume's confrontation only happens when a unionist leadership has reached agreement and attempts are made to overthrow it through mass mobilisation. It is that mobilised threat to agreement that must be confronted, and successfully withstood, for the first time.

There is no similar challenge to nationalists, other than that they stop the violence. Nor is there any clear shared sense among nationalists of where they are going. Unionists know what they want. They want the Union and the border, and they want to stop the growth of the nationalist advantage over them. Nationalists do not seem to know what they want, and they have the luxury of not yet having to say what they want. The moment of truth for them will come when demographic change creates the opportunity of a nationalist majority making a clear decision on the future, whether to go into a united Ireland or not, for instance. Until that day arrives, and it may still be a very long way off, they simply don't have to declare themselves. To unionists, who are constantly being challenged on what they will accept, nationalists seem, therefore, to be riding in the wake of republicans, leaving it to history to open greater opportunities for them. By leaving it to republicans to be the cutting edge of nationalism, and declaring no preference for any other outcome themselves, they squander their hopes.

True, nationalists would argue that there is no visionary unionist on the other side to meet them in a coalition against republicanism. There is no one declaring a love of reconciliation or powersharing. But that is not the whole of the problem for them. There is no actual parity between the positions of unionists and of nationalists. Unionists have to declare their limits every day, nationalists never have to declare them at all. The unionist sin is that they are so unwilling to relax their demands and trade, the nationalist sin is that they are unwilling to declare their demands and trade.

The IRA is not at the centre of the dispute between nationalism and unionism. Addressing that ruptured relationship does not necessarily mean appeasing the demands of the IRA. Skewing the process of reconciliation in the direction of appeasing the IRA may actually make the problem worse.

Sinn Féin regards the unionists as being under a moral onus to help bring IRA violence to an end. In July 1997, after it was clear that Sinn Féin would be admitted to talks, Mitchel McLaughlin said that there was a danger of us sliding back to the old violence if unionists didn't take their responsibilities for peacemaking seriously. John Hume sees it in the same terms. This could only be so if the violence of the IRA was a necessary or inevitable result of unionist behaviour or the Northern Irish past. This is the significance of the Hume argument that all trouble comes out of Bombay Street. It is essentially a nationalist vision in which the unionists are in the wrong. They can hardly be expected to see it that way themselves. This is the result of seeing the problem as a conflict requiring conflict resolution. It is possible to see that there has been huge injustice in Northern Ireland without holding it responsible for IRA violence. It is also important to see that the IRA campaign was honed to be an efficient party political instrument for preventing reconciliation, rather than delude ourselves that it is merely a symptom of the pain of excluded people.

I do not want my children and theirs to be taught in their schools that the IRA campaign was a necessary phase in the readjustment of the constitutional anomaly created in 1921. I will tell them myself that it was a wasteful and horrid business. But the price of ending it may be a reassessment of our history to allow for it. We will argue that the need for it has passed, rather than that there was never a need for it.

EPILOGUE

I am back in a corner and this time my accuser is a supporter of the SDLP. She is furious with me because of an article I have written about the party. 'You are perverse,' she says, as if she thinks I only ever write to get myself into trouble. I have had many people say to me: How could someone like you, who came out of the same background as the republicans, turn so comprehensively against them, when you should have understood what made them? It is a cut closer to home when friends in the SDLP tell me I should know better, that I should have sufficient sense of responsibility not to undermine the peace process by carping at it.

My problem is with the thesis that underpins the SDLP strategy for wooing republicans into political negotiations. This accepts that they were trapped in history. They weren't, at least not in any history but that of their own tradition, and they were not trapped in circumstance. They had always made choices and they had often made bad or inappropriate choices. They had made many choices that were calculated to limit the potential of the SDLP itself.

The SDLP efforts to help Sinn Féin into talks, of course, had been pragmatic, rather than ideological. In a way it didn't matter what arguments were used to explain it. Most Catholics saw hope in it and wanted it to work. Most Protestants, however, saw a new Catholic ethnic solidarity that might threaten them even more than the IRA campaign had done. Some republican sceptics actually tended to a similar vision: they feared that this pan-nationalist front would eclipse and alienate Sinn Féin. On the other hand, some in the SDLP feared that the alliance would give too much credibility to Sinn Féin. These tended to say nothing for fear of sounding as if they preferred to preserve their own party intact than to have peace. But how, I asked my SDLP friend, could the growth of Sinn Féin and the deepening of division between nationalist and unionist actually produce peace? 'Your job as a party is to fight these people,' I said. 'Instead, Sinn Féin grows within a space created for it by the SDLP.'

To my reading, republicans will no longer need armed struggle when they have cleared a political path to producing the result that armed struggle produces – that is, when political action alone can veto an internal settlement, and that comes when Sinn Féin overtakes the SDLP. Fighting Sinn Féin and denying them that opportunity doesn't mean that you prefer that republicans stick with violence; it means that you have a distinctive ideology and that you assert your right to proclaim it, no matter what anyone else does. 'You might lose out to them, in the referendum, or in elections to a devolved assembly?' I said to her. 'We won't' was her apparently confident reply.

Bernadette McAliskey has her own term for the pan-nationalist front. She calls it a Hibernian alliance. In a speech in St Louis, Missouri, on 13 October 1995, she said: 'The problem with the Hibernian alliance is that Sinn Féin's bottom line is everyone else's top line. What Sinn Féin says is not negotiable is the first thing everyone else wants to throw out.'

The notion that the SDLP's top line is Sinn Féin's bottom line is not one that Unionists put much faith in. They don't believe that the SDLP has a top line. Many in Sinn Féin also think that the SDLP will accept anything that republicans can manage to win for them, that there is no limit to the nationalist programme for shafting the Unionists. They think that the SDLP is a party of compromise for the sake of peace and quiet, but that every raising of the nationalist potential will cheer them. Does the SDLP mind if republicans succeed in sapping the will and morale of Unionists and dragging them grudgingly into a united Ireland; do they have a political interest in preventing that?

202   It's down to this for Northern nationalists who vote for the SDLP:

what's your price for turning on the Provos, and how good will you feel about yourselves afterwards, if in pitching it too high you only make things worse?

Like the old tradition of flattering the dangerous fairies by calling them the good people, *na daoine maithe*, nationalists flatter the Provisionals by calling them peace makers and honouring their efforts, for fear that if they cease for a moment to speak well of them, they will sour their milk, dry up their wells, maim their firstborn sons, close off the roads, bring buildings tumbling upon them, set neighbour against neighbour and wreak general havoc in the land.

I wonder if nationalists are too long used to the luxury of having no responsibility in Northern Ireland. In the 1960s, which was the decade of my teens, there was a prevailing ethos among Northern Irish Catholics. They had a strong sense of being disadvantaged within a sectarian state, and they had little sense that they could do anything immediate about that. The problem was that Unionists regarded Northern Ireland as a Protestant state. The coupling of a religious, ethnic character with the policy of government was selfish and exclusive. Catholics could pit their own culture and institutions against the state's; they could develop a Catholic polity in which Catholics could be educated, get jobs and live out their lives without regard to Protestants, or they could decide that however wilful and exclusive was Protestant sectarianism, they would not match it in kind, but would simply try to shame it out of existence.

I had thought for a time, when I was eighteen, that life and energy and love and intelligence were all about questioning your past and throwing off the shackles of religion and ethnic chauvinism. For me this was natural and glorious, it was like being born again. The enemy were the old romantic and conservative fools who dwelt on history, who told you, if not literally, that your path was ordained. The revolution, as I saw it, was a spiritual one; it was an individual one; it was about finding out all the special ways in which everything that they said was true did not apply to you.

Discovering that for others the revolution was about shagging the Brits and blowing up barber shops came as a serious disappointment. Only one political movement in Ireland ever excited my 203 naïve younger self with a sense of thrilling radical potential, and that was the SDLP at its beginnings, out of the civil rights movement. That exhilaration had much to do with the enjoyment of seeing Unionists outclassed in articulation and wit, an indulgence I now regard as sectarian. The republican agenda was not a project to accelerate the growth of justice and nonsectarianism in Northern Ireland, but the precise opposite. It was a calamitously inappropriate monopolisation of popular feeling. Had the IRA simply emerged out of the coalescence of anger and humiliation among Northern Catholics it would have been more organic, more adaptable and more amenable. From the start, however, republicans sought to abort the prospects for harmonisation of Protestant and Catholic, to overthrow the apple cart entirely, not to help it run smoothly on balanced wheels. The two possible courses open to Catholics – towards insisting on Irish unity and towards conciliation within Northern Ireland – were not equally exclusive of each other. The exclusiveness comes only from one option: the insistence on Irish unity, especially when pursued through violence. Conciliation does not rule out a united Ireland in the long run, but the insistence on a united Ireland rules out conciliation. The only sensible way forward in Northern Ireland was to uncouple ethnicity and polity, not to match a unionist Protestant polity with a Catholic one.

I told my friend that I didn't like the suggestion that ethnic bonding had first call on my allegiance; that I didn't like this nonsense about a nationalist consensus; that I didn't like to hear SDLP members argue that nationalists are entitled to seven seats in parliament, as if the qualification for a seat was ethnic rather than ideological. I didn't see how a nationalist veto pitted against a Unionist veto would ever dissolve two communities into each other. It looked to me like a device for defining our separateness for ever. 'Are Catholics in Northern Ireland always to have a greater interest in sticking together?' I asked.

'You have to start from where you are at,' she replied. 'It is Unionists who make this an ethnic contest. You can't just pretend that they haven't and go your own way.'

The SDLP has always been inhibited from dealing any serious

damage to Sinn Féin by the complexity of their relationship. Republicans are – literally – cousins and siblings of SDLP members and voters. They know each other well. The history of animosity is measured out for many on both sides in sullen Christmas dinners and rancorous wedding receptions that have pulled them un-willingly together.

I reminded her that Sinn Féin had never had any problem regarding the SDLP as collaborators and sell-out merchants. 'We are approaching the end of this and things will become clear,' she said. 'Sinn Féin will have to sign up to a compromise or they will be exposed as the ones who don't want peace.'

I conceded that the strategy of the SDLP in working to get Sinn Féin into talks did inhibit Sinn Féin. The theory had been that a taste of the need for ordinary political pragmatism would teach them how to compromise. Something like this had been seen already in local councils where Sinn Féin members had taken office. After the July 1997 ceasefire, Sinn Féin was hampered in its political dealing by its violent past. It had a clear incentive to break from the past if it was to make political progress. It became impossible for them to make statements about their position without these being read as implying threats. When leading members said that they would accept no settlement short of a thirty-two-county Irish republic, those who heard had little guidance on whether to interpret this as a prediction of resumed violence if the goal of a united Ireland was not achieved. Sinn Féin had an interest in being clear about its relationship with the IRA if it wanted to be understood.

Its insistence on distancing itself from the IRA, and speaking only for itself, could create confusion over republican intentions, to Sinn Féin's own disadvantage, whereas previously the same tack had been a shelter for criticism. They insisted that they had done enough to inspire confidence by securing a ceasefire from the IRA, but the doubt about their intentions was not so easily dispelled, nor does it seem clear that they had ever really wanted to dispel it. Their ambi-guity could be an irritant to others in the talks, but they could not maintain it and at the same time reassure anybody of their benign intentions. 205

The IRA was tied after the elections of 1997 into a mandate to make peace, and could not risk going back to political violence without squandering the Sinn Féin vote. The most likely price of a withdrawal from talks would be a loss of community support. At least, any resumption of political violence would have to be negotiated in such a way as to ensure that their support base did not blame them for it and could see the logic in it. Otherwise the violence would not be seen as community inspired, but as the sort of conspiracy that the British always said it was.

Support for Sinn Féin and the IRA was now becoming two different things, even if the organisations were still effectively one, as community pressure built on Sinn Féin to distance itself from the violence. The Sinn Féin support base now liked to imagine that it was part of a larger thing called the New Nationalism, symbolised by President Mary McAleese, a Catholic woman from Ardoyne. It might imagine a continuing partnership between Sinn Féin and the SDLP exercising the right to demand concessions from Unionists. It had invested its morale in the new relationship with the SDLP and had much to lose without it. At the same time it had little power to keep the SDLP on side. It could argue that if the SDLP went its own way, republicanism would have little choice but to resort to violence, but a community support base that saw little point in violence might simply desert them.

As the talks progressed, many voices urged nationalists to put forward their toughest demands. They said that this was the only way to make a deal that could endure. 'You can't build bridges from the middle' – the caption of an Ian Knox cartoon – became the slogan for those who said that nationalist unity and stridency would actually take us to a more dependable compromise. Essentially this was a challenge to the SDLP to hold firm on united nationalist ground. The Irish government was seen to have balked first when, on 1 December 1997, Foreign Minister David Andrews apologised for suggesting that a cross-border secretariat might have powers like government, and Taoiseach Bertie Ahern was thought soft and failing in his partnership with Northern nationalists when he said the constitution could be changed. Another problem for the

Provisionals was that any violence after their ceasefire would have a different meaning to any before it. The violence would have to continue if it was to be represented as a product of an unresolved problem. Sinn Féin wanted to be seen as the ones who understood the roots of violence and the route to ending it, but they didn't want to be seen as blackmailers who would switch it on and off to get their way. And how could they avoid that?

Bombs would no longer signal simply the background rumble of seismic forces in a society that couldn't knit together; they would be read as signalling fundamental changes in republican policy, for which Sinn Féin was more accountable than it had been for any previous violence.

The trouble with guns was that their stain stayed. Having made themselves, with their violent agitation, an indispensable partner in any government's plan for peace in Northern Ireland, the Provisionals had wedded themselves to a murderous methodology. The shadow of the gun would always be over them. They could get a limited credibility for their peaceful intentions by stopping the violence, but they could never get credit for a serious change of heart unless they disowned their own past, and they weren't going to do that.

They were dealing with a government that had successfully pushed responsibility for solving the problem back onto Northern Ireland parties. Any failure in that effort would present the Provisionals and the loyalists with no logical course but to fight a sectarian war. The genius of Blair's strategy was that it let him off the hook, and much as loyalists and republicans might be able to justify slugging at each other, republicans would be handicapped in finding a rationale for another ersatz anti-imperialist war. They were in danger of being left with no war to fight but the least desirable and dirtiest – a purely sectarian exchange of murders.

Their own theology was likely to compel them into such a war, however, as loyalist violence increased. No republican could argue that Catholics should be defended by the British army or the RUC, no matter how well they were doing that job. Republicans would have to provide the only legitimate defence available, according to their view, even if this made things worse, and even at the cost of their own political freedom of action. This paradox would challenge their absolutism, and expose their fundamental philosophy as untenable if they had the courage to read its implications. Otherwise, they would have to go through 1970 again: first fight the Protestants, then fight the army and the police when they tried to intervene. Then they would have to argue plausibly that the security measures against them proved that the British were the real enemy. And what would they be fighting the British for anyway, but the freedom to get at the Protestants? How could they sell that idea to communities that were tired of violence?

Ironically, the Ulster Unionists also found themselves trapped within a logic which compelled them to make excuses for the political representatives of loyalist paramilitaries, even when they were said by the RUC to be breaking their own ceasefires. Unionists knew how to tell when the IRA was issuing veiled threats and were quick to say so, but similar hints from loyalists had to be treated as thoughtful mediations from an aggrieved community with limited options. The talks process was going to be a nightmare for everybody.

Did the Provos see all this complexity ahead of them? One of the most succinct descriptions of a possible IRA conspiracy running through the peace process is contained in Henry Patterson's reissue of *The Politics of Illusion*. The strategy was, he said, 'a rational wager on the inflexibility and lack of imagination of the Unionist leadership'. Having challenged the Unionists to make a deal and having seen them back out of the talks, the drift of political reform would then be further towards joint sovereignty, and away from devolution. This is a theory that integrates the confrontations over parades with the talks strategy; however, Patterson didn't reach this conclusion. He said that Gerry Adams had moved closer to a partitionist settlement and that his real problem would be holding his own movement together. On 1 December 1997, when the *Belfast Telegraph* printed the text of exchanges at the end of 1996 between the British Prime Minister John Major and Gerry Adams, which had taken place between the ceasefires, it was clear that the British had very little faith in Adams as a peace maker. Nor did he encourage them to think more highly of him. The replies which he gave to their questions were formulaic restatements of the party line.

Adams had a clear line of communication direct to the head of government at a time when he was looking for assurances, and what is striking about his answers to Major's questions is that they are evasive and minimalist, as if phrased to make Major's job more difficult, not easier. The accompanying article by Martina Purdy quotes a briefing for the prime minister from Sir Patrick Mayhew, the then secretary of state for Northern Ireland, in which he says: 'We have to be careful not to fall into the trap set for us. It remains very difficult to see what Adams and McGuinness are up to.'

Like Patterson, David Sharrock and Mark Devenport, in their biography of Adams, *Man of War, Man of Peace?*, show an unwillingness to conclude firmly that the peace strategy was purely tactical: 'If violence persists there may be those who will argue that Adams did his best. But many others will point to the evidence that he was merely playing on people's aspirations towards peace to indulge in a grand tactical experiment.' But which do they themselves think it was?

If it was a tactical experiment it was one that some republicans were hugely sceptical of. Bernadette McAliskey saw it as a strategy that would cost republicans dear and would squander the fruits of past efforts. 'I am not intellectually incapable of understanding the peace process,' she said in the *Irish Reporter* in February 1996, before the Canary Wharf bomb. 'I understand it, and I reject it, because it has from its embryonic stages in the original Dublin Forum, created by C.J. Haughey, and the resulting Anglo-Irish Agreement of 1985, been a process whose aim is to eradicate republicanism, not violence.' By her reading, the SDLP had indeed roped republicans into something which they would be trapped in. Not that she wanted them to go back to war, nor believed that they intended to. The Canary Wharf bomb, she thought, was no act of tactical sophistication either. She saw the bomb simply as a grasp for credibility with the militants and the disaffected: 'I think finally the leadership took a calculated risk in the Canary Wharf bombing in order to reassert its own authority within its military ranks. In my opinion, they made the assessment that if they did not move at that time they were heading toward a real possibility that some element of their own organisation or people who had drifted away from it would, out of frustration, make some military move on their own.'

What makes it tempting, however, to attribute sophisticated planning to the Provisionals is that they have gained so much from their moves. That bomb at Canary Wharf cleared the way for Sinn Féin to compete with the SDLP in three elections in the coming year. It enabled them to mark progress against the background of continuing armed struggle, and to trust that voters supported political violence as an ingredient of the peace strategy. If they had sustained the ceasefire through the elections they would have been faced with the argument that the vote for them was a vote against armed struggle. They skirted that problem by getting their vote up at a time when there was no ceasefire.

These were, apparently, incidental, unplanned gains. No one foresaw that the bomb would serve them so well?

One argument against the conspiracy theory is that it credits the Provos with implausibly sophisticated long-term planning. I have heard different community workers say: 'You don't want to credit these guys with too much savvy; they're not that bright.' When they found themselves in the talks process, their demands having been met, they were left with few options of their own. If they had planned for their entry into talks, they had not planned far beyond the start of negotiations.

They would always have opportunities to draw occasional propaganda advantage, as when Alex Maskey turned an offer of state protection into an opportunity to humiliate the RUC, to refuse them access to his home. He challenged the government virtually to acknowledge the legitimacy of his fears that the RUC would set him up for assassination. They would pick up phrasings from journalists and repeat them as if they were the summation of long-wrought policy; hence they could argue that a corps of 'securocrats' was obstructing peace, not because they had worked this out for themselves but because they had read the idea in Brian Feeney's column in the *Irish News*.

Who is holding whose tail here? I wonder. Have Sinn Féin trapped the SDLP into their strategy, or have the SDLP trapped Sinn Féin into a process that doesn't suit them, but which they can't back out of without disgrace? I asked my friend in the SDLP: 'Do you know yourselves what the Provos are up to? Has Adams told you something he has told no one else? Isn't that what we are all banking on?'

But she didn't have to answer. What choice do any of us have but to put faith in the good intentions of the IRA? That's the trouble with guns, you have to give the benefit of the doubt, over and over again, to the people who hold them.

BIBLIOGRAPHY

Adams, G. *Before the Dawn*, Heinemann in association with
 Brandon, 1996
Adams, G. *The Politics of Irish Freedom*, Brandon, 1986/1995
Adams, G. *Cage Eleven*, Brandon, 1990
Beresford, D. *Ten Men Dead*, Grafton, 1987
Berne, E. *What Do You Say After You Say Hello?* Corgi, 1975
Bishop, P. and E. Mallie. *The Provisional IRA*, Corgi, 1987
Bowyer Bell, J. *The Irish Troubles: A Generation of Violence*, Gill and
 Macmillan, 1993
 The Gun in Politics: An Analysis of Irish Political Conflict, 1916–1986,
 Transaction, 1987
Breen, R. 'Who Wants a United Ireland', in R. Breen, P. Devine
 and L. Dowds, (eds.), *Social Attitudes in Northern Ireland*, Appletree
 Press, 1996
Bruce, S. *The Red Hand: Protestant Paramilitaries in Northern Ireland*,
 Oxford University Press, 1992
Buckley, A.D. and M.C. Kenney. *Negotiating Identity: Rhetoric,
 Metaphor and Social Drama in Northern Ireland*, Smithsonian,
 1995
Burton, F. *The Politics of Legitimacy: Struggles in a Belfast Community*,
 Routledge and Kegan Paul, 1978
Clarke, L. *Broadening the Battlefield*, Gill and Macmillan, 1987
Cline, R.S. and Y. Alexander. *Terrorism as State-sponsored Covert
 Warfare*, Hero Books, 1986
Clutterbuck, R. *Protest and the Urban Guerrilla*, Cassell, 1973
 Living with Terrorism, Faber and Faber, 1975
Collins, M. (ed.). *Ireland after Britain*, Pluto, 1985
Conroy, J. *War as a Way of Life*, Heinemann, 1988

Coogan, T.P. *The IRA*, Fontana, 1987
 The Troubles, Hutchinson, 1995
De Baróid, C. *Ballymurphy and the Irish War*, Aisling Publishers,
 1989
Devlin, P. *Straight Left: An Autobiography*, Blackstaff Press, 1993
English, R. 'Green on Red', in D.G. Boyce, R. Eccleshall and
 V. Geoghegan (eds.), *Political Thought in Ireland from the
 Seventeenth Century*, Routledge, 1993
Gearty, C. *Terror*, Faber and Faber, 1991
Guelke, A. *The Age of Terrorism and the International Political System*,
 Tauris Academic Studies, 1995
Hart, P. 'The Geography of Revolution in Ireland, 1917–1973, in
 Past and Present, no. 155 (May 1997)
Heskin, K. *Northern Ireland: A Psychological Analysis*, Gill and
 Macmillan, 1980
Holland, J. and S. Phoenix. *Policing the Shadows: The Secret War
 Against Terrorism in Northern Ireland*, Coronet Books, 1996
Hume, J. *Personal Views*, Town House, 1996
Jackall, R. (ed.). *Propaganda*, Macmillan, 1995
Keena, C. *A Biography of Gerry Adams*, Mercier, 1991
Lee, J. J. *Ireland: 1912–1985*, Cambridge University Press, 1989
Mallie, E. and D. McKittrick. *The Fight for Peace: The Secret Story
 Behind the Irish Peace Process*, Heinemann, 1996
McCann, Eamonn, *War and an Irish Town*, Pluto, 1974/1993
McClung Lee, A. *Terrorism in Northern Ireland*, General Hall,
 1983
McGartland, M. *Fifty Dead Men Walking*, Blake Publishing,
 1997
Morrison, D. *West Belfast*, Mercier Press, 1989
 The Wrong Man, Mercier Press, 1997
Oakes, G. 'The Cold War System of Emotion Management:
 Mobilising the Home Front for the Third World War', in
 R. Jackall (ed.), *Propaganda*, Macmillan, 1995
Ó Dochartaigh, N. *From Civil Rights to Armalites*, Cork University
 Press, 1997
O'Brien, B. *The Long War*, O'Brien Press, 1995

O'Brien, C. Cruise. *States of Ireland*, Hutchinson, 1972
  'Thinking about Terrorism 1', in *Passion and Cunning and Other Essays*, Weidenfeld and Nicolson, 1988
O'Doherty, S. *The Volunteer*, Fount, 1993
Omer, Y.E. *International Law: Documents Relating to Terrorism*, Cavendish, n.d.
Orr, J. 'Terrorism as Social Drama and Dramatic Form', in J. Orr and D. Klaic (eds.), *Terrorism and Modern Drama*, Edinburgh, 1990
Packard, V. *The Hidden Persuaders*, Penguin, 1957/1991
Paletz, D. and A. Schmid (eds.). *Terrorism and the Media*, Sage, 1992
Patterson, H. *The Politics of Illusion*, Hutchinson, 1989
Rubenstein, E.R. *Alchemists of Revolution: Terrorism in the Modern World*, Basic Books, 1987
Said, E.W. *Peace and its Discontents*, Vintage, 1995
Schelling, T.C. *Arms and Influence*, Yale University Press, 1966
Sederberg, P.C. *Terrorist Myths: Illusion, Rhetoric and Reality*, Prentice Hall, 1989
Sharrock, D. and M. Devenport. *Man of War, Man of Peace? The Unauthorised Biography of Gerry Adams*, Macmillan, 1997
Smith, M.L.R. *Fighting for Ireland: The Military Strategy of the Irish Republican Movement*, Routledge, 1995
Stevenson, J. *'We Wrecked the Place': Contemplating an End to the Northern Irish Troubles*, Free Press, 1996
Sutton, M. *Bear in Mind These Dead: An Index of Deaths from the Conflict in Ireland, 1969–1993*, Beyond the Pale Publications, 1994
Toolis, K. *Rebel Hearts*, Picador, 1995
Townshend, C. *Political Violence in Ireland*, Oxford University Press, 1983
Urban, M. *Big Boys' Rules*, Faber and Faber, 1992
White, R.W. *Provisional Irish Republicans: An Oral and Interpretive History*, Greenwood, 1993
Williams, J.W. 'Terrorism as Mass Communication', paper presented to the conference on 'International Perspectives on Crime, Justice and Public Order', Dublin Castle, Dublin, Ireland, 17 June 1996

INDEX

MALACHI O'DOHERTY was born in Donegal in 1951 and grew up in Riverdale in west Belfast. He went to school with the Irish Christian Brothers and studied at the Belfast College of Business Studies, entering journalism first as a columnist on the now defunct youth magazine *Thursday* and later as a staff reporter on the *Sunday News*. He lived abroad through most of the 1970s, working for a time as a sports reporter in Morecambe, a hop-picker in Worcestershire, a ghost writer for a guru in India, where he also published several short stories, and as a language instructor to the Libyan Air Defence Forces. He has been a popular free-lance journalist and commentator in Belfast since the mid-eighties, as a regular contributor to several BBC radio and television programmes. He has been a columnist for the *Irish News* and currently writes 'O'Doherty's Outlook' in the *Belfast Telegraph*. He also writes frequently on Northern Irish affairs for the *Scotsman* and occasionally on cultural and literary matters for the *Sunday Times*. He has presented several acclaimed television documentaries on political and social affairs for Channel 4, the BBC and UTV, and he is a research student in the Department of Politics at Queen's University Belfast.

Malachi O'Doherty is married and lives in south Belfast.